To MaryAnne

Retribution!

with best wishes

Elizabeth Ducie

Elizabeth.

A Chudleigh Phoenix Publications Book

Copyright © 2024 Elizabeth Ducie

Cover design: Berni Stevens

The right of Elizabeth Ducie to be identified as the Author of the Work has been asserted by her in accordance with the Copyright, Designs and Patents Act 1988.

All Rights reserved. No part of this publication may be reproduced, stored in a retrieval system or transmitted in any form or by any means without the prior consent of the author, nor be otherwise circulated in any form of binding or cover other than that in which it is published and without a similar condition, including this condition, being imposed on the subsequent purchaser.

ISBN: 978-1-913020-22-4

Chudleigh Phoenix Publications

For Margaret James,
who told me Charlie deserved another story.

ACKNOWLEDGMENTS

I am once again very grateful for all the support provided by my friends in the thriving community of writers and readers, both in Devon and beyond. My thanks go to Morgen Bailey (morgenbailey.wordpress.com) for her patience and editing skills; and to my faithful band of beta readers who never fail to find the mistakes I've missed (or tried to hide).

This series was supposed to be a trilogy, but my characters had other ideas and six years on, here we are again. Rereading the first three parts, I was reminded once more of all the friends I made across the world during my thirty years on 'the day job' and I am grateful for the way their (real) stories have become entwined with my (fictional) ones.

Berni Stevens (bernistevenscoverdesign.com) is responsible for the cover (redesigned for 2024). Julia Gibbs (@ProofreadJulia) made sure the final text is as error-free as possible. My thanks go to both of them. As ever, I owe a huge debt of gratitude to my sisters, Margaret Andow and Sheila Pearson, for their analytical reading skills and ongoing cheerleading. Last but not least, my thanks go to my husband Michael McCormick, my fiercest critic and strongest supporter, who keeps reminding me not to get distracted.

PROLOGUE: DUBLIN, JULY 2021

"And you're absolutely sure it's the same woman?"

"Oh yes, I'm sure alright. Her hair was very different when I knew her. And she was quite a bit older than in your picture. But I'll never forget those eyes. Beautiful eyes she had. When she gazed up at you, like she's doing there, you'd think you were the only person in the world."

The woman took a long drink from her glass, shuffled her bum along the seat so her thigh pressed more tightly up against his, and pointed at the photo lying on the table between them. "But that's not you in the photo, darling. Why did you say you're carrying her picture in your wallet?"

"I didn't." The man in the leather jacket was beginning to get tired of her already and wondered how he'd got himself into this position. Drinking late at night with a woman who looked old enough to be his mother. Although judging by the way she was running her brightly-painted chipped fingernails along his arm, the thoughts she was having about him were anything but maternal.

If he'd not crossed the Ha'penny Bridge spanning Dublin's Liffey River. If he'd not found this dimly lit bar, smelling of stale beer. If his brother hadn't been so late in turning up. If he'd not smiled at the lonely-looking woman sitting on the bar stool next to his. And if he'd not dropped the picture from his wallet when he'd paid for his drink.

If none of those things had happened, he'd never have heard her say, "Why have you got a picture of Charlie Jones in your wallet?"

He'd stolen the picture from his father's desk drawer. No-one knew he had it. It was creased with age. He'd cut away her companions, just kept her. Everyone had told him she was dead. He'd kept that knowledge in his heart, a comfort in the darkest times. A reason not to hate her, when all he wanted to do so very badly, was exactly that. But this woman, Kitty Campbell, she knew too.

"Who's Charlie Jones?" The question had been out of his mouth before he could stop himself. And it opened the floodgates in the woman.

"Her, in your picture. She's the woman who brought me halfway across Europe on a wild-goose chase then left me to fend for myself while she went off with someone else. I was only a kid, barely eighteen, and she was twice my age. I trusted her. But she dumped me, like that!"

Kitty had gone on to tell some long rambling tale about being held against her will in Greece, and how this Charlie Jones had helped her escape, given Kitty hope of a future together, then gone back on her word. How Kitty had tried to track down her former friend but how she'd disappeared completely once they reached London.

He'd switched off, trying to find an excuse to finish the conversation and slip away. But then Kitty had pushed her badly dyed red hair out of her eyes and tapped him on the arm. "Of course she didn't call herself Charlie Jones when I knew her. I only found out her real name when there was all that publicity a couple of years later about that civil servant who was supposed to have killed himself, but really ran off to South America. She was all over the news for a while then. No, I knew her as Rose Fitzpatrick."

Her words had ripped through him and suddenly the last thing on his mind was leaving Kitty Campbell alone. All he wanted to do was to hear everything she knew about Charlie Jones, Rose Fitzpatrick, the only name by which he'd ever known the woman in the picture. He'd suggested they move to one of the booths around the edge of the room, and Kitty had quickly agreed.

"Any idea where she is now?" He tried to make the words sound casual, a disinterested question. Certainly not the most important piece of information she could possibly give him. Her drink, the third he'd paid for in rapid succession, was finished, and Kitty was searching in her purse. Pulling out a lipstick, she turned to the cracked mirror on the wall behind them and pouted. He nudged her arm. "I said, do you know where she is now?"

"What?" She finished touching up her makeup, closed her purse and looked back at him. "Why are we still talking about that woman? Come on, darling, let's go somewhere quieter." The leer she gave him sickened him and he had to stop himself from pushing her away.

"We're not going anywhere. I want you to tell me what you know about the woman in the picture." He realised his voice was louder than he'd intended. A couple of people across the bar stopped their conversation and looked over at his table. "I mean," he made a conscious effort to calm down and lower his voice, "please tell me what you know and then we'll go wherever you want to."

Kitty sighed theatrically and dropped her bag back on the table. "She and that partner of hers," he could almost taste the bitterness in her voice, "shacked up in London. She worked with her sister, Suzanne, in some kind of consultancy. They seemed to move around quite a lot. There was that business in Africa of course. Then they were in South America for a few months. And they worked in your part of the world for a while."

"What do you mean – my part of the world?"

"Russia, Ukraine. That's where you're from, isn't it?"

"Certainly not." He shook his head firmly.

"Sorry. My mistake. I thought with your accent… So where are you from then? Romania? Bulgaria? Somewhere like that?"

"Yes, somewhere like that." He smiled at her, trying to get her back on track. "So she's still in London, is she? Still travelling around a lot?"

Kitty shook her head. "No. She stopped all that when Annie had her kid. Worked in computers for a while. Then a few years ago, they packed up and headed west."

"What? To America?"

"No, darling. Nothing so adventurous. They moved to Devon. Running a pub down there, they are. Not sure where. Always meant to go down there and see them. Talk about old times, you know." Kitty was starting to slur as the evening of drinking finally hit her. "But somehow, I never got around to it." She smiled at him. "Can we go now, darling?"

As he desperately tried to think of a way of letting her down gently – she looked like she'd been let down plenty of times already in her life – a shadow fell across the table.

Looking up, the man in the leather jacket was relieved to see his brother. Finally!

Hopefully, between them, they could find a way to get rid of Kitty. Gently if possible. But forcibly if necessary. Once he'd revealed to his brother the information he'd just learned, they were going to have a lot to discuss. A lot of planning to do. And the last thing they needed was any witnesses.

PART 1

CHAPTER 1: DEVON, APRIL 2024

The hairs on the back of her neck were rising. Charlie Jones stopped at the crossroads and leaned back against the wall of the department store as though waiting for someone, casually scanning her surroundings in all directions. It wasn't the first time she'd felt like this. As she'd got into the car that morning to leave The Falls pub. When she reached the Park and Ride car park. Boarding the bus for Exeter. And as she alighted from the bus on Fore Street. Each time she was convinced she wasn't alone. Someone was observing her, following her.

She had absolutely no proof of her suspicions. And each time she glanced back or stopped to check the reflections in a shop window, there was no-one in sight, apart from other folk going about their everyday business. No-one seemed to be watching her or acting strangely. But in her former life, her safety and that of her associates had depended on her keeping alert. And she'd developed a sixth sense about that sort of thing. A sixth sense that was working overtime.

She carried on walking and turned into the first coffee shop she came to. It was still relatively empty and she had her pick of seating. Once her pot of peppermint tea was ready – they didn't serve instant coffee and she couldn't stand the real stuff – she settled into an easy chair at the round table in the window. It gave her a clear view along the high street in both directions, plus she could see anyone who came through the door.

Pulling out her phone, she pretended to scroll through messages, while keeping a close eye on everything going on.

And finally, she recognised a familiar face; or at least a face she'd seen earlier that morning as they'd queued for the Park and Ride bus. A man in a leather jacket was strolling slowly, almost aimlessly, down the street from the same direction she'd come. As he drew level with the coffee shop he caught Charlie's eye and immediately looked away.

Nothing strange there. Brits were generally not good at making eye contact with strangers in the street. Although he didn't look like a local to Charlie. He had the small stature and dark complexion of an Eastern European. But that meant nothing these days, even in a county like Devon where cultural diversity was still a relatively new concept.

He walked on a few more steps, drawing level with the shop window opposite. Then he made a great point of pulling out his phone and comparing the time on the screen with the time shown by the hands of the large clock above the shop door.

Having apparently satisfied himself that his device was accurate, he continued walking down the street and disappeared around the corner. Charlie watched him go. Why make such a big thing about checking the time on his phone? Especially as he'd not so much as glanced at the showy gold wristwatch poking out from below the cuff of his leather jacket.

And yet, Exeter was a small city. It wasn't at all unlikely that she would see the same person more than once during a visit. Was she imagining it all? Just one of those coincidences that happens all the time? Part of her wanted to believe it was all in her head. It was years since she'd been involved in any of the international projects that led to her being followed or kept under observation. These days, apart from an occasional spot of amateur sleuthing, she lived a quiet safe life with Annie and their daughter Suzy. And she wouldn't want it any other way.

But a part of her, the part that was trained to suspect everyone and trust no-one, the part that didn't believe in coincidences, was convinced there was some basis to her concerns. And that part of her still had enough influence to make sure she didn't take any risks.

After pouring the last drops of tea from the pot and draining her cup, she wandered through the tables to a corridor that ran from the side of the counter to the rear of the premises. The two doors to the toilets were on her left. To her right were the entrances to the kitchen and staff room. Ahead, a door stood ajar, leading to the outside. Taking the opportunity of an empty corridor, Charlie peered through the gap.

A tiny yard and a battered wooden gate, which swung open on squeaking hinges, gave way to a narrow alleyway running down the back of the shops. To her right, Charlie could see the main road; to her left, another alleyway, more or less level with the point where her possible pursuer had disappeared. Charlie decided crowds were the best option.

She turned right out of the yard and in moments was back in the main street, which was more crowded as the morning progressed. A quick scan of the area told her the man in the leather jacket was nowhere in sight.

With her appetite for shopping gone, Charlie zig-zagged through the crowds, changed direction several times and finally found her way back to the bus stop. Rather than joining the queue, she entered the nearest shop, a stationers, and positioned herself in the window, running her fingers through a selection of birthday cards while keeping an eye on the road.

When she saw the bus approach, she hung back until the last minute before dashing across the pavement and jumping on as the doors closed. Waving her return ticket to the driver, she ran up the stairs and grabbed a seat near the back.

As the bus pulled away, she glanced down at the pavement and was in time to see the short man in the black leather jacket skid to a halt beside the bus stop.

Charlie pulled back from the window. Had he seen her? Was he really following her? She toyed with the idea of talking it all through with Annie when she got back home. But something cautioned her to keep quiet. If it was all a figment of her overactive imagination, she didn't want to upset Annie for nothing. Especially when they were due to tie the knot in just a few weeks.

CHAPTER 2

By the time the man in the leather jacket returned to the lodgings they'd rented in the little backstreet in Newton Abbot, his feelings were in turmoil and he didn't know whether to laugh, cry or hit someone.

He'd been parked under the trees at the side of the village green in Coombesford when she'd left that morning. He was confident she hadn't noticed him as she'd driven out of the pub car park. Confident enough to queue up within touching distance of her at the Park and Ride bus stop. And once they'd arrived in Exeter, he'd faded into the background, allowing her to get quite a way ahead of him as they walked along the main street.

He'd missed her turning into the coffee shop, and it had given him a jolt to see her sitting in the window staring straight at him when he walked past. He thought he'd carried it off well. No nod of recognition, even though they'd travelled on the bus together. A few more steps, a casual consultation of his phone, and then a turn into the tiny alley from which he would be able to see her leaving the coffee shop.

Except she didn't leave. At least not by the front door. He was certain of that. He'd waited for ages. Just how long could she make one drink last? Maybe waiting for someone? Intending to make a day of it?

But when he'd strolled back along the street a while later, her seat was empty and she was nowhere to be seen. Nor was she on the obvious route back to the bus stop. He was fairly certain she was on the bus that was pulling away as he reached the stop. Certainly, by the time he returned to the Park and Ride, her car had gone.

He didn't bother to try to find her again at that point. After all, he knew exactly where she lived, she and that Scottish woman with the pink hair. It was a case of observation; getting to know Charlie Jones, her behaviour, her habits, her regular journeys. Far too soon to make a move.

But in case she had spotted him, maybe he'd get his brother to take on the surveillance side of things from now on. No, that wouldn't work. He was a much bigger man, and found it difficult to blend into the background. Plus he was such a man of action, he hated hanging around, just watching.

No, the best thing to do was to lie low for a while. There was no point in arousing her suspicions, and if she caught sight of him again, that was what would happen. And there were plenty of other things they could be getting on with. There was still a lot more preparation to do. There was that daughter of theirs, for a start. Now she'd be much easier to keep an eye on. Kids that age weren't aware of anything beyond their screens and their mates.

He took a deep breath and forced himself to relax. The plan was definitely coming together. And he'd waited all these years.

Their landlord's cat, a huge ginger tom with one eye and a damaged ear that spoke of an unsuccessful late-night fight, was sitting on the doorstep glaring at the man. He stooped and collected a handful of gravel from the path, but he didn't even need to pretend to throw it. The cat, having learned from experience, shot up and disappeared over the wall and down the side alley.

Congratulating himself on this minor victory, the man opened the front door. A smell of damp mixed with burnt toast assailed his nostrils and he pulled a face as he ran up the two flights of stairs to the second-floor flat. Ugh, he'd be glad when they could leave this place, this town, this country, and head back home to the wide open spaces and clean air he was used to. But the room was cheap, and so long as they paid on time, the landlord asked no questions and didn't seem to care who they were or what their business was.

The dingy attic room was empty, and the man looked around it with distaste. At one end, two single beds were tucked under the eaves. His was neatly made; the other was rumpled and covered in discarded shirts and socks.

At the other end of the room, where light struggled to filter through the dirt on the Velux windows, was a table and two chairs. Dirty crockery among piles of papers. His brother was such a pig. He looked forward to the time when they no longer had to live in such close proximity. Strolling across to the table, he idly glanced at the papers, as he began to gather the crockery together. What he saw made him curse softly to himself.

Not only was his brother a pig, but he was also an idiot. Photos of Charlie Jones, her family and friends lay scattered in full view, together with a map of Devon, with Coombesford circled in red. Newspaper cuttings of local murders in recent years overlapped with printed reports of international events from two decades before.

Everything they'd spent weeks collecting and collating, all exposed for anyone to see. Not that he really expected anyone to come into their temporary home of course, but that wasn't the point. It wasn't the expected they had to watch out for. And it was stupidity like this that could land them in prison, or even get them killed.

As he gathered all the papers together and returned

them to the hiding place they'd set up behind the rafters in the darkest corner of the room, he wondered for the first time whether having his brother with him was really an advantage. Would he be better off without him? And if the answer was yes, was there any way he could get rid of him without wrecking everything he'd prepared so far and everything he was planning to do?

But the more he thought about it, the more he realised it wouldn't work. The two of them made a good unit. He had the brains, the vision and the patience to see a plan through to the end. His brother was the muscle on the team. No subtlety, but no fear either. It was he who'd managed to dispose of the woman in Dublin – and the man in the leather jacket didn't need to know the details of what had happened. He just knew that if this plan was going to succeed, he couldn't do it alone.

But he also knew his brother wouldn't survive without him. And they were going to have sharp words about security – and good housekeeping – when he got back from wherever he was.

CHAPTER 3

"Oh sugar drops!" Annie walked out of the bathroom and threw her glasses down on the bed.

"What's up?" Annie knew Charlie was amused by her imaginative alternatives to swear words – a habit she'd adopted after they caught their daughter Suzy, while still a toddler, solemnly asking one of their friends what a very rude word meant, and realising where she'd picked it up from. But Annie assumed Charlie knew better than to laugh at her.

"I've left my book behind the bar! I took it over there this morning, thinking I was going to get a quiet moment or two before the lunchtime rush, and forgot to bring it back with me when we closed up."

"You could always read something else." Charlie pointed to the overflowing bookcase under the window. Like every other room in The Folly, their little upside-down house in the grounds of The Falls pub, they'd filled the space not taken up by bedroom furniture with more book storage.

But Annie sighed and shook her head. "No, I've got to finish this one. It's for tomorrow's book club, and you know how prickly Olga gets if anyone's failed to finish it."

"Would you like me to go and get it then?" Charlie almost managed to make her offer sound genuine, but Annie doubted if she really wanted to leave her warm and comfortable bed, and get dressed again.

"No, you're fine. I'll go." Annie pulled her dressing gown on over her Mickey Mouse pyjamas and tightened the belt around her tiny waist. "We've only got one couple staying over there tonight and they've been in bed for hours. I can go like this. I'll be in and out in no time." She pulled open the door and slipped into the hallway.

"Take a torch. The ground's a bit rough at the edge of the beer garden," Charlie called, as Annie reached up and took the Maglite off the hook behind the front door. She clicked on the hall light and let herself out into the garden.

It was dry and still in the darkness and despite a slight breeze, not uncomfortable. Stepping outside the circle of light radiating from the front door, Annie paused and looked up. The moon, little more than a hazy ball on the horizon, was eclipsed by the brilliance of the magnificent show above her head.

With little or no light pollution, the sky was filled with constellations. Some, like the Plough and Orion's Belt, were familiar to her. Others she was unable to put a name to. It was one of the best things about moving out of London and down to the southwest.

She was immediately transported back to summer nights on the Isle of Skye when her grandfather would take her down to the side of the loch and they would sit, with their feet dangling in the icy water, as he pointed out the stars to her.

Her eyes prickled with tears as she briefly mourned the loss of her greatest childhood influence and so much else from those days. Then shaking herself mentally, she remembered that she'd gained so much more than she'd lost when she'd thrown in her lot with Charlie Jones. And it had been her choice.

With the torch on, she swiftly crossed the beer garden

and the small patio leading to the rear of the pub.

When she reached the corner of the yard, she paused and cast a rueful look at the old shed in the corner. If she got her way, it was going to be converted into a one-bed annexe for The Falls. An extra room would be useful at busy times – profitable too. She'd wanted to get it done before the wedding but they were running out of time and Charlie was being so stubborn. And it wasn't as though she ever used that old motorbike these days. Annie resolved to have another go at changing Charlie's mind the next day. She continued on her way across the yard.

Slipping the key into the keyhole, she was surprised to feel no resistance. The back door was unlocked. Surely she hadn't left it open? No, it was Charlie who'd been the last to leave. She must have forgotten. That wasn't like her.

The corridor was lined with strip lighting and Annie knew it took a while to fully warm up. So she didn't bother switching it on; she just kept the torch on as she crossed to the bar door and slipped through. Now where had she left her book? She tutted as she realised her glasses were still lying on the bed in The Folly. Squinting, she found what she was looking for. Yes, there it was, on the shelf under the till.

The noise, when it came, was so slight, she wondered at first if she'd imagined it. But the rest of the building was so silent, it stood out more than it might have done during the day. A dull thud, followed by a gentle metallic rattle. Then she realised why it sounded so familiar. It happened every time she crossed the kitchen in too much of a hurry. An unwary toe hitting the shelving in the corner, making the hanging utensils swing.

Annie froze. The noise had definitely come from the kitchen. Was there someone in there? Maybe one of the guests had woken and come down for a drink. Unlikely. They had everything they needed in their room. And besides, they would surely have put the light on. She was pretty certain if there was someone else downstairs with her, they were up to no good.

She reached into her pocket for her phone, her first instinct being to call Charlie. But no, she'd left that on the bedside table. There was no help from that direction. Should she hide or confront whoever it was? She heard another faint scuffling. Maybe she'd be able to see what was going on from the restaurant.

She tiptoed across the bar and into the large dining area set out with tables and chairs, keeping her torch pointing towards the floor. Peering round the door into the corridor, she thought she could see shadows moving, wavering across the ceiling opposite the kitchen. But without her glasses she couldn't be certain.

Suddenly there was a low growl and the scratching of claws on slate. A small ball of fur flew out of the kitchen and came hurtling down the corridor towards her, skidding to a stop only when it collided with her legs.

"Bertie! For goodness sake. What were you doing in there?" Annie bent down and picked up the squirming Jack Russell, rubbing her face against his silky ears, waiting for her heart to stop racing and her breathing to return to normal. "You gave me a real fright."

Bertie had been living with them ever since his previous owner had been 'detained at His Majesty's pleasure' as the saying goes. Annie had been dead set against taking on a pet on top of everything else going on in their busy lives. But as Charlie and Suzy had pointed out, it was their fault the dog was homeless. And now Annie was as fond of him as the rest of the family, although she insisted he slept in the pub after ejecting him from their bed multiple times in the first week.

His night crate was in the utility room, next to the boiler, and usually he went there quite happily each evening when they locked up, and remained there until they let him out the next morning. Charlie must have forgotten to shut him in that night, as well as leaving the back door unlocked. What was she playing at?

Annie walked down the corridor to the utility room, shut Bertie in his crate and made sure the door was properly closed. As she did so, she was certain she heard another quiet sound behind her. Turning, she ran up the corridor and pushed open the back door. All was still and silent. She quickly returned to pick up her book, locked the back door and hurried across the garden to The Folly.

She couldn't shake off the feeling she'd not been alone in the pub. Maybe she'd get Charlie to come back with her and have a final check on the place, to be sure.

But Charlie was already asleep and Annie didn't want to disturb her. She was obviously exhausted, which could explain why she'd forgotten to lock up properly. And with all the wedding preparations going on, it wouldn't do to give her something else to worry about.

Telling herself she was just imagining things, Annie climbed into bed and waited for sleep to claim her too.

CHAPTER 4

They'd been sitting in this dingy pub in the back streets of Bristol for hours. The man in the leather jacket's first pint was sitting in front of him barely half drunk, and he'd spent most of the evening drinking soda water. He'd caught the landlady looking at him askance a couple of times, but his brother had been drinking alcohol steadily since they arrived, enough to stop them from being thrown out.

It was about as far from the fancy wine bars he was used to at home as you could imagine. The low ceiling was still stained brown with an accumulation of nicotine, nearly twenty years after the smoking ban had been introduced. Wooden beams and benches around the walls were made of blackened oak. The chair seats were a faded green tapestry marred by goodness knows what spillages over the years. And there was carpet to match.

In one corner, a silent TV screen showed a continual diet of quiz shows, the youthful faces of the celebrity contestants revealing the age of the programmes themselves. In the other corner a couple of one-armed bandits were separating the punters from their money. It was a dive. It was perfect.

It had been quiet when they'd first got there but as the evening wore on and the offices and shops all closed down for the night, the place slowly filled up. The brothers knew exactly what they were looking for; someone on their own, preferably out of work or, better still, homeless. Certainly down on their luck. Willing to take a few risks for a cash bonus, without asking questions. They'd identified a couple of targets, watched them for a while then rejected them.

One had arrived on his own, placed his order without an unnecessary word or a smile for the bar staff and spent an hour or so reading the newspaper while nursing a single drink. He looked unkempt and in the time they watched him, he didn't take out a phone to check the screen once. Unlike most of the clientele. But as the brothers were about to approach him and try to start up a conversation, the doors flew open and a noisy group of friends arrived, surrounding him and clamouring for his attention. Definitely not a loner, that one.

Another shuffled in mid-evening. Obviously short of money, he counted out enough small denomination coins for a half pint, and took it to the end of the bar. But once that was finished, he gradually worked his way through a group of apparent regulars, cadging drinks from each one in turn and growing more garrulous by the minute. That was the last thing they needed. Someone who was unable to guard his mouth after a few drinks.

But finally, their patience was rewarded. A thin-faced youth, possibly in his early twenties, slipped into the bar around nine-thirty. He smiled and raised an eyebrow at the landlady who acknowledged his presence with a slight nod. Instead of going to the bar and ordering a drink, he wandered over to one of the noisier tables and started collecting empty glasses. After depositing them at one end of the bar, he set off for one of the other tables.

Over the next half hour, he made two full circuits of the pub before exchanging his final load of empties for a half pint for which he made no payment and which he drank, in a corner, talking to no-one.

As they watched, the performance was repeated twice more before time was called and everyone started heading home. The young man collected the final glasses and handed them across the bar then disappeared in the direction of the gents. The brothers rose to leave.

"Good little worker you've got there," the man in the leather jacket said to the landlady as they passed the bar.

"Who, young Stana? He's not bad. Bit unreliable though. Only turns up when he feels like it." She grinned as she wrung out one of the bar cloths. "But he's cheap, doesn't expect paying. So I mustn't grumble."

"Local lad, is he?"

"Shouldn't think so. His English isn't very good." She shrugged. "But he doesn't need to say much when he's only collecting glasses."

Once outside the door, the brothers crossed the road, stepping into the shadows of a shop doorway. The bulb on the nearest street light was broken. They could see the pub perfectly well but were themselves fully hidden.

It wasn't long before the pub door opened one more time and the young man came out. He turned up the collar of his shirt against the wind and walked along the road that led to the suburbs.

"He won't live far from here," said the man in the leather jacket. "He'd pick a reasonably close pub to 'work' in."

He pulled the car keys out of his pocket and handed them to his brother. "You fetch the car but don't get too close. We don't want to spook him. I want to see where he lives, make sure he's on his own. I'll follow him on foot and you can join me when we get to his place." He paused, remembering how much his brother had been drinking. But he knew his capacity for alcohol was as huge as his frame. And it had never affected his driving before. "Just keep your speed down and don't do anything to attract attention." Then he set off after their young quarry.

He'd been right in his assumption that Stana would live near to the pub. After less than five minutes, he saw the young man turn left into a narrow side road. Hurrying to catch up with him, he was just in time to see him climb the steps of a rundown hotel, more of a hostel really. Through the open door, he saw Stana cross the empty foyer and stretch over the desk to pull a key off the peg labelled with a large 5.

Crossing to the other side of the road, the man watched the windows on the second floor. A light came on and Stana appeared at the window, pulling the cheap curtaining materials across to shut out the night.

As he waved to his brother, who was just edging the Renault around the corner, the man in the leather jacket was as sure as he could be that they'd found what they needed. Yes, they would be paying young Stana a visit any day now and making him a very tempting offer.

CHAPTER 5: MAY 2024

Sitting on the back seat of the Renault, Stana closed his eyes and tried to concentrate on the money they'd promised him. More money than he'd ever had. Enough to pay his rent at that lousy hostel for three years. Or better still, enough money to let him find somewhere nicer to live. Maybe improve his English, get some training, a decent job. Finally start getting his life together. Yes, the money was definitely what he needed to concentrate on.

When the man in the leather jacket had knocked on his door and walked straight into his room just before midnight the previous week, he'd panicked. No-one ever came to visit him, especially not at that time of night. The man's smile had helped to ease some of his fears. Some, but not all.

He'd sat on the rickety old armchair with his legs crossed, looking completely at ease, while Stana had perched on the edge of the bed. He was closer to the door than his visitor, but somehow Stana knew that if he made a run for it, he wouldn't get very far.

And then the man in the leather jacket had spoken to him in his own language. "You seem like a nice lad. Hardworking and honest." Stana must have looked confused because the man went on. "We've been watching you work. Down at the pub. The landlady seems to rate you." He'd paused and pulled a face. "But not enough to pay you a decent wage for what you do, am I right?"

Stana had nodded, then shaken his head, unsure how to answer the implied question. But the man was talking again. "I've got a little job I need some help with. And you look like the sort of person who'd be perfect for it. It's nothing difficult. A spot of surveillance work."

"But I don't have no training—"

"That's not going to be a problem. All I want you to do is follow someone for me. I'll tell you where and when. You only need to keep an eye on them and tell me what they do."

"I'm not very good at writing—"

"You don't need to write anything down. We can meet up when you're finished and you can tell me everything you saw."

"And that's it? Follow someone and tell you what they do?"

"Exactly."

"Why?"

"What do you mean, why?"

"Why do you need me to do this? Why can't you do it yourself?"

"The person in question knows me, Stana. It's a friend of mine. I'm planning a little surprise for her and if she sees me, it'll spoil the surprise."

The man in the leather jacket went on to name a sum so huge that it blew all other possible questions out of Stana's mind and he'd agreed straight away.

Now, sitting in this car parked outside Bristol Temple Meads station, those questions were clamouring for space in his head. Was there anything illegal about what he was doing? Was he in any danger? What would happen if the person realised he was following her?

But he was too scared to ask the questions. Not only

because the man in the leather jacket was being so nice to him and seemed to be relying on him. Nor because he'd already spent the advance he'd been given on his fees. But also because of the very large man sitting in the driver's seat. A man of very few words but a huge presence. So Stana closed his eyes and thought of the money once more, until a voice broke into his thoughts and brought him back to reality.

"Okay, Stana, there she is." The man in the leather jacket pointed to a taxi, pulling up outside the station. As they watched, a tall middle-aged woman got out of the back seat and paid the driver with a laugh and a joke. She looked fit for her age, casually dressed and with long dark hair tied back into a ponytail. "Right, here's your ticket. Tell me again what you're going to do."

"I'm going to make my way to platform 12 and wait for the 16:45 to Penzance. I'm going to make sure I can see her, but not get too close. When we get on the train, I'm going to find a seat in the same carriage as her, where I can see her. And I'm going to watch her, see whether she talks to anyone and so on. When she gets off at Newton Abbot, I'm going to follow her again and see who meets her. Then I'm going to get the next train back here and wait for you to contact me for my report."

It was the most he'd ever said in this man's presence so far and at the end of the speech he found himself sweating and panting as though he'd run a race.

"Good man." The man in the leather jacket nodded at him. "Right, off you go. The train's due in fifteen minutes. Oh, and take this bottle of water with you. If you get thirsty on the train, you won't have to leave your seat and risk missing anything."

Stana grabbed the bottle, jumped out of the car and without looking back, made his way into the station. He panicked slightly when he realised he'd lost sight of the woman, but made himself walk to the barrier and slip his ticket in the machine. Once down on the platform, he was relieved to spot her immediately.

She was carrying a large cardboard box, cradling it in her arms as though it contained the Crown Jewels. Stana leaned against the wall and watched her through half-closed eyes. He gave a little giggle. He'd always fancied himself as a private eye.

The train arrived on time and Stana watched the woman enter carriage B. He could see there were plenty of free seats in there, so he let a few people get on before him and then followed them into the carriage. The woman had settled herself in the window seat at a table for four. Stana positioned himself on an aisle seat, two rows down, and began his assignment.

By the time they reached Tiverton Parkway, his water bottle was empty. The water had tasted of lemon and ginger, with a hint of almonds in the background. When they reached Exeter, not only was his bladder bursting, he was also experiencing urgent turmoil in his guts. The man in the leather jacket had told him to stay put. But it wouldn't hurt to nip to the toilet. He'd be back in a couple of minutes. No-one would know. And nothing was going to happen in that short time, surely.

As soon as the train left Exeter St David's station he jumped to his feet and hurried to the end of the carriage.

CHAPTER 6

The 18:09 train to Penzance pulled out of Newton Abbot station exactly on time. Train conductor Sid Norfolk looked at the clock in his tiny cubbyhole and allowed himself a small smile of satisfaction. They'd be in Plymouth in just over half an hour. His shift finished there, and he'd be gone. Shirley had promised him a special meal for his dinner, seeing as how it was his birthday, and he didn't want to miss that. Smashing cook, was his Shirley. Not bad at other things too, he mused with a throb of anticipation.

The sound of running feet, followed by a bang on his door, pulled him out of his daydream.

"Quick, come quick. Someone's collapsed in the toilet." The young woman standing outside his cubbyhole was smartly dressed. Looked like a businesswoman on her way home from a day of meetings in Birmingham. He'd spotted her in First Class when he'd checked tickets. She'd been tapping away at her laptop and barely glanced up as she waved her ticket in front of him. But now she was really looking at him.

And she wasn't as immaculately turned out as previously either. There was a tear in one of her tights and her hair looked like she'd been running her fingers through it. She reached forward and pulled on his arm. "Please, come quickly."

She turned and fled back along the corridor and hit the button to open the sliding door.

Sid followed her through the First Class carriage, aware of curious eyes following his back. But all such thoughts left him as he reached the toilet cubicle. The woman pressed the button, and the circular door swung open.

"Okay, madam, thank you for calling me. You've been very helpful. I'll take it from here. You go back to your seat."

Sid watched the woman hurry away before turning his gaze back on the scene in front of him. He'd got some training in first aid. He'd better check if there was anything immediate he could do.

"Right, sonny, let's see what's wrong, shall we?" He stooped next to the prone body then grabbed a shoulder and pulled the motionless male onto his back. Sid gasped when he caught sight of a dark pool of liquid seeping from the man's chest.

The young man spreadeagled on the floor looked to be in his early twenties. His denim jeans were old and torn at the knees. His tee-shirt, extolling the virtues of a 1990s punk band, was very grubby, although the dirt was mostly hidden beneath the large spreading bloodstain.

Sid gently placed two fingertips below the man's stubbly chin. He wasn't surprised to find no pulse at all. He reached for his radio and called the driver.

"Rhonda, we've got an incident in the toilet outside the First Class carriage. This train isn't going further than Plymouth, I am afraid, and neither, I suspect, is anyone on board. I'll radio the station and warn the passengers there's going to be a delay. And I'll warn Totnes we won't be stopping there today."

After alerting his bosses there was a body on board and telling them to have the British Transport Police waiting when they arrived in Plymouth, Sid taped an out-of-order notice on the cubicle and locked the door. He headed back to his cubbyhole to check the correct wording for informing passengers of an emergency on the train. He also reminded himself there was another important call needed. He wasn't going to be eating Shirley's cooking or enjoying her other home comforts any time soon, that was for sure.

Sighing, Sid pressed the button on the intercom and made the announcement that would ruin everyone's evening.

CHAPTER 7

Most of the passengers on the much-delayed train were just relieved to be home at last. Many of them didn't give the deceased young man another thought once they'd finished complaining to their nearest and dearest about their terrible experience on the bloody rail service and the stupidity of someone who could get themselves killed on a busy Saturday evening train.

But for at least two of the passengers, there was a long sleepless night ahead.

***

The woman who originally found what she later realised was a crime scene and alerted that conductor, Sid, had never seen a dead body before. Nor had she ever had anything to do with the police.

Once the train arrived in Plymouth, there was so much going on, what with having to tell her side of the story not once but twice to different young police officers, while avoiding all the questions from her fellow passengers whenever they were left on their own for a few minutes, that she'd not had time to process the sight that had met her when she opened the toilet door.

Now, as she lay in her lonely bed in her lonely

apartment just outside Redruth, the memory of that sight came back to her, and she quietly sobbed into the darkness.

***

And for the killer, there was a lot of soul-searching and unanswered questions buzzing around, making sleep impossible. These were all questions the man in the leather jacket would ask and would expect answers for. And he wasn't the sort of person to cross. In fact no-one ever did that more than once.

Would the bundle of soiled clothing thrown out of the window between Exeter St David's and Newton Abbot lie undiscovered long enough for the elements to destroy any forensic evidence? Better still, would it be washed out to sea? Would the hidden knife be discovered and the planted DNA do its job satisfactorily? Would the significance of the key ring fob be recognised?

And most importantly, had the young man died instantly, as intended, or had he remained conscious long enough to give any information to that woman? It had been such a shock meeting her in the corridor just before they'd pulled into Newton Abbot. Maybe a visit to Redruth was in order.

It had been an easy enough task to find out her address while they were all stuck on the train. So many people had been asking her questions, she'd seemed like a hunted puppy sitting in the corner of the compartment. A friendly word, an entreaty to everyone to leave her alone, and then a few gentle words of encouragement were all it had taken. It had been a huge risk, of course, but she'd seemed so grateful for someone to look after her and didn't seem to connect her rescuer with the crime scene at all.

But now, in the quiet of the night, what if something the young man had said gave the game away? Or what if she remembered seeing him in the corridor? Yes, on reflection, it looked as though a quick trip down to Redruth was the best option. Not part of the original plan;

and maybe unnecessary. But it was always better to take precautions.

When the man in the leather jacket asked for a report, as he would before very long, it was imperative all the answers given were accurate. Otherwise, there would be consequences. And the killer had no intention of ending up as the next victim. No, not at all.

CHAPTER 8

Dealing with the aftermath of a murder was always a difficult task for the police. But when the crime scene is a moving train and the culprit could be any one of the three hundred-plus people on board, not to mention the people alighting at the earlier stations, that made the task so much harder.

Once the British Transport Police had been alerted to the situation, they'd instructed the control room to slow the train, so they had a chance to get to Plymouth station before it did. On arrival, the entire train was designated a crime scene and taken out of service. Only one door was unlocked, and two officers were stationed there to control all entry and exit, while two of their colleagues began the long task of interviewing everyone.

It was therefore a couple of hours before all the details had been taken and the last passenger was allowed to continue their journey. No-one had admitted to seeing anything suspicious, although several people reported noticing the young man board the train at Bristol Temple Meads.

Several said they thought he was alone, but one person reported watching a short altercation between the man and a middle-aged woman on the platform in Bristol while the train was pulling into the station. They thought the two then boarded the train together.

As the body was being transferred to the trolley for removal to the mortuary van, one of the scene of crime officers spotted something lying on the floor where the young man had fallen. It was the figure of a tiny green alien with huge round black eyes, wide spreading pointed ears and a cream space suit. A metal ring affixed to the head suggested it was the fob from a key ring. But what did a model of Baby Yoda have to tell them about the crime committed there?

Once the body had been dispatched to the mortuary, the scene of crime officers began the huge task of examining all six carriages, starting at either end and moving towards the toilet compartment where the body had been discovered. There was a plethora of fingerprints and other DNA but it was doubtful if it would tell them very much.

They photographed the area around the seat where the murder victim had been sitting, and checked for unclaimed luggage, but found none. As they headed off for the night, it was clear that their task was going to be long and probably frustratingly unproductive.

***

On the Sunday morning, the on-duty pathologist began work. The young man had no identity on him, not even a wallet or a ticket for the journey he was taking when he was killed. His clothes were cheap, poor quality, and probably bought off a market stall or in a charity shop. His teeth were in a bad way and it was unlikely anyone would be able to identify him via dental records.

He'd been stabbed in the chest, although there was no sign of the murder weapon.

The officers detailed to identify the victim ran the dead man's fingerprints through the system. There was no match at the National Crime Agency. Maybe he was a foreigner? Possibly a migrant. That meant a call to Interpol and Europol. But the chances of finding anyone at their desks on a Sunday morning were slim, so that would have to wait until the next day.

Turning his attention to the other samples collected from the scene, the pathologist processed the fingerprints taken from the tiny plastic Baby Yoda. There was a partial print only, and that was not the dead man's. It was, however, registered in the Police National Computer database. One Charlotte Jones.

Not on file because of a criminal record, but due to her former role as a member of MI6, the Secret Service. Now that was an interesting piece of information to follow up. Just as well, since, as expected, all the other DNA samples spoke of numerous people being present in the area, although not necessarily at the time of the murder.

With nothing else to go on, the police pulled up the CCTV footage from Bristol Temple Meads around the time the train had passed through there. They quickly found a reasonable shot of the young man waiting to board the train. Copies were sent to all the local newspapers and television stations in the southwest; the picture was also posted on social media.

After that, it was pretty much a waiting game. With no identification of the murder victim and no witnesses to the crime, there was nothing for the police to go on.

CHAPTER 9

"Major Crime Investigation Team, Exeter. DS Smith speaking. Can I help you?"

"Smithie, how's it going? Still sneaking off for cooked breakfasts when the wife's not looking?"

"Sorry, who is this?" Derek Smith had a good idea who his first Monday morning call was from but wasn't going to give her the satisfaction of admitting that.

"Come on, Smithie, surely you recognise my dulcet tones. It's not that long since we pounded the streets of Bournemouth together."

"DS Laura Manning. I thought the voice was familiar. How are you?"

"Oh, you know. Same old, same old."

"Still based on the south coast, are you?"

"No, actually, I'm a lot closer to home than that. Plymouth. Transferred to the British Transport Police a couple of years back." There was a pause then he could hear the glee in her voice as she went on. "And it's DI Manning these days."

"So you did beat me in the end! You always said you would. Well done, you." He hoped his voice sounded more sincere than he felt.

"Thanks. But I didn't call just to rub your nose in it. We've got an odd case. One I'm hoping you can help us with."

"Go on."

"We had a stabbing at the weekend – on the Penzance train."

"Yes, I heard about it. What's it got to do with us?"

"There's someone up in your neck of the woods whose name's come up in connection with the case. I wondered if you could get someone to have a shufti. It's probably nothing, and it would save us a journey."

"Sounds fair enough. Who's the party in question?"

"Some woman called Jones, Charlotte Jones. Lives in a place called The Falls in Coombesford? I guess it's a local pub."

"That's right. It's a pub with rooms."

"Oh, you know it, do you? Have you come across this Ms Jones then?"

"Charlie? Yes, I know her quite well. I've never heard her called Charlotte before. She's helped us on a couple of cases in the past few years. Been quite useful, she has. Although I'd never tell her that to her face, of course."

"Apparently she's ex Secret Service. Retired back in 2006. That's why she was on the database."

"Really? She kept that quiet – but I guess she would, wouldn't she? So what exactly do you want us to ask her?" There was a long pause. "Laura, are you there?"

"Yes, still here. I was just wondering – if she's a friend of yours – whether we should come up and do it ourselves."

"Now, steady on. I said I knew her. I didn't say she was a friend. But I'll take my DC with me when I go and talk to her. She can act as an independent witness, if you think it's important. What's Charlie's connection to the case anyway?"

"We think she might have been at the crime scene. We've got her DNA placing her there. She could have been a witness. Or even involved in the incident."

"What, Charlie? No. I don't believe it. There must be some other logical explanation. It's a train, for goodness sake. There must have been thousands of people's DNA at the scene. I doubt they get thoroughly cleaned that often." He paused and shrugged. "But we'll go and see her and ask. I'll give you a ring later on. What time do you go off shift?"

"Three pm. Oh, and there's one other thing. We found part of a key ring at the scene. It's a tiny model of Baby Yoda. Off the telly. Don't mention it to anyone at the moment, but if you get a chance, have a look at her keys, will you? Thanks, Smithie. I owe you one. Just let me know if there's anything I can do for you in return."

You could start by calling me Derek instead of Smithie, he thought, as he put down the phone. Derek Smith had been very much one of the lads when he and Laura Manning had started out together. But that was years ago, and as someone who was hoping to make it up the next rung of the ladder himself in the near future, he was starting to think about his dignity and demanding a bit of respect from his colleagues.

"So, what do you think, Sarge?" Detective Constable Joanne Wellman said, as she turned the car onto the A38 and headed south towards Coombesford. "Could Charlie have been involved in this stabbing?"

"I shouldn't think so for one moment, Jo. There has to be a perfectly good explanation. I've never known Charlie Jones to show the slightest hint of violence."

"I guess you've known her longer than I have." His colleague's voice held a heavy level of scepticism. "But didn't DS Manning say she was some sort of undercover agent?"

"Yes, that was news to me, I must admit. But it was a long time ago. Before she came anywhere near Devon. She used to be in the Secret Service; MI6 apparently."

"Doesn't that make her a trained killer?"

"Well, yes, I suppose that's true in theory. But again, only in self-defence."

"Maybe she's still undercover? Maybe the pub's just an elaborate front?"

"What? And Annie and Suzy are part of her cover story? Come on, Joanne, you've been reading far too many spy novels. Anyway," he continued, as Joanne left the bypass and headed down the narrow road towards the village, "we'll know in a few minutes."

They pulled into the car park of The Falls and stopped close to the door. It was mid-morning and there were no other vehicles around. "Good, we should be able to have a chat with Charlie before the lunchtime rush. I'm sure we can sort all this out quite quickly."

CHAPTER 10

Charlie Jones was standing behind the bar, stacking clean glasses on the shelves when the two detectives walked in. Her face lit up in a warm smile, convincing Derek Smith, if indeed he'd needed convincing, that the pub owner had nothing to hide.

"Detective Sergeant Smith, how lovely to see you, and you too, Detective Constable Wellman. What brings you out this way? The restaurant's not open yet, I'm afraid, but if you want an early lunch, I'm sure Annie will be able to put something together for you."

Derek Smith checked the time on the huge backwards clock behind the bar and nodded. "Thanks, Charlie, we may well take you up on that. But we need a word first, if that's okay."

"Sure, what can I do for you?" Charlie winked. "Always glad to help the boys and girls in blue – even the ones out of uniform. Got another murder you want our help to solve?"

"It's funny you should mention that, Charlie. It is a murder we want to ask you about, but not around here."

"Oh?"

"Yes, it's about the stabbing on the Penzance train at

the weekend?"

Charlie's grin faded immediately. "Stabbing? What stabbing?"

"It was around six on Saturday evening. They think it happened sometime between the train leaving Exeter St David's and arriving at Newton Abbot."

"Good grief. That's terrible." She paused. "Wait a minute. Six o'clock on Saturday evening. That sounds like it might have been the train I was on."

"I think it probably was. I'm surprised you hadn't heard about it. It's been all over social media."

"We try to restrict our screen time at the weekend." She cocked her head in the direction of the house she shared with the rest of her family. "We're trying to set a good example to our resident internet junkie." Charlie stacked the final glass on the shelf and gave her full attention to the two detectives. "So what do you want from me?"

"You see, Charlie, we had a call from the team down in Plymouth. They seem to think you might have been at the scene, and might have witnessed something." DC Wellman consulted her notes. "The train left Exeter at 17:49 and arrived in Newton Abbot just before 18:10."

"Yes, that definitely sounds like my train. I got on at Bristol Temple Meads at a quarter to five and we reached Newton Abbot at ten past six. But I don't think I saw anything that would help with the enquiries. Who was it who got stabbed?"

"I'm afraid we don't know the identity of the victim as yet." DS Smith reassessed his approach to the situation. He'd been convinced there was no way Charlie could have been involved. But if she was on the train at the time the murder took place, which it appeared she was, then he had to take this much more seriously.

Glancing at DC Wellman to make sure she was taking notes, he began again. "Why don't you talk me through your journey, Charlie. Maybe start with why you were on the train."

"I had to go up to Bristol to collect a sculpture I'd had commissioned as a wedding present for Annie." Charlie broke off and gave a shy smile. "You do know we're getting married on Saturday, don't you?" The DS nodded and Charlie continued. "You know how horrendous it can be, finding parking in Bristol, especially at the weekend. The sculpture was only light, so I decided to let the train take the strain, as the saying goes. I parked the car in Newton Abbot, in the little car park round the back of Queen Street, took the quarter past eleven train up to Bristol, grabbed a bite to eat, collected the sculpture and got the quarter to five train from Bristol back to Newton Abbot."

Derek Smith pulled his phone from his pocket and showed Charlie a picture of the stabbing victim. "Any chance you know this young man, or saw him on the train?"

Charlie shook her head. "Never saw him."

"Which carriage did you travel in?"

"The second one. B, I think it was. I remember it was next to First Class."

"And did you leave your seat at any time?"

"I don't think so." Charlie paused and clicked her fingers. "No, wait, I did go down to the refreshment carriage to grab a coffee. Just as we left Tiverton. I reckoned I had time to let it get cold enough to drink before we got to Newton Abbot."

"Okay, Charlie. We'll leave it at that." As the DS put away the phone, he glanced at the shelves at the back of the bar. Peeping out from behind one of the bottles, he spied a small, rotund, blue and white robot. Further down the row was a gold-coloured metal man. He pointed to the models. "Who's the Star Wars fan?"

Charlie laughed. "That would be Annie. And Suzy, too, these days. They're still trying to convert me. Suzy even put a Baby Yoda keyring in the Christmas stocking she made for me last year." Charlie turned to look behind her. "Hang on, I've got it here. It's on the spare keys for the bar."

She picked up a large bunch of keys and riffled through them. "That's strange. It's gone. I must have lost it somewhere. How annoying. I'll have to get hold of another one before Suzy realises it's missing." Charlie put the keys back on the hook. "Right, well, if that's all you wanted to ask me, why don't we go through to the kitchen and you can say hello to Annie. You can tell her what you want for lunch at the same time."

As Charlie led the way through the door and down the corridor towards the kitchen, DC Wellman looked at her sergeant and raised one elegant eyebrow. Derek Smith shrugged and pulled a face. He didn't want to suspect Charlie of being involved in a crime of this nature, but she'd been quite happy to admit she was on the same train. And the toy found at the scene matched the one missing off her key ring.

Derek decided he'd simply report back to DI Manning in Plymouth and leave her to proceed as she wished. He was still convinced there was a logical explanation for all this.

In the kitchen, Annie McLeod was her usual welcoming self, pushing her bright pink fringe out of her eyes and waving to the two detectives from her position in front of the stove.

"Wow, what a lot of knives." DC Wellman was looking at the row of wooden blocks lined up against the wall. "How do you keep track of them all?"

"We don't," Annie said with a puzzled look. "We use so many during the day, we never seem to have enough. And Charlie keeps pinching them to cut lemons in the bar. Every so often, we invest in another rack of them. To be honest, I've lost track of how many we have in total. They're a bit pricey, but they're certainly the best. Decent knives are a cook's best friend, you know."

"I'm sure they are." DC Wellman looked pointedly at her sergeant. "I'm sure they are."

CHAPTER 11: JUNE 2024

Detective Inspector Laura Manning sat at her desk and ran the video footage one more time. It showed a tall casually dressed middle-aged woman with long dark hair standing on platform 12, holding a large, but apparently light, parcel. The display on the station announcement board behind her showed the time as 16:35 and the next train as the 16:45 to Penzance.

The woman was joined by a slight man in torn jeans and a grubby tee-shirt. He appeared to be asking her for something, but without success, as she shook her head and turned away. DI Manning wondered if he was begging. He certainly looked to be down on his luck. But without sound, and in the absence of any witnesses close enough to hear, they'd probably never know.

What was clear was that the woman wasn't interested in talking to the young man. At one point, he reached out and touched her arm, only for her to angrily shake off his hand. An altercation resulted, which looked to become quite heated as the train arrived at the platform.

The young man jerked open the door of the nearest carriage and jumped up onto the train. DI Manning could see from the sign on the side of the train that he'd entered the First Class compartment. Somehow, she very much doubted he'd have a ticket for First Class, or any ticket at all, for that matter. Certainly, there was none found on the body when the scene of crime officers had searched it. The next minute, she saw him leave the First Class carriage and move to the standard class next door.

The woman hesitated and looked from one end of the platform to the other, before jumping on the train behind the young man and pulling the door closed. Once the train started moving, DS Manning stopped the video and reran it from the beginning. She paused it at the point where both people were standing so their faces were fully visible.

The young man was very definitely their victim, currently lying in the Plymouth mortuary. Following the widespread coverage the previous weekend, they now had a first name for the young man: Stana. This had come via a phone call from a pub landlady in Bristol who'd recognised the young man as an occasional helper of hers. But she'd been unable to provide any further information. Local police were following up on that at the moment, but the general consensus was that he was probably in the country illegally.

More importantly, after long consideration and comparison with photos provided by MI6 and the Major Crime Investigation Team in Exeter, DI Manning was ninety-eight per cent convinced the middle-aged woman was Charlotte Jones.

The woman who admitted being on the train, but was adamant she'd never seen the young man. But whose DNA was at the scene of the crime, and whose fingerprints were found not only on the toy discovered under the victim but also on the recently discovered murder weapon.

DI Manning picked up her phone and called DS Derek Smith in Exeter. "Smithie, it's Laura Manning. I've been looking at a video someone took on their phone at Bristol Temple Meads station last Saturday. We've got our chap getting on there. And we've also got someone who looks very much like your friend Charlie not only getting on at the same time as him, but also getting into a bit of a verbal scrap with him on the platform."

"But she said she didn't see him. That doesn't sound too good, does it? What do you want to do, Laura?"

"I think we have to get Ms Jones in for a more formal interview. It would appear she lied to us about not seeing this guy. At the very least, we need an explanation for that." She paused. "And there's another thing, Derek. I told you her DNA was at the scene? Well, the SOCOs did another search of the train and found the knife hidden inside one of the seats. It's got the victim's blood on it and a couple of partial fingerprints."

"Charlie's?"

"Got it in one. So how do you want to play this? Do you want to bring her in, or are you happy for me to come and do it? I need to be there for the interview anyway."

"I'm happy for you to take the lead." He paused. "The only thing is, Laura, Charlie's getting married today, right about now in fact. The place is full of their friends and family. Do we really have to ruin her big day?"

"I know it seems harsh, but we're talking about murder here. Do you know if they're planning a honeymoon?"

"Ah yes, good point. I believe they're taking a trip to Latin America. Leaving tomorrow morning, I think Charlie said."

"There you are then. We don't have a choice. We need to bring her in. But let's leave it until this evening. No point disrupting the wedding itself."

CHAPTER 12

Charlie Jones gave a deep sigh of satisfaction as she stood at the bottom of the slope by the waterfall and gazed at her partner of more than twenty years – now her wife. Annie's bright pink hair matched her dress and contrasted beautifully with the blossoms of gypsophila and honeysuckle in her bouquet and woven into a circlet around her head.

Suzy had worked wonders with the floristry. In fact their daughter, having begged to be given the role of wedding planner, had taken all her duties very seriously indeed. Every detail of the day had been planned and organised to the nth degree, much to the amusement of close friends and family.

And to give credit where it was due, the day had gone off without a hitch. Even the weather was perfect.

Neither Charlie nor Annie had any religious beliefs, so they'd decided against holding the wedding in Coombesford Church, tempting as it was to take up the Rev Rosemary's offer to officiate. Instead, they turned to Olga Mountjoy.

Three years after the death of her husband, the Ukrainian woman was well settled into her role of lady of the manor, and having trained as a secular celebrant, was much in demand at less traditional weddings, funerals and other special occasions in the area.

Having started the day with a short legal ceremony in Exeter Registry Office, Charlie and Annie had made their way to the grounds of Mountjoy Manor.

Watched by a small crowd of close friends and family, the couple had publicly pledged themselves to one another with vows they had written themselves. Afterwards, Olga had switched roles from officiating celebrant to gracious hostess and laid on an elegant wedding breakfast. There was much chatter and laughter among the group which included Charlie's sister Suzanne, who'd travelled from Kent with her husband, Steve. Suzanne Ford-Jones was representing their parents, neither of whom was well enough to travel from their retirement home in Wales.

Suzanne seemed to greatly enjoy the role of not only sister to one of the brides, but more importantly, aunt and chief assistant to the wedding planner and maid of honour. Annie, who was estranged from her own family, was delighted to share her day with these people she'd considered family for so many years already.

With her aunt's help, Suzy had managed to pull off some wonderful surprises for the couple in the form of guests who'd arrived unexpectedly in the past few days. Friends and colleagues from their time in Africa, South America and the Former Soviet Union region.

And of course, no Jones sisters celebration would be complete without their good friend Francine Matheson who arrived from France, with not only her husband, Anton, but also his sister Lydia, who they'd rescued during a desperate car chase through the Russian and Ukrainian night so many years before.

Once the food was finished and the speeches delivered, everyone had retired to their rooms for a brief rest before reassembling in the garden of The Falls for an open house. For once, neither Charlie nor Annie was allowed anywhere near the kitchen or behind the bar. The food was in the hands of Esther Steele from Steele Farm and Celia Richardson from Cosy Corner Café, while Celia's husband Roger was pouring the drinks, together with friend and former detective Rohan Banerjee.

The garden was packed; it seemed as though everyone in the village – and many from elsewhere as well – wanted to congratulate the popular couple on finally tying the knot. Local musicians played in the background and there was even a small dance floor in one corner for those who wanted to strut their stuff.

As the sun started to sink below Chudleigh Rocks in the distance, Charlie and Annie strolled hand in hand along the side of the stream, reliving the day and some of the highlights.

"Charlie, where are you?" they heard Suzanne call from the top of the slope leading down from the beer garden. "Can you come up here, please. There's someone to see you." She sounded serious, but there'd been so many surprises so far, she could have been acting.

"I wonder what she's going to spring on us this time," Charlie said, as the couple reached the top of the hill. Then she grinned when she saw who was standing next to her sister. "Why, if it isn't our two favourite detectives. What a pleasure to see you – for the second time in less than a week. I do hope you're off duty and can have a drink with us."

But DS Derek Smith didn't return Charlie's cheery greeting. Nor did he even crack a smile.

Suzanne was shaking her head at her sister. She glanced across at a dumpy-looking woman standing next to DS Smith. Charlie had never seen her before and held out her hand to introduce herself.

The stranger ignored Charlie's outstretched hand. "I'm DI Manning from the British Transport Police." She nodded to DC Wellman who stepped forward with an apologetic look on her face. "Charlotte Jones, I am arresting you on suspicion of murder…"

PART 2

CHAPTER 13

Suzanne Jones flopped down onto the padded bench running under some of the windows in the bar of The Falls. She kicked off her shoes and wriggled her toes to get the circulation back into them. How had she allowed herself to be persuaded into high heels? And by Charlie of all people. Charlie! Suzanne's stomach flipped as she thought back over the events of the past few hours.

When DS Smith and DC Wellman, accompanied by DI Manning from the British Transport Police, had arrived at The Falls just after six o'clock, Suzanne had assumed they were coming to wish the happy couple well. Several people had acknowledged Derek Smith, so he had to be well known in the village.

But their stern faces had quickly dispelled her assumption. They explained they needed to speak urgently to Charlotte Jones (Charlotte!) and no, it couldn't wait until the next day, as they knew about the couple's travel plans.

Suzanne had walked them across the beer garden and called down to Charlie and Annie where they'd been snatching a moment or two of calm before the dancing and drinking began in earnest.

Charlie had also jumped to the wrong conclusion initially, but as soon as she'd heard DI Manning's words, she'd been eager to go with the detectives to Exeter police station, "to sort this all out." Not that she had much choice in the matter.

Several people, including Annie, Suzanne, Suzanne's husband Steve, and Rohan, offered to go with her. But she was adamant they stay in Coombesford.

"I don't know what this is all about," Charlie had said, as she hugged Annie and Suzy, "but I'm sure we'll be able to clear it up very quickly. In the meantime, you guys are in the middle of a party. You've got guests to look after. As Arnie says," she'd paused and tapping the tip of Suzy's nose, adapted a broad Austrian accent, "I'll be back."

Obviously the party hadn't continued as planned. No-one felt in the mood for dancing without one of the two principle players, but Charlie was right. There was a garden full of people, some of whom were local, but some had travelled a very long way to be there.

Everyone needed feeding. And the food was there anyway. So a much-subdued crowd had eaten and drunk their fill before helping with the clearing up. The locals then headed home, taking with them some of the visitors who were lodged all over the village. The guests staying at The Falls gradually drifted away to their rooms, and now all was quiet.

Suzanne looked up as Rohan entered the bar, accompanied by his landlady and very close friend, Esther Steele.

Esther took one look at Suzanne and headed for the coffee machine behind the bar. "Right, I know it's late but I think we could all do with a shot of caffeine. Americanos all round?"

"Or maybe something stronger?" asked Rohan.

Suzanne shook her head. "I don't want anything to drink in case I have to go into Exeter to collect Charlie. So, yes please, Esther. Coffee would be great." Suzanne looked around. "Are we the last ones up?"

"I think so. Annie and Suzy have gone back to The Folly. The poor kid's so distraught, Annie's letting her sleep in their bed tonight and is staying with her, although I doubt if she'll get much rest. All the clearing up's finished. Everyone pitched in. So at least the kitchen's clear for the morning. Not sure where your Steve is."

"Oh, he's gone to bed too. Said he wanted to be fresh for the morning, once we know what help we can be. He knew I was going to stay up as long as necessary."

Once the three were settled around a table with their coffees, Suzanne turned to the former detective. "Okay, Rohan, you start. What did you manage to get out of DS Smith?"

"He couldn't tell me much. The DI was listening. But he did manage to say they had some pretty incriminating evidence against Charlie. Something about fingerprints and a video."

Suzanne's phone rang. Grabbing it, and seeing the name on the screen, she hit the button. "Charlie! What's happening? Are you finished? Do you want me to come and collect you?" She listened in growing horror to her sister. When the torrent of words at the other end subsided, she instilled as much confidence as she could into her voice. "Okay, sis. Hang on in there and try to get some sleep. We'll sort this out, I promise. Goodnight, sweetheart."

There was a buzzing in her ear. "Charlie? Charlie, are you still there?" But her sister had gone. Suzanne turned back to her two companions. She only realised she had tears running down her cheeks when Esther jumped up and ran around the table to hug her.

"What is it, Suzanne? Why isn't she coming home?"

"She says they are... They want to..." She stopped and took a deep breath. "She's been charged and will be kept in custody pending a magistrate's appearance on Monday morning. Apparently the police believe they've enough evidence to prove she committed murder."

"Evidence? What evidence?" Esther asked.

"DNA, for a start."

"But I thought that was all sorted earlier in the week. Charlie never denied she was on the train. And there must have been thousands of other fingerprints there as well. Why are they focusing on hers?"

"Because they weren't just on the train, but at the murder scene – even though Charlie swore she never went in there. They say her fingerprints are not only in the cubicle but also on the knife. And apparently they have some video footage of her with the murder victim. They showed her pictures of her arguing with the young man and following him onto the train."

Suzanne stopped and took another deep breath. "And when they moved the body, he was lying on a fob from her key ring!"

Rohan had been pacing around as he listened to Suzanne talk. He stopped and returned to the table. Sitting back across from the two women, he spoke quietly, but his words dropped loudly into the silent bar. "So the police are convinced they've caught the killer?"

Suzanne nodded.

"Which means they won't be looking for anyone else?"

Suzanne shook her head.

"But we know Charlie's innocent, don't we."

Suzanne looked up sharply. "Of course we do. What are you suggesting?"

"I'm not suggesting anything, Suzanne, other than the fact that your sister and our friend is in a very bad situation." He turned and raised an eyebrow at Esther. "And if the police aren't interested in proving her innocence, then I guess it's up to us."

Suzanne smiled at the pair, as Rohan continued. "So I suggest we all go and get some sleep. We'll reconvene in the morning and start planning. Charlie needs us."

CHAPTER 14

The following morning, Annie appeared in the kitchen of The Falls as the clock in the bar was chiming seven. Rohan was switching on the ovens and beginning to heat the water, in preparation for breakfast. He took one look at her white face and the dark circles under her eyes and turned her gently but firmly around and marched her out of the kitchen.

"Back to the house you go, Annie. I've got this."

"Don't be silly, Rohan. Who's going to cook breakfast? We've got all those guests. And who's going to get everything ready for opening? Sunday lunchtime is one of our busiest sessions of the week. We need Charlie."

Rohan wondered if he should remind Annie the pub wasn't due to open that day at all, and she wasn't even supposed to be there that morning. She and Charlie should be in a car on their way to Heathrow for an afternoon flight to Rio de Janeiro. But by the look of it, Annie was already suffering enough. He didn't want to increase her pain more than he had to. Suzanne would be up soon. She was the one who'd spoken to Charlie the previous night and she should be the one to bring Annie up to date on what was happening to her new wife.

"Esther will be here in a few minutes. She's just sorting out her dad's breakfast at the farm then she said she'd come and act as my sous chef." He paused. "Besides, all those guests, as you call them, are family and friends. No-one's paying for their rooms, so they can all muck in, like they did last night with the clearing up. You go and spend some time with Suzy. I'll give you a shout when the food's ready." A thought struck him. "Unless you'd rather eat over there. We can get something brought over for you."

"No, that's fine." Annie gave him a wan smile. "We'll come over and join you. But, if you're sure, then I really would rather be with Suzy. She's very upset." And with a little wave, Annie wandered back across the beer garden to the little upside-down house in the paddock.

"I can see she's not the only one," muttered Rohan as he went to the fridge in search of bacon and sausage.

It was a very sober crowd that met for breakfast in the restaurant a couple of hours later. Suzanne and Steve sat in the corner with Annie and Suzy. Suzanne had brought her sister-in-law up to speed on what was happening in Exeter. Rohan had heard them agreeing not to tell Suzy all the details. But he could see from the young girl's face that she was bursting with questions. He had an idea.

"Esther, can you keep an eye on things for a few moments?" he asked. Then grabbing his phone, he headed out into the car park. "Hello, Olga. Yes, it's me, Rohan. No, no news yet. Or at least no good news. She's still at the station." He listened to the voluble stream of words at the other end of the phone and grinned, despite the severity of the situation. "No, I'm afraid we can't do that, Olga. This is England. We don't behave like that."

Then he returned to the question at hand. "Yes, of course we will. No, I don't know what's going to happen." He paused. "Olga, can I ask you a favour? Would you pop into The Falls in a little while and invite Suzy to come over to your place? Maybe suggest a swim or something? I suspect Annie needs to concentrate on Charlie, and she can't do that if she's worrying about their daughter as well. You will? Olga, that's great. See you in a little while."

Back inside, he joined Esther in keeping the hot and cold buffets topped up for the rest of the guests who were seated at a couple of the large tables, chatting quietly and occasionally casting glances across at the group in the corner. Then the two of them grabbed their own plates and began eating. For a while silence reigned.

When the front door burst open, everyone looked up, probably expecting – or maybe hoping – it would be Charlie returning. Instead, they were faced with the sight of a slight middle-aged but very well-preserved woman with magnificent breasts and a startling tan. Since everyone had been at the wedding the previous day, they all recognised Olga Mountjoy, widow and owner of Mountjoy Manor, where the ceremony and family meal had taken place. There were smiles from all around the room.

"Annie, Suzy, my darlings, I am so sorry."

Rohan knew Olga's Ukrainian accent always got stronger when she became emotional. Today, even he had difficulty understanding what she said. But it didn't matter. He knew why she was there. She swooped across the room and enveloped first Annie then Suzy in a tight hug.

Rohan also knew Olga fancied herself as a bit of an amateur thespian and, despite the circumstances, he had to suppress a giggle as she carried on speaking. "Suzy, sweetie, I want you to come with me. I need you – and Bertie – right away."

Suzy stared at their friend then looked across at Annie, shaking her head. But Olga ignored that and continued. "Please, my little friend, I really need you."

She wrung her hands and gave a theatrical shudder. "I think there's something under my garden shed. I can hear scrabbling every time I go in there."

Rohan had seen Olga's 'garden shed' the previous day at the wedding. It was a beautiful octagonal wooden building in the grounds of Mountjoy Manor. And while it did indeed have a sign over the door with the words 'Olga's Shed' burned into the wood in italic letters, he was fairly certain nothing as prosaic – or grubby – as a garden tool would ever be allowed in there.

Around the edge was a built-in seat covered in thick cushions whose white and green covers reflected so well the view through the windows. There was a table in the centre, containing a pile of the latest novels and glossy magazines, and a tiny built-in fridge, just large enough to hold a chilled bottle of Chablis or rosé wine. Rohan didn't know how Olga spent her time in there, but he was sure she wouldn't be doing any gardening. His reverie was disturbed by Annie's voice.

"Suzy, go and get Bertie, please."

"But, Mama Annie—"

Annie reached across and pulled her daughter to her. "Yes, poppet, I know you're worried about Mama C – we all are. But there's nothing we can do for the moment. And I promise you, I'll call you as soon as there's any news. Please, for now, just go and help Auntie Olga. After all she did yesterday, it's the least we can do." As she hugged her daughter again, Rohan saw her catch Olga's eye and mouth, "Thank you." Olga nodded.

Within moments, the assembled group watched through the windows as a strange procession crossed the car park and turned right towards the village green. The slim Ukrainian woman led the way, not glancing back, as if she knew her followers were with her. Trotting behind was Suzy, looking over her shoulder as though still torn between her concern for Charlie and her love of an adventure – especially one involving nature, and even rats were nature in her book.

And finally, bringing up the rear, the small black-and-white Jack Russell who was obviously delighted to be out in the fresh air, but whose progress was delayed by the urgent need to stop and sniff every single plant and other interesting smell he encountered.

"Right, everyone." Annie jumped up and pulled the group's attention back to the matter at hand. "Suzanne has brought me up to date on the call from Charlie last night. I'm going into Exeter in a little while to see if I can find out exactly what's going on. But it's pretty obvious the police are convinced they have the true murderer. Which means they'll stop looking."

She paused and looked around the room. "Which means we're going to have do our own investigation, to prove Charlie's innocence. Rohan, Esther and I have some experience of that, after the past few years," she said somewhat modestly, "but fortuitously we have a much more experienced team here, plus many of you have worked with Charlie over the years. So I'm going to hand over to Suzanne and Steve to take the lead on this."

For a moment, her voice seemed to break, and Rohan wondered if their friend would be able to carry on. But then she coughed to clear the tears from her voice and pushed back her shoulders. "Let's do this, people. Let's bring Charlie home."

Annie reached across and gave Suzanne a hug, then sat down, indicating that her sister-in-law had the floor.

Suzanne blinked rapidly a couple of times, then stood and clapped her hands.

"Okay, folks, let's get started."

CHAPTER 15

Suzanne looked around the room at the group of friends assembled before her. They spanned so many years, and so much geography, and yet they were all in this one place at the same time. But it was just as well they were. She was convinced that between them, they held the key to Charlie's situation and therefore were the ones able to break the deadlock and get her sister released.

Suzanne and Steve had woken early, and had spent a couple of hours reviewing the situation. Now, she began to outline their conclusions to the group.

"The situation is this. Charlie has been arrested for the murder of an unknown man, possibly of Eastern European origin, in the toilet cubicle on the train from Bristol. The police have video footage of Charlie arguing with the man and following him onto the train. Charlie's fingerprints were originally identified at the crime scene, on part of a key ring, and later also on the knife."

Suzanne paused and smiled ruefully. "So not looking good. However, Charlie swears that although she was definitely on that train, she never saw the young man, and she certainly didn't argue with him on the platform. Nor did she visit the toilet during her journey."

"And you believe Charlie's version of events?" The question came from Steve, who was standing at the back of the room, leaning against the wall. "The evidence is pretty damning."

Suzanne smiled at her husband. She'd known he was going to play devil's advocate. In fact, she'd specifically asked him to. She nodded and turned back to the rest of the group.

"My dear sister has been many things in her life. There have been times when she and I haven't seen eye to eye on things. And there have been times when I've had no idea where in the world she was, or what she was getting up to. But she's never lied to my face and I trust her absolutely on this. If Charlie says she's innocent, I believe her."

"That's good enough for me," said Steve.

There were murmurs of assent all around the room. Suzanne slowly released her breath and felt herself relax slightly.

"So if the evidence isn't real, Charlie's being framed. And in a pretty spectacular way."

Suzanne turned to Rohan and Esther sitting close together at one of the tables. "Guys, I know you've worked with Charlie and Annie on a number of murders in recent years. And you certainly know this village and the surrounding area better than the rest of us. Is there anyone locally who would have the resources and abilities to organise all this?"

"I've been wracking my brains to try to come up with someone who'd fit the bill," said Rohan. "But I don't see it myself. All the cases we've worked on together have turned out to centre on individuals with personal reasons for carrying out the crimes they did."

"And the culprits are all either dead or in jail," Esther added.

"So would you concur with the conclusion Steve and I came to earlier?" asked Suzanne. "This is much more likely to be someone from Charlie's past; either from the work we did together or from her days in the Secret Service."

Rohan and Esther looked at one another and nodded.

"Yes, we agree," Rohan said. "And, in that case, we're not going to be much use to you, at least initially. So I've got a suggestion to make." He stood and looked around the room. "Annie's going to have her hands full worrying about Charlie, and keeping Suzy calm. You guys are the best hope of clearing Charlie's name. So Esther and I will concentrate on running The Falls in the interim."

"And we'll help with that in any way we can," came a voice from the door. Rohan's face split into a huge smile as Roger and Celia Richardson entered.

"We weren't eavesdropping," Roger continued, then paused, "well, I guess we were," there were smiles and quiet laughs around the room, "but we just came over to see how we could help."

Suzanne walked over and gave Celia a quick hug. "That's settled then. Rohan, you and the Coombesford gang concentrate on running The Falls and keeping us fed. And the rest of us will start working on clearing Charlie's name."

"How long are you planning on staying?" asked Esther.

"As long as it takes, Esther. As long as it takes." Suzanne had a thought. "What are the bookings like next week? Will we be okay to stay on in our room for the moment?"

"I'll check the reservations and let you know."

"If there's a problem, we can always find you somewhere else to stay in the village," Celia said. "We've got a spare room. And Olga's got a whole manor house to herself."

"That's very good of you." Suzanne could feel her eyes pricking with tears again.

"Don't be silly. Charlie and Annie are part of the Coombesford family. And families take care of each other."

As Rohan and his friends hurried off to work out how

they were going to cover The Falls as well as their other commitments, Suzanne turned back to the rest of the group.

"Okay, guys, let's start pooling information. I'm conscious some of you have planes to catch in the next couple of days, so let's make sure we gather every idea we can while we're all together."

Wilberforce Businge cleared his throat. "Suzanne, may I make a suggestion? We all met you or Charlie at different times of your lives. Shall we start by constructing a timeline of which years, and parts of the world, we cover. That way we can identify any gaps."

Suzanne had originally met the big Ugandan with an ebony walking stick and sparkling gems on his cufflinks and tiepin when she was working for the International Health Forum, trying to slow the rapid growth of the counterfeit trade in Africa. Charlie had gate-crashed that project and had hit it off immediately with WB, as he was universally known.

"Excellent idea, WB. Does anyone have any paper we can take notes on? Or better still, a flipchart?"

"I think I can go one better than that."

Suzanne looked to the door where Esther was standing, holding a large canvas bag.

"I've just fetched my laptop from the farm. Why don't we go to the function room. There's a projector in there and a screen. You guys talk, I'll make notes and we can project them up on the screen so everyone can see them."

Suzanne frowned. "But I thought you were going to help run The Falls."

Esther shook her head. "There's three of them out there working on the plan for the next few days. And every few minutes someone pops their head around the door or phones to offer to help. They don't need me. I'm free until we start cooking lunch."

"In that case, I think that's a great idea." Suzanne stepped back. "Lead the way."

CHAPTER 16

By the time Rohan, accompanied by Celia, arrived with coffee a couple of hours later, the group in the function room had made quite a bit of progress. The screen was lit up, showing an elegant timeline prepared by Esther, and the table was littered with bits of paper, covered in scribbled notes.

"Looks like you've been busy," Rohan said, as he placed the tray on a side table and started filling the cups. An enticing aroma wafted across the room. Celia placed a large plate on the centre of the conference table.

"Celia, we've only just had breakfast," Suzanne protested.

"But Celia's chocolate chip cookies are legendary," Steve said. "I'm not going to miss out on the chance to try them." He bit into one and grinned appreciatively. "Oh yum. The rumours are true!"

"So how far have you got?" Rohan asked.

Suzanne walked over to the screen and pointed out the coloured lines. "We've covered the period from 2004 to 2010 pretty well. 2004 was when I went to Africa and Charlie followed me. And from then until Suzy was born, the two of us worked together. She was no longer working for the Secret Service. I know all the projects she was involved in. Plus we've got folks here," she indicated the other people in the room, "who were with us in southern Africa, Latin America, and in Russia and Ukraine."

"So we think we can investigate anything that came out of that time period pretty thoroughly," Steve chipped in. "Where the difficulty comes is in the years before that. The years when Charlie was working undercover."

Suzanne nodded. "She told no-one else in the family what she was doing. We all thought she'd gone off the rails. Sometimes she was missing for months at a time – once she disappeared for over a year. So getting a handle on what happened during that time is going to be very difficult."

Suzanne paused and exhaled deeply. "But that's what we've got to do, folks. I'm sure this whole thing stems from Charlie's past, and probably not from anything we were involved in together. Otherwise, why not target me rather than her. Or even both of us for that matter."

Steve looked at her in alarm and she held out her hand to him.

"It's alright, Steve, I know that's still a possibility. We'll take all the precautions we need. I'm not going to do anything rash."

"So what's the next step, Suzanne?" Celia had been standing quietly at the back of the room and Rohan had almost forgotten she was there.

"We're going to take a two-pronged approach. Those of us who worked together in the noughties are going to cover those years. I know I just said we don't think the source of all this comes from there, but we have to be sure. At the same time, we need to start looking at the earlier years in more detail. And for that, we're going to need some pointers."

"From whom?"

"For a start, we have one guest here who knew Charlie back in the 1990s. And there's her contacts in Germany.

We can try to work on them. But most of all, we need to get Charlie to open up. She's always been very close-mouthed about her undercover days. I know she thought she was protecting the rest of the family but this time she has to see she's only doing more harm than good by keeping everything to herself."

"The question is: who's going to be able to convince her to let go of her secrets?" This came from Esther who had been quietly tidying up the timeline on the screen. "Annie's too close to her, and too emotional. Do you think she'd talk to you, Suzanne?"

"Possibly. We weren't always the best of friends, but that's all a long time in the past. She *might* talk to me." Suzanne stopped and looked across at Rohan. "But I think I've got a better idea. Rohan, you were an undercover cop, weren't you? Back in Manchester, before you became a private investigator?"

"Until my cover got blown in a very public court case, yes. Why?"

"Because I think you're probably the best person to talk to Charlie and get her to open up. You've been there. You know what it's like to be playing a role, maybe doing things you'd never normally consider doing, in order to maintain your cover."

"And it doesn't always make for comfortable reflection, I can tell you."

"Precisely. And I suspect that's part of Charlie's reluctance to tell us about her past. Yes, there's the whole Official Secrets thing. Plus the need to protect her family and friends from the people she dealt with. But also, deep down, I guess there's an element of shame about the things she's not telling us."

"And we have to break through that?" Rohan nodded. "I think you might be right."

"So, here's what I think you should do." Suzanne consulted the notes she'd been scribbling on her pad. "I want you to make an appointment to see Charlie. We don't think she'll be released at the moment, but they can't deny her visitors. Especially if you tell them you're acting on behalf of her lawyer – we still need to decide who we're going to appoint to that role, by the way. Then you need to do whatever it takes to make Charlie start talking. We need as much detail as we can get about her days in the Secret Service. We need the names of anyone she can remember who might bear her a grudge. In fact, anyone she can remember at all. And any contacts she might still have."

Suzanne held up a hand as Rohan opened his mouth to voice an objection. "Yes, I know it's more than twenty years ago, but I'm sure there'll be someone in the background we're not aware of."

Suzanne looked around the room. "And once we have that information, the hard work really starts."

CHAPTER 17

The meeting broke up soon after that. Everyone had their assignments to work on, and they agreed to reconvene later in the day to report back on progress so far.

Suzanne's first task was to talk to Felix Sousa. She'd worked with the lithe, athletic-looking man nearly twenty years before when, as the Trio de Paulo, he and two friends had helped the Jones sisters trap counterfeiter Michael Hawkins and attempt to arrange his transport back to Britain to stand trial. But it had been a decade earlier that Charlie had first met him, when he was an aid worker being held by terrorists in Lebanon and she was part of the team that went in to rescue him and his fellow hostage.

"Felix, you spent more time with Charlie back in the 1990s than anyone else we've got here. Isn't there anything you can remember? Anything at all that might give us a clue?" She paused and her shoulders slumped. "Because, to be honest, I'm beginning to think we've got nothing, nothing at all."

Felix pulled a face. "I've been through everything already, and really can't think of anything."

"Let's try it once more, shall we? Talk me through the

whole thing, even the smallest detail. Maybe there's something in there that you don't realise you know."

"Okay, I'll try. Although you have to remember it's thirty years ago."

"Do your best. It's to save Charlie."

"Okay. It was 1991. The Lebanon hostages situations had been going on for nearly ten years. We'd been snatched seven months previously. I was an aid worker and was being held with a British nurse. Charlie was part of a team sent in to extract us. Someone managed to smuggle a message in to us, so we were expecting an attack of some kind, but had no idea what would happen or exactly when.

"It came around four in the morning. There was a crash, some yelling, lots of gunfire, a scream, an explosion and then silence. A terrible silence. We thought at first the rescue had failed. But afterwards, we realised we were temporarily deafened by the explosion.

"The next thing we knew, the door flew open and the room was full of masked people in combat fatigues. We were grabbed and hustled out, pushed onto the floor of a lorry and driven away into the night. We drove for ages then stopped at a deserted farmhouse in the hills behind Beirut."

"And that's when you first met Charlie?"

"Yes, that's right. It was only at that point we were really sure we'd been rescued. Before that, we thought our captors might have been moving us because their hideout had been compromised. But our hearing was starting to come back and Charlie told us who they were, and that we had to lie low for a few hours as it was too dangerous to move any further during daylight.

"Once the adrenaline had eased, the fear set in. We were out, but we weren't safe. What would happen if we were discovered before we managed to reach the Jordanian border? We tried to sleep, but we were too terrified. I really believe, if Charlie hadn't stayed and talked to us, we'd have gone mad with fear. That's a strange thing to say, I know, after everything we'd endured during captivity, but I think it was being free, but not free, if you see what I mean."

"Of course." Suzanne didn't want to prolong this conversation more than she had to. She could see reliving the experience was taking its toll on the Brazilian who had presumably worked hard to shut this period of his life out of his memory. "Felix, do you think there's anyone left in Lebanon from those days who would bear a grudge against Charlie?"

"I really don't think so." Felix shook his head slowly. "All our captors were killed during the rescue attempt. There might be some relatives left, but would they really have waited thirty years to take revenge? And why only go for Charlie? She wasn't even leading the team. She was just one of the foot soldiers." He shook his head again.

"Okay, Felix, let's leave it there. I'm so sorry I've had to put you through this." Suzanne stood. "I'll leave you in peace, but I'll see you before you head off for the airport tomorrow morning."

As she headed for the door, Felix called out to her.

"There's just one thing that occurs to me. I don't know whether it's worth considering or not."

"Anything. We're getting desperate."

"We've been concentrating on the people Charlie was working against. But what if it's someone she thought she was working with?"

"What do you mean? One of her clients?"

"No, one of her colleagues in the Secret Service." He shrugged. "It's a long time ago and I may be misremembering, but I got the impression she didn't get along with the rest of the team. There was one other woman in particular. I heard the two of them having a real verbal spat just before we left the farmhouse and finally drove into Jordan. Nearly came to blows. Although I have no idea what it was about."

"Do you know who she was?"

"No, I never knew any of the names. Except the team leader, of course. He was older than the rest, so he might be dead, but it's worth a try, surely. I remember his name because it seemed so funny and yet so appropriate. Strong, his name was. Cyril Strong."

CHAPTER 18

"So that's where we've got to so far." Rohan had been talking for nearly fifteen minutes, bringing Charlie up to date on what they'd done since she'd been arrested and remanded in custody. "And no matter how we look at it, everything's pointing back to your days in MI6. So you need to tell us everything you can remember, no matter how small, no matter how insignificant you think it might be."

Charlie Jones stared at her friend and felt her heart break a tiny bit more. She couldn't argue with the logic in anything he'd said. In fact, the thought processes she'd been through during the long lonely hours she'd had to herself had brought her to the same conclusion. But she couldn't, she just couldn't talk about that part of her life. It was locked tight in a sealed box buried deep in the back of her memory and there was no way she was going to bring it to the surface.

To do that would be to risk everything she'd built up in the past twenty years. The respect of her friends and colleagues, the friendship she'd re-established with her sister. And most importantly, the love she gave and received in her little family unit. No, losing her freedom –

once again – was not such a major issue when balanced against losing Annie and Suzy. And if they knew, really knew, about her past, that was what would happen.

Slowly, she shook her head. "You know I can't do that, Rohan. I signed the Official Secrets Act. I can't talk about anything that happened back then."

"But it could mean the difference between you being found guilty of a murder you didn't commit, and going to prison for a long time, or allowing us to find out what's really going on here and pointing the police in the right direction."

"Yet I'd still go to prison – just for a different crime. One I'd actually be guilty of."

"Charlie, we're not suggesting you betray all the people you worked with, the ones who were on your side. Or even betray national security. All we're asking for is a few names, people we can investigate, people who might bear you a grudge."

Charlie reflected that some of the people who might bear her a grudge could well be the people Rohan described as being 'on your side'. But she wondered if she could provide a few pointers, something to keep her supporters busy for the moment. She was pretty certain whoever was doing this to her would break cover at some point. After all, what was the purpose of gaining retribution – and she was sure that was what this was all about – if the people involved were unaware of who was exacting revenge upon them and for what.

"Okay." She rubbed her hands over her face and sat back as though agreeing with everything Rohan had said. "You already know about Felix, who's here in Devon. I reconnected with him in Brazil in 2007, but our original meeting was more than fifteen years earlier in the Middle East."

"Yes, Suzanne spent a long time talking to him yesterday. Not sure how useful it was, but she certainly took a load of notes."

"Right. Well, then there's Tomas Braun, in Berlin. Suzanne will remember him. I went to visit him in 2011 before we tracked down Michael Hawkins in Russia. His gang was the reason for the major undercover operation I did in the late 1980s. He's always had a great network across that part of the world. Get Suzanne to use her contacts to find him. If he's still alive."

"Time's up." The rap on the door and the shouted message made them jump.

Rohan gave the prison guard at the door a thumbs-up, gathered his notes together and pushed them into his pocket.

"That gives us something to be getting on with." Standing, he pulled Charlie into a rough hug before letting her go and walking rapidly to the door. Charlie felt her eyes prickle with tears and swore she saw the same reflected in her friend's face. "I'll be back in a couple of days. See if you can come up with some more suggestions, will you?"

Charlie nodded and smiled. She sat calmly waiting. Moments later, the young guard returned from escorting Rohan out and collected Charlie to return her to her cell.

As the door closed behind her and she heard the lock fall into place, she wondered just how long it would take her friends and family to track down Tomas or whoever now led his gang.

She also wondered how long it would take them to realise she'd given them leads to the late 1980s and early 1990s. How soon would they start pushing to find out exactly what she had been doing in the period after that? A time when the twenty-something-year-old Charlie Jones was very different from the one around now.

Somehow, she suspected it wouldn't take them very long at all.

CHAPTER 19

The guests from Africa left Coombesford on the Wednesday after the wedding. WB travelled to Heathrow in a chauffeur-driven car, accompanied by Chibesa and Sara Desai.

Chibesa had been the logistics expert for Suzanne's anti-counterfeiting project in Southern Africa when she was working for the International Health Forum in the early 2000s. And it was Sara, reeling from the death of her sister from fake insulin, who'd provided significant leads to the counterfeiters. Fleeing her native Swaziland to escape revenge from the gang and taking refuge in Lusaka, she'd rekindled her friendship with Chibesa, a friendship that had quickly turned to love and they'd married a couple of years later.

The couple from Zambia had initially baulked at the extravagance of a chauffeur-driven car and suggested they all take the bus from Exeter. But WB had scoffed at the idea of trying to fit his large frame into a narrow seat and being confined to someone else's timetable for four or five hours.

Then they'd offered to pay their share of the cost. But when WB confessed that the driver was a mate of Rohan's and all he was being asked to pay for was petrol, they gave in and allowed themselves to be transported in luxury.

There was another surprise waiting for them when they checked in. WB, whose network of contacts was legendary, had managed to get their seats upgraded to business class. Travelling with the well-connected Ugandan definitely had its perks.

The three flew to Nairobi together before finally separating: WB taking a short flight to Kampala, Chibesa and Sara facing a long journey to Lusaka. And while flying over the waters of the eastern Mediterranean and the sands of the Sahara, they whiled away the hours discussing the events of the past few days, and wondering if there was anything they could do.

"Although, to be honest," Chibesa took off his glasses and was polishing them with the hem of his brightly coloured shirt, "I can't believe we're going to uncover anything down here. Counterfeit drugs are still a big problem in Africa. Bigger even than in the days of the International Health Forum, I'm afraid to say. But that operation was twenty years ago. Stefano Mladov is dead. Kabwe Mazoka is dead. Michael Hawkins is in Belmarsh prison. Anyone left from their gang will have moved on. I doubt if anyone even remembers the name Charlie Jones."

WB nodded and sighed. He knew Chibesa was right. But he felt so helpless, and he suspected his friends did too. It had felt like desertion, leaving Suzanne and the others trying to work out what was going on. He'd arranged to have a Zoom call with the team in Coombesford at the end of the week, and he desperately wanted to have something to report back, even if it was assurances that they could find no indication of a plot against Charlie originating in southern Africa. Suddenly he had a thought.

"What about the Harawa family? I've not spoken to them for a while, but I think they're still in the Copper Belt. They were always pretty well connected."

"Good point." Chibesa turned to his wife. "They were the family who took us in after Suzanne was abducted from Mazokapharm." He grinned at WB. "I seem to remember it was Suzanne rather than Charlie who made the biggest impression in that family."

"Yes, but that was years ago, as you said. Suzanne's happily married and I believe Nathan is too. But it might be worth having a chat with them. Do you want to do it, Chibesa, or shall I?"

"I'll leave that one to you. I'm going to talk to my contacts in Zambia and see if they've heard of any international conspiracies that might stretch as far as the UK. Although, at the risk of repeating myself, I really can't see that we're going to uncover anything."

Not for the first time, WB thought what a beautiful young woman Annette Harawa must once have been and how easy it must have been for a young Zambian farmer to fall in love with her and breach all the social mores of the time. The silver-haired woman on the screen was no longer young but she still had an air of health and vitality about her.

"I'm so sorry to hear about Charlie's troubles." Annette looked genuinely upset at WB's news. "But I don't think there's anything I can do to help you."

"I just thought that with all the local people you talk to in your clinic…" He paused. "You're still working, aren't you?"

"Oh yes, still working." Annette laughed. "I've cut back my hours and don't do house calls any longer. I have a young intern who covers that. But doctors rarely retire, you know. Especially in a country where we are so thin on the ground." She winked at him. "And I have to admit that I often hear things that maybe I shouldn't, about some of the things my patients – or their children and grandchildren – get up to."

She shook her head. "But I haven't heard of anything major for some years. And certainly nothing that stretches as far as England. I'm sorry, WB. I'd love to help you and

Charlie, of course, but I don't see how I can."

WB realised he'd hit a dead end with Annette Harawa. But there were other members of the family. Maybe they could help. "How's the younger generation doing, Annette?"

"Lily's working in Geneva. I only hear from her occasionally and she hasn't been home for several years. She's working at the university there. Developing quite a name for herself in the IT world apparently."

"And Nathan?"

"Nathan's fine. He's normally in and out of here most days. But he's away right now. He's taken the family to Europe for a trip. In fact–" she turned away from the screen and stretched across to pull some papers off a side table, "according to this schedule, they're in France this week. Then they're heading over to Switzerland to visit Lily before flying home."

She dropped the papers back on the table. "He'll be sorry to have missed you, WB. But I'll tell him you called and get him to ring you when he gets home. Maybe he'll have heard something from his business contacts that can help you."

CHAPTER 20

As his satnav took him off the main highway and up into the hills overlooking the Pacific, Damien Bradley Smithson III began to get a bad feeling about this trip. And when he arrived at the address his assistant had logged into his phone, he assumed she'd made some sort of mistake, although that wasn't like her.

Damien had been one of the first clients to engage the Jones sisters when they set up their consultancy back in 2007. Concerned about the effects he'd observed on athletes taking a new health drink, he'd persuaded Suzanne to investigate the manufacturing company in São Paulo that had introduced the product to the marketplace. The company had been run by slick businessman Nigel Atkinson and, despite his vigorous denials and threats to her to back off, Suzanne had uncovered irregularities resulting in the product being removed from the marketplace and Atkinson going to prison in the US.

When Suzanne Jones had called him, saying her contacts told her Nigel Atkinson had been released and was living in California, Damien had readily agreed to go and talk to him, to see if he could get any hint of an involvement in Charlie's trumped-up murder charge. But this wasn't the office block or fancy condo Damien had been expecting.

This was a converted barn by the side of a dirt road. Little more than a rickety roof propped up with rough trunks of wood, it was open to elements on three sides. At the closed end there stood a small table with candles at the corners. A battered old piano stood to one side. An expensive-looking microphone, amplifier and stack of speakers next to the table looked out of place. Rows of mismatched wooden chairs stretching back from the table looked much more in keeping with their surroundings.

But there was no sign of the disgraced businessman he'd come to meet.

The only occupants of the barn were a couple standing by the front row of chairs. A heavily pregnant young woman, barely more than a girl, was sobbing in the arms of an old man. He was patting her back and whispering in her ear, although whether he was trying to reassure her, or increase her distress, it was impossible to tell.

Finally, her tears stopped. The old man put his hand on her forehead and muttered a few words. With a watery smile at her companion, she turned and left.

The old man sighed, and walked slowly through the chairs towards Damien.

Damien had seen a lot of things during his fifteen years in politics, firstly at local level but for the past three years as staffer to the US Senator for California. He'd trained himself to expect the unexpected and be able to respond to whatever was thrown at him or his boss – sometimes literally, sometimes metaphorically – as they toured the state or the halls of power in Washington DC.

But his first sight of Nigel Atkinson since Damien had watched him being led from the court house to start an eleven-year prison sentence back in 2009 almost caused him to give away his sense of amazement. He thought back to the tall muscular man who'd spent half his time in the gym and the rest glad-handing business contacts, surrounded by a bevy of beautiful women. It was hard to reconcile that picture with the one before him now.

Atkinson had been in his early fifties when the latest in a series of business scams had caught up with him and landed him in prison. Now, he was only in his mid-sixties, but he looked at least ten years older. His hair, grey streaked with white, was long and lank, pulled back into a ponytail that fell well below his shoulders. He looked as if he'd not shaved for several days.

He was wearing a grubby white caftan shirt over faded denim jeans, and on his bare feet he wore battered Jesus sandals. Around his neck, suspended on a thick cord, was a rough wooden cross.

"May the Lord be with you, my son!"

As the first words from the mouth of a convicted criminal, they were unusual.

Damien stepped forward and offered his hand. "Mr Atkinson, thank you for agreeing to see me. I won't take up too much of your time."

Atkinson shook his head. "My time is the Lord's time. I spend it as He wishes. And today, He wishes me to spend time with you." He released Damien's hand, and pointed to the nearest row of chairs. "Sit, sit."

Once seated, Damien opened his mouth to explain why he was there, but Atkinson held out a hand and stopped him.

"I like to start all conversations with a prayer. You don't mind, do you?" His eyes bored into Damien's and for the first time, he thought he saw the old Nigel Atkinson peering out from inside this disguise.

"Of course not. Go ahead."

"Oh Lord, You put us on this earth and gave us time to use as we please. In Your wisdom help us to spend that time wisely, in Your name, Amen."

"Amen." Damien hadn't been inside a church for many years, but as always, found it impossible not to echo the closing word. "I must say this is a surprise, Mr Atkinson."

"Please, no more Mr Atkinson. That name belongs to a different life. A very different life; and a different person. I'm just simple Brother Nigel now." He spread his hands wide, gazing around at the battered premises. "This is my new life, my new world."

His hand, wrinkled and speckled with age, gripped Damien's arm, and he realised there was still some of the old strength in there somewhere. "Do you know how long eleven years is, son? When you have nothing to do but stare at a wall and think? No, of course you don't."

Damien was pretty certain the prison Atkinson had been incarcerated in was considerably less stark than the picture being painted, but he decided it wasn't worth arguing the point.

Atkinson was staring into space, rubbing his hands, as though trying to wash away his sin. "You know, I have to thank you, my son. You and those clever Jones sisters. I hated you at first, obviously. You destroyed my life. Took away my freedom. But gradually I came to realise that you had been doing God's work all along. I had strayed from the right path and you were His instruments to bring me back." He grasped Damien's hand and shook it vigorously. "Thank you. Thank you. Thank you."

There were tears in Atkinson's eyes, and Damien suddenly had a picture of this man, addressing a crowded barn on a Sunday morning, appealing to the consciences of his congregation.

Damien cleared his throat. "Well, Mr– I mean, Brother Nigel. It's one of the Jones sisters I've come to ask you about." He explained Charlie's predicament and Suzanne's request that he talk to their old adversary. Surveying their surroundings, he finished, "Obviously, your new life shows me there is no way you would be involved in a scheme like this. But we wondered if you had heard anything, through your contacts in the er... criminal fraternity, that might help us find out what was going on."

Atkinson was shaking his head even before Damien

had finished speaking. "I found God while I was in prison, or should I say, He found me. After all, I was the one who was lost, not Him. But when I walked out of those gates four years ago, I didn't look back. And I have no links to anyone I might have met in there." He stood and held out his hand. "I'm sorry, my son, there's nothing I can do to help you. Now, if you will excuse me, I have to work on my sermon for this coming Sunday. The Lord's work is never done, you know." He walked away without looking back.

Damien returned to his car. It was clear to him that he wasn't going to get anything more from this old man. Where he was parked, the road was too narrow to turn. He had to drive nearly half a mile before he found a turning place on the brow of a hill, with views stretching to the ocean on one side and open slopes reaching upwards in the other. As he was reversing, the sun glinted off something bright and metallic hidden under a stand of trees some way off the road. It was a large gold-coloured Lincoln Navigator.

Damien whistled. He'd passed no other buildings on his way there, and there were none in sight further along the road. If this vehicle belonged, as he suspected, to Nigel Atkinson, then finding God was much more lucrative than his outward appearance would lead people to believe.

As he drove back past the barn, Damien caught sight of Nigel standing by his altar, talking into a mobile phone. At the sound of the car, he rapidly pushed the phone out of sight into the pocket of his caftan.

CHAPTER 21

Rohan parked the car in front of 19 Cherry Tree Lane and made a few rapid assumptions about the person he had travelled to meet. The neighbourhood, on the outskirts of Dorchester, spoke not of sumptuous or conspicuous wealth, but certainly of a kind of smug well-to-do-ness. The houses were mainly semi-detached, and of the style commonly produced by building companies in the 1930s.

The garden was neat and suggested a lot of work had gone into it: a central lawn mown into neat stripes, surrounded by a narrow flowerbed bursting with colour. Not a place where a weed would be welcome – or indeed survive. This looked like the home of a retired army officer. Rohan envisioned a checked shirt and tweed tie, even on a day of relaxation.

The figure that opened the door to him was therefore a bit of a surprise. Very short, probably less than five feet, and as round as a football. His bushy black beard contrasted sharply with his shiny bald head. His skin was deeply tanned. But if his appearance was unexpected, his initial response to Rohan's request to talk about 'the old days' was exactly as expected.

"I don't know how you got hold of my address – and I

don't want to know. But I can't talk to you about anything that happened in my past. Official Secrets Act and all that. In fact, I shouldn't even admit who I am." He began to push the door closed and it was only Rohan's quick thinking and size nine boot that stopped him being shut out altogether.

"Charlie Jones is about to go down for murder. And she's innocent. We need your help!"

Rohan's shout caused the door to fly open.

"Why didn't you say so? That makes all the difference." The man held out his hand. "The name's Strong, Cyril Strong." He gave a high-pitched giggle that Rohan found somewhat disconcerting. "But I guess you know that already. Come in, Mr Banerjee, come in."

Rohan followed Strong into the front parlour – no other word would do for the prissy 1950s-style of furniture and interior design. Rohan caught a glimpse of someone peering through a partly open door at the end of the corridor. Apparently Strong did too, as he paused and called out: "It's alright, Edith, nothing for you to worry about."

Once in the room, Rohan sank into the enveloping cushions of a leather-covered sofa, while Strong perched on an upright armchair next to the fireplace. Strong laid a finger to his chin and smiled. "Right then, tell me all about it. I've not heard from Charlie since she resigned from the service twenty years ago. What's she been up to?"

"She spent about a decade working with her sister, investigating counterfeiting operations and other criminal activities in the pharmaceutical industry. Then in 2010 her partner, Annie, had a daughter."

"Annie? Are you saying Charlie's gay? I had no idea. She certainly wasn't–" but he broke off and shrugged. "Sorry, shouldn't have interrupted. Do carry on."

"Becoming a parent had a big effect on Charlie. She gave up travelling the world, gave up investigating international criminals. She got a job in computing in

London."

"And how did that go?"

"She hated it."

"Yes, I should think she would."

"But she kept at it for quite a while, she'd do anything for her family. Then when Suzy – that's their daughter – was about eight, she and Annie sold up and moved down to Devon. Bought a pub, in a tiny village called Coombesford. And they've been there ever since."

"Country life, eh? I wouldn't have thought that was up Charlie's street at all."

"Oh, you'd be surprised. They've settled in pretty well. The pub's the hub of the village and they're very popular." Rohan paused and then reminisced. "Mind you, it's not been a completely quiet few years. They've got involved in solving several local murders along the way. That's how I came to live down there, in fact. I knew Charlie from years back and she called me in to help with some undercover work. And I sort of stayed in the area."

"But from the sound of it, things have taken a turn for the worse?"

"That's right. Charlie and Annie got married a couple of weeks back. And at the wedding reception, she was arrested for murder. The police reckon they've enough evidence to convict her, and they don't have any other lines of enquiry, so they're not looking for anyone else."

"But what makes you think it's something to do with Charlie's time in the Secret Service? If she's been investigating international criminals with her sister, and local murders with you guys, isn't it more likely the source of this problem lies closer to home?" Strong shook his head. "I'm sorry, Mr Banerjee, I can't see anything in what you've told me so far that would justify my breaking the Official Secrets Act." He stood. "I don't think I'm going to be able to help you. I'll show you out."

When Rohan didn't move from his seat, Strong turned back towards him and tutted. "I said, I'll show you out, Mr

Banerjee."

"I'm not going anywhere, Mr Strong. My friend and your former colleague is in trouble. And you may be the best lead we have at the moment. Please listen to what I have to say. And then I'll get out of your hair." Rohan gulped, realising that might not be the most appropriate saying to use in the circumstances. "I mean, I'll leave you in peace. You'll never hear from any of us again."

Strong sighed, sat, and folded his hands across his rounded belly. He glanced at the carriage clock on the mantelpiece. It was approaching six pm. "You've got five minutes to convince me, Mr Banerjee. Then I'm going to switch on the television for the evening news and you can show yourself out. So you'd better get on with it."

Rohan took a deep breath and tried to get his thoughts in order. He had just one shot at this. "Let me start by asking you a question, Mr Strong. You knew Charlie Jones very well. Did you ever know her to tell a lie?"

"She's a spy, Mr Banerjee, or at least she was. We all were. Lying was our stock in trade." He paused and gazed out of the window for a long time before appearing to come to a decision. "But if you're asking me whether I think Charlie Jones would lie to her friends and family, then I'd have to say no. She was one of the most honest people I ever met. Sometimes too honest for her own good."

"In other words, you'd agree that if Charlie Jones says she didn't commit this murder, she's telling the truth."

"The balance of probability says yes."

"Then the evidence against her, by definition, must be false."

"It would certainly appear so. Why, what have they got?"

"Fingerprints at the scene of the crime and on the murder weapon. Part of her key ring on the floor under the victim's body. And a film of her arguing with the victim on the station platform while waiting for the train."

"Hmm. All of which can be faked, of course."

"Obviously. But not by the sort of local criminals we've been dealing with in Coombesford – all of whom are either dead, or in prison, anyway."

"Fair comment. But what about all the time she was working with her sister. Suzanne, isn't it?"

"Yes, Suzanne. She and her husband Steve, plus their friend Francine Matheson, are looking in great detail into those years and those cases. But so far they've uncovered nothing."

"Which leaves her time with us, in the service."

"Precisely. And at this moment, that's a blank page."

Cyril Strong cleared his throat and brought his hands up to his mouth. There was a long silence. Finally he turned to Rohan and nodded.

"Alright, Mr Banerjee, I'll tell you what you want to know. But I need you to promise that everything we say remains in your head; not written down. And that you share the information with as few people as possible. Charlie was a good friend, as well as a colleague, and I wouldn't want to let her down. But you have to understand that other people's secrets – and their lives – are in danger here."

Rohan jumped up and held out his hand. "Mr Strong, I'll promise anything you need me to, if it'll help Charlie. And my name's Rohan."

Strong held out his hand in return and spoke without a trace of irony.

"Lofty. Charlie and the rest of the gang always called me Lofty. You can do the same."

CHAPTER 22

"So, in short, you're telling me you've got nothing. Nothing at all?" Suzanne watched as Annie ran her hand through her short pink hair, her frustration plain to see on her face.

"Not nothing, Annie. Not a huge amount of something, that's true. But certainly not nothing." Suzanne felt her tongue beginning to twist so stopped to take a breath.

Her sister-in-law rounded on her. "It looks like nothing to me. Lots of charts and lists," Annie pointed to the papers littered across the table, "but no clues as to who's doing this or why." She glared at the group sitting at the conference table. "You really are lost without Charlie, aren't you?" And she strode out of the function room, slamming the door behind her.

Esther rose to follow her, but Suzanne placed a hand on her arm to stop her.

"Leave her. She's upset. When she calms down she'll realise she's being unfair and she'll be back here apologising. Trust me."

"Mind you," said Esther with a sigh, "she's got a point. It's two weeks since Charlie was arrested and we're still no nearer to proving her innocence."

The three of them stared at the screen and the papers in silence for a few moments. Then Suzanne jumped to her feet. The other two looked at her in surprise.

"Do you realise we've been sitting struggling with this for five solid hours! And it's really stuffy in here. It's no wonder we're running low on energy." She clapped her hands. "Right, this is what we're going to do. Rohan, you open all the windows and doors, let's get some fresh air in here. Esther, you pop to the kitchen and get a new jug of coffee and some clean cups. Meet me out in the beer garden in fifteen minutes. We're going to change the view, see if that gives us a different perspective."

Fifteen minutes later, they were seated at one of the benches in the beer garden, when Annie walked out of The Folly and crossed the paddock towards them. She stood staring at her feet and cleared her throat nervously.

"Look, I know you're all trying your best. I'm sorry. I just want–" She stopped, seeming to run out of words.

Esther jumped up and hugged her. "Don't be daft. We understand. Goodness, if I had to put up with what you're going through right now, I'd be yelling at everyone. And probably trying to break down the door of the prison as well."

"Sit down, Annie." Suzanne patted the bench beside her. "We've spent ages trying to work out who's doing this to Charlie. So we're going to start from the other end. Who do we know, or strongly suspect, is *not* involved? And if we explain it to you as we go along, we can check our own logic and you can tell us if there's anything obvious we're missing. A fresh pair of eyes is often very helpful."

"We're fairly certain it's not anyone connected with the crimes here in Coombesford." Esther pulled a clean sheet of paper towards her and divided it into four quarters headed: Yes, No, Maybe and Unknown. "Too complex, too sophisticated, and since all the main players are in prison or dead, it would require a strong network on the outside world." She wrote 'Locals' in the No section.

"From what Damien told us after his trip to California, do we think Nigel Atkinson is in the clear or not?" Rohan scratched his head. "Suzanne, you knew him in the old days. What do you think?"

"My gut tells me Brother Nigel isn't involved, at least not directly. He was always very keen to keep his own hands clean; would use someone else to do the dirty work. And he doesn't seem to have much in the way of resources at this church of his."

"Although there's the car Damien spotted."

"Yes, Esther. And his furtive behaviour as Damien was driving away. I'm pretty sure Nigel's up to something. But it's probably as straightforward as fleecing his parishioners with promises of forgiveness. Let's do the Christian thing and give him the benefit of the doubt."

Esther nodded and wrote Nigel's name in the Maybe section.

Rohan went on to relate to Annie the call they'd had with WB earlier that day. "We've also got no indication that there's anything coming out of southern Africa."

Esther put 'African gangs' in the No section, as Suzanne took up the narration once more.

"We've yet to hear from Walter Mukooyo who's trying to make contact with Tomas Braun in Berlin. Put him in the Unknown section, Esther."

"Plus there's the leads Cyril Strong gave me on Tuesday," said Rohan. "It's a bit difficult to chase them up as he was really cagey about the information he was willing to release. But there are a couple of names I'm following up on." He pursed his lips. "Esther, can you just put Ms Y and Mr Q in the Unknown section for now, please."

Esther gave a giggle. "Very James Bond!"

"Yes, I know, but Lofty was adamant people's lives were at risk, so I promised him I wouldn't write down anything that might compromise anyone."

"And then there's Francine's attempts to reach Stefano

Mladov's daughter."

Annie slapped her hand on the table. "I'm *so* sorry. That's what I came out for. There's a message on the answerphone at The Folly. Francine tried to get through. She wants you to ring her back. Said she'd be free all afternoon but was going out this evening."

Suzanne grabbed her phone and checked the time on the screen. "It's just after four-thirty. They're only an hour ahead in France. Maybe we can catch her before she goes out."

Her call was answered at the first ring and Suzanne put her on speakerphone.

Francine got right down to business. "We talked to Marina Mladov last night. The poor thing's in a terrible state. She left Kyiv with the kids just after the war started. But her husband had to stay in Ukraine. He's a doctor, so she thinks he's spending most of his time on the frontline."

"She *thinks*? Doesn't she know?"

"She's not heard from him for several months. She doesn't even know for sure if he's still alive."

"Poor Marina," said Annie. "What an awful situation to be in. At least I know where my Charlie is."

"Yes, well, I'm not sure how much help Marina was able to be there." Francine paused and there was a rustle of paper as though she was checking her notes. "Since Nico was killed and Stefano died in the fire, her brother Mikhail has turned the company businesses pretty much legit." There was a snort from Suzanne. "Yes, I know it's hard to believe, but apparently Stefano always knew the next generations didn't have the same appetite for crime as he did. So despite what he was mixed up in when he died, there was a basis there for Mikhail to get out of crime altogether. He and Marina's family were reconciled and spent quite a bit of time together. Of course they're still in Russia, so she's not sure what's happened to them. But she was adamant that they wouldn't be behind the plot to frame Charlie."

The call ended with promises on both sides to keep in touch. Suzanne, Rohan, Esther and Annie stared at the phone for a few seconds as though hoping it would magically give them the answers they so desperately needed. Annie spoke first.

"So that's it. Another loose end tied off. Better put the Mladovs in the No section, Esther."

But Suzanne shook her head. "I'm not so sure." There were murmurs of surprise from the others. "No, I'm not doubting what Marina said. Mikhail was the elder of Stefano's sons, but he was much less inclined to violence and law-breaking than his brother and father. I can quite believe there's nothing coming from that part of the world. Especially in the middle of a war." She paused and groaned quietly. "But there's another strand to that particular period of our lives. A major strand in fact. It looks like I'm going to have to make a trip up to Belmarsh."

"Suzanne, you can't—"

"Yes, Annie, I can. I'm going to have to go and see Michael Hawkins."

CHAPTER 23

"Suzanne, my dear, how lovely to see you."

If it weren't for the fact that they were seated in a stark grey room furnished with just a table and two chairs. Or the fact that the man in front of her was dressed in prison uniform rather than a smart suit. Or the fact that she was free to leave at any time while he was handcuffed to the table and would only be able to move from there to his own room at the behest of the guard standing outside the door. If not for those three facts, Suzanne could almost believe she was back in her old boss's office waiting for the great Sir Fredrick Michaels to tell her why he'd requested this meeting.

It was so surreal a situation that Suzanne could do nothing more than go along with it.

It was over a decade since she'd been this close to Michael Hawkins, although she'd seen his picture on the news when he was extradited from Russia. At the time he'd looked like a little old man, the effects of five years in a Siberian prison obvious in his stance and his shuffling walk. Now he looked fit, relaxed and younger than the mid-seventies that she knew him to be.

"Hello, Michael. Thank you for agreeing to see me."

"Not at all, not at all." He grimaced. "It's not as though my diary is very full these days. It's nice to see an old friend."

He was really pushing it there. Work colleagues, mentor and mentee, adversaries; even captor and prisoner at one point. They had been different things to each other at different times over the years, but friends? Not so much. She wondered if he was delusional or just playing with her. And catching the ironic gleam in his eye, she suspected she knew which. Needing to make the most of the short time she'd managed to squeeze out of the prison authorities, she cleared her throat. "Michael, I've come to ask for your help."

"Ask away." He spread his hands as far as the cuffs would allow in a gesture of open-handed generosity.

"Charlie's in trouble. She's been framed for murder and we're hoping you might be able to shed some light on who's doing it to her."

"That's terrible." Hawkins reached a hand towards her. "You must be devastated." He raised an eyebrow. "But why would you think I might have anything to do with it?"

"We don't think that, Michael." She was quick to give an assurance she really didn't believe. She didn't want to risk offending him. "We just thought you might have heard something, through your contacts…" Her voice trailed off as he began laughing, quietly at first, but then gradually louder.

He wiped his eyes and shook his head at her. "I think you've been watching too many spy movies. And you've forgotten just where I've been for the past twelve years. I know little more than you do." He paused and licked his lips. "Although I must admit that I already knew about your sister's little problem."

She opened her mouth but he held up a hand to forestall her. "I said I knew about Charlie's arrest. That was on the news. But I have no idea who's behind it."

"I see." Suzanne felt a weight descend on her shoulders

once again. She'd pinned so many of her hopes on this interview.

"Pity really." Hawkins looked directly at her and his face hardened. "I really would love to know who's managed to trap the high and mighty Charlie Jones. I'd like to meet him and shake him by the hand!"

Suzanne gasped. It was as though he'd physically struck her.

Hawkins continued, his voice getting harsher with every word. "Did you really think, after everything you and your precious sister did to me and my friends, that I would so much as lift a little finger to help you? I always knew you were naive, Suzanne, but I didn't think you were stupid." Suzanne stood and nodded across at the guard outside the door. "Going so soon? What a pity. We were having such a nice little chat."

As she walked out of the room on legs that could barely carry her, Hawkins called after her. "Give my best to Charlie and tell her I'm looking forward to seeing her once more. I'll take her under my wing and show her around."

His mocking laughter followed Suzanne down the corridor.

Her hired car and driver was waiting for her outside the gates of Belmarsh prison when Suzanne came out. Barely acknowledging his greeting, she directed him back to the apartment on Victoria Embankment and spent the whole of the journey staring out of the window, her mind in turmoil. She just hoped the guys in Devon had come up with something while she'd been away.

Arriving at the apartment block, she came to a decision. Steve was waiting for her inside. It was too late to head to Paddington that evening. They'd have one evening of relaxation before they headed back to the southwest and Charlie's predicament.

A long hot shower, to wash away the dirt of a prison

visit and being in the same room as Michael Hawkins. Maybe a curry at Sanjay's across the road. And an early night. The following day was soon enough to tackle their problems.

But as she opened the door to the apartment, she heard voices, two, both male. In the lounge with its huge windows overlooking the Thames, Steve was sitting facing the door, and his smile lit up at the sight of her. Their visitor was on the sofa with his back to the door. She had the impression of dark close-cut curly hair and broad shoulders in a well-cut casual jacket. Then he stood and turned towards her with a smile and an outstretched hand.

"Hello, Suzanne. I came as soon as I heard. What can I do to help?"

It was twenty years since Suzanne had last seen Nathan Harawa. She was dismayed to realise that he could still make her stomach lurch just as easily now as he had during those four steamy days in Lusaka.

PART 3

CHAPTER 24

For the second time that afternoon, Suzanne felt as though her legs were about to give way. There was a loud buzzing in her ears. Looking between her beaming husband and his smiling companion, she was momentarily lost for words. Then she gathered her senses and held out her hand.

"Nathan, what a wonderful surprise. I had no idea you were in Europe." Mentally, she kicked herself. What a stupid thing to say. Why would she know where in the world he was, given how long it had been since they'd seen each other?

"The whole family's in France. But I spoke to Mum on the phone last night and she told me about Charlie's arrest so I flew over to see what I could do to help."

"And how did you find us? Here, in our home in London?"

"Mum got Annie's contact details off WB and I spoke to her before I left France. Sounds like the poor woman's holding it together pretty well."

"Yes, she is." Suzanne wasn't at all sure she wanted to discuss her sister-in-law's mental well-being with this man from Zambia. "So how does your wife feel about you dashing off at a moment's notice to help a complete stranger?"

"Hardly a complete stranger. It may be a long time ago, but I've never forgotten the goings-on back then or the role you and Charlie played."

Suzanne wasn't sure whether Nathan was talking about the counterfeiting gang they'd all helped to bring down, or something more personal. But now wasn't the time to examine that in any detail. Besides, Steve was looking at her with confusion on his face.

"Suzanne, what's got into you? Nathan's come all this way to see if he can help. You should be welcoming him with open arms, not interrogating the poor man."

"I know." Suzanne gave a heavy sigh, threw herself into an armchair, and smiled at their visitor. "I'm sorry, Nathan. It's been a long, and very frustrating, day." She brought the two men up to date on her visit to Belmarsh and the lack of co-operation she'd met from Michael Hawkins.

"And I have to say," she concluded, "I'm inclined to believe him. The Michael Hawkins we used to know was always very full of himself. If he'd had anything to do with Charlie's incarceration, he'd not have been able to stop himself from crowing."

"So another dead end then?" Steve sounded almost as defeated as she felt.

"Afraid so. I guess it's back to Devon and back to square one." She stood. "But not tonight. I'm off for a long shower, then we'll grab some supper. We can leave first thing in the morning. Can you check the train timetable, Steve?"

"No need for that, my love." She looked askance at her husband. "We've got a surprise for you. Nathan flew over in his own private jet and he's offered to take us down to Devon tomorrow. We'll be travelling in style." He paused. "And in return, I've offered him the spare room for the night."

"But if you'd rather I got a hotel room…" Nathan was

looking at her uncertainly. Maybe he finally realised just how strange and unsettling his sudden appearance was to Suzanne.

"No, of course not." Suzanne forced her face into a perfect smile. "The spare room is always made up and you're most welcome." Picking up a copy of a takeaway menu from a side table, she handed it to Steve. "And you can ring Sanjay's while I'm freshening up. My usual, please. You do like Indian food, don't you, Nathan?"

Of course he did. She knew he did. But as she walked towards the main bedroom to grab her dressing gown, she reflected that the last thing she could do was explain to her wonderful, but sometimes somewhat naive, husband just how she knew that, and why she was less than delighted at the new arrival in their lives. Although she had to admit, flying to Devon by private jet would be a real treat.

CHAPTER 25

Despite Suzanne's misgivings, the evening with Nathan was not so bad. Steve obviously enjoyed the other man's company and kept the conversation flowing with lots of questions about life in Zambia.

The following morning, they made the short journey to London City airport and the even shorter journey, at least time-wise, to the West Country. Landing at Exeter's XLR Executive Jet Centre meant they didn't have to fight their way through the crowds in the main terminal, and within just a few minutes of touchdown they were in Rohan's friend's car, cruising southward along the M5 towards Coombesford, an early lunch and a catch-up with the rest of the team.

And it was as that catch-up session was drawing to a close that Suzanne's phone rang. It was Walter Mukooyo. An adversary of Suzanne's when she'd first worked in Africa many years earlier, he had become a friend over the years and she now had a good deal of respect for the wily former politician turned regulator, who lived these days in Geneva, close to the headquarters of the World Health Organisation.

"I've found him, Suzanne," were his first words.

"Tomas Braun. He's living in a small village in Bavaria. Apparently he's retired and has no further involvement in crime – or so he was eager to insist. Although if he's living out his later years in comfort, it's presumably due to his less-than-legal lifestyle in the past."

"But did he know anything, Walter?"

"Ah well, that's the bad news. He wouldn't talk to me. Said he was only willing to talk to one of the Jones sisters directly. And he's insisting you do it in person."

"Oh, for goodness sake." She thought hard. "Whereabouts in Bavaria? Is it going to be difficult to get to, did he say?"

"He's not going to let you go to see him there. He wants to protect his hideaway. He said if you go to Munich, he'll meet up with you there."

"I suppose that's not so bad. Let me make some enquiries about transport and get back to you." She was already trying to work out whether a plane or a train was going to be the fastest option. "And, Walter, thank you."

"Anything for Charlie, my dear. Give her my love when you talk to her next, won't you." He paused, and Suzanne thought he'd disconnected the call. But then she heard a quiet cough.

"Suzanne, be careful. I don't know why, but I got the distinct impression Tomas was scared of something – or someone. And from what Charlie's said in the past, that's definitely not the Tomas Braun she knew back in the old days in Berlin."

CHAPTER 26

"I'm not sure it's such a good idea, Steve."

"But why not? The guy's here, he's offered to help. And you have to admit, a private jet is the quickest and easiest way to get from Exeter to Munich."

Suzanne and Steve had been making plans all morning. Or at least, Steve had been making plans, together with Nathan, and Suzanne had been looking for ways to derail them. She desperately needed to get out to Munich to meet Tomas Braun, but she wasn't at all sure about using Nathan's plane.

Finally, she'd suggested to her husband that the two of them go out for a walk to clear their heads. They'd taken one of Celia's pasties to split between them and drove the car to Stover Park.

Midweek, the park was practically empty, and it felt good to get away from the stressed atmosphere at The Falls for a little while. Having strolled around the lake in the sunshine, Suzanne and Steve found themselves a picnic table and benches under the trees. Inquisitive squirrels and quarrelsome ducks crept closer as the couple sat watching.

But as soon as they'd finished eating and thrown the

final crumbs to their animal friends, Steve was back in planning mode and Suzanne was forced to defend her objections once again.

"I just don't like it. He turns up out of the blue, like a knight in shining armour. It seems too much of a coincidence."

"Are you saying you don't trust him? You surely don't think he's got something to do with Charlie being framed?" Steve looked frankly disbelieving at this and Suzanne had to admit it was a very unlikely scenario.

"No, of course not. But what's his family going to say…"

"His family's quite happy sunning themselves in the south of France. He spoke to his wife last night and she insisted he stay as long as he needs to."

Suzanne could see this was an argument she was not going to win. But as she finally agreed to the plan and gathered together their belongings to head back to the car park, she couldn't help feeling uneasy. And it made it even worse that she had no idea why.

They'd parked against a bank separating the car park from a steep gully. As they reached the vehicle, they found an elderly woman pacing up and down, wringing her hands. When she saw them, she rushed towards them.

"Thank goodness. Can you help me? It's my Angus. He's gone down into the gully, and he can't get out." She pointed over the bank. "Please hurry. He's only young and he gets so frightened."

Glancing at Steve, Suzanne climbed up the bank and looked over. Halfway down the slope lay a very sad-looking poodle. The hair on its head was pulled into a pom-pom, tied with a bright red ribbon, matching the collar around its neck. Both the ribbon and the collar were very muddy. As was the dog itself.

When it saw Suzanne looking down at it, it wriggled frantically. And Suzanne realised its collar was snagged on a broken branch, stopping it from moving either up or down.

Steve climbed the bank and threw himself on the ground next to her.

"Have you contacted the rangers?" Suzanne called to the woman.

"No, I don't have a phone."

The dog gave another whimper and its owner moaned in sympathy.

"I've got one," Suzanne said. "You can use that." She began to climb back down the bank but Steve stopped her with a hand on her arm and pointed at the collar. Every time the dog moved it seemed to tighten the pressure around its neck.

"If we wait for the rangers, it could be too late. The poor little thing will strangle itself." Steve hauled himself to his feet and pulled the belt out of his raincoat. "Here, you hold this end. I'm going to go down and release it. If I attach its lead to the belt, you can help me guide it out."

Before Suzanne could say anything, he was over the top and down the slope. She knew her husband, a part-time vet and full-time animal lover, had a wonderful way with dogs. So she wasn't surprised to see him quickly calm the puppy and release him from the branches.

When she felt a tugging on the belt, she pulled gently and guided Angus back up the slope, over the top and into the arms of his sobbing owner.

"Okay, Steve. All clear. You can come back up now." She leaned over the bank and looked down at her husband. His big smile lasted as long as it took to put one foot on the bank above the broken branch. Then it turned to a look of horror at the sound of a crack and a roar, as his legs slipped out from under him.

The side of the bank collapsed and tumbled to the bottom of the gully, throwing Steve down with it. It was brief, only a matter of seconds. And then all was silent.

CHAPTER 27

Rohan's phone rang as he was walking up the lane from the centre of the village towards the farm. It had been a long day on top of a long week, the third such long week they'd been through. And they were nowhere closer to finding out what was going on. He leaned against the fence and hit 'accept'.

"I understand you're trying to get hold of me?" The voice was female, hoarse, as though from a lifetime of smoking, and sounded a long way away.

"Who is this?"

"It doesn't matter who I am. A little birdie tells me you're trying to find me." There was a pause. "And that worries me. I don't want to be found. So when I hear of some young investigator asking after me and leaving messages all over the place, it worries me. Who are *you*, Mr Banerjee and why do you so desperately need to talk to me?"

Finally, the penny dropped for Rohan. "It's Ms Y–"

"I said my name doesn't matter. Now I'm running out of patience, Mr Banerjee. Tell me who you are and why I should talk to you."

"It's about an old colleague of yours – Charlie Jones.

She's in prison, awaiting trial for murder."

"It couldn't happen to a nicer woman!" There was an unpleasant chuckle at the other end of the line. "I always knew she'd fall off that high horse of hers one of these days."

"No, you don't understand. She didn't do it. The police are convinced they have the right woman and they've closed their investigation. But she was framed. Her friends are trying to find the true culprit."

"And you thought of me? Charming. Although how you even heard about me, I have no idea."

Rohan paused, wondering if he was about to make things worse, not better. But he didn't seem to be getting anywhere, so it was worth a try. "It was Lofty, I mean Cyril Strong. He gave me your details. Said you knew Charlie well back in the day. He thought you might have some ideas."

It was the caller's turn for silence. Rohan began to wonder if she had disconnected. But finally there was a sigh. "Yes, Charlie and I spent a lot of time together back then. Late eighties, early nineties it was. We were never bosom pals or anything like that. She didn't approve of some of my methods, and I thought she was too prissy for words. But she was a good operative, one of the best I've ever met. And for what it's worth, if she's saying she's innocent, I'd be inclined to believe her too. The Charlie Jones I knew would never lie about something like that."

"So do you have any suggestions for who might be behind this? It's got to be a fairly sophisticated set-up. Some of the evidence they've faked is very convincing."

"Not really. Most of the operations we worked on together were small scale, one-offs. I suppose you know about the extraction of hostages in Lebanon?"

"Yes. In fact Felix, the young aid worker, was here in UK the other week, so we had a chance to talk to him."

"And then, there's the major operation in Berlin…"

"We're following up on that."

"In that case, I'm stumped, I'm afraid. I'll ask around. I still have a few contacts from the old days. But I wouldn't hold out much hope." There was an intake of breath. Rohan assumed she was taking a drag on her cigarette. "Of course, once she left for Albania, I never saw or heard from her again."

"Okay. Well, I appreciate your talking to me. I know it's difficult when you're trying to stay hidden. Must be scary coming out into the open, even on the phone."

"Don't be silly, dear." She gave another cackle, this time of pure mischief. "I'm not hiding from my past. I can't stand people in general. I've got a nice little home and a nice little life away from the crowds, where no-one bothers me and I don't bother them."

Rohan grinned. He felt he would like this woman if he was ever to meet her. But there was one more question before he let her go. "Can I just ask – are you still in contact with Mr Q?"

"Oh, yes, I see him every week. In fact, I'm going to visit him this afternoon."

"But I thought you said you didn't–"

"Poor Mr Q is living in a retirement home. He thinks he's Titania, Queen of the Fairies. And every week, we plan how he's going to get revenge on his cheating husband, Oberon. I'm afraid there's nothing left of his memories." There was a pause. "I hope you manage to find the answers you're looking for, Mr Banerjee. And give Charlie Jones my best. Goodbye."

As Rohan finished walking along the lane, he sighed. It looked as if he'd come up against another couple of dead ends. He just hoped the others were having more luck.

CHAPTER 28

By the time the emergency services had rescued Steve from the gully and transported him off to hospital, it was late afternoon. Suzanne followed the ambulance in their car and waited with him while a succession of nurses popped in and out, checking his stats, arranging an X-ray, and promising a doctor's attendance at some point in the evening.

Steve had remained conscious throughout, and despite his obvious pain his main concern was the effect his accident would have on their proposed trip. Suzanne had already decided she would go on her own, but knew a hospital A&E department was the wrong place to have an argument, so kept her own counsel.

They finally arrived back at The Falls around one in the morning. Steve was protesting that he didn't need to be in a wheelchair, but Suzanne was ignoring him, saving all her puff for pushing. Annie met them in the car park.

"Suzy wanted to stay up and check how you were, but she finally crashed out just before midnight."

"I'm fine, thanks." Steve was wan, and Suzanne knew he was anything but fine. "I just feel so stupid."

"But the owner of little Angus doesn't think you're

stupid," Suzanne reminded him. "She thinks you're a hero." She turned to Annie with a wink. "And I'm going to put my hero to bed, Annie. Although," a sudden thought hit Suzanne, "it's going to be difficult for him to manage the stairs with a cast. He may have to go up backwards on his bum."

"We've already thought about that." Annie grinned. "If we can get the wheelchair across the garden to The Folly, Steve can have Suzy's room. She's in with me tonight. Then we'll come up with a better solution from tomorrow."

Next morning, Suzanne, Steve and Annie were joined at the pub's breakfast table by Nathan. And it was quickly obvious to Suzanne that her husband and his new friend had been plotting behind her back.

"Nathan's going to fly you out to Munich and go with you to meet Tomas." Steve swallowed a couple of painkillers and grimaced as he tried to settle his leg in a more comfortable position.

"But—"

"No buts, Suzanne. We have no idea what this trip is going to result in, and if I can't be there to support you, at least I know Nathan will have your back."

Suzanne looked across at Annie, hoping for some female solidarity, but her sister-in-law was nodding in agreement with Steve. And as she swallowed her pride and her discomfort at being alone with her former lover, Suzanne realised they were right. And this wasn't about her. It was about helping Charlie.

Suzanne smiled. "Okay. You've convinced me." She turned to Nathan. "If you're really sure you can spare the time, I'd be delighted to accept your offer."

Two days later, just after noon, Suzanne and Nathan left the jet at Munich Airport and strolled across to the Hilton Hotel. Tomas had told them to book a table in the

Mountain Hub café. They ordered hot chocolates and sat sipping their drinks, watching the continual flow of people.

"Fascinating, isn't it, wondering where everyone's going to or coming from."

The soft voice made them jump. The elderly man standing behind them was, on first sight, nothing like the former gangster they'd been expecting. Completely bald and clean-shaven, dressed in expensively casual clothing, he looked like a retired businessman on his way to a game of golf or a day sailing with his friends.

But, glancing down, Suzanne spotted the trademark snakeskin boots. And when she looked up at his face and was hit by the full force of his brilliant emerald green eyes, she knew for sure that she was in the presence of Tomas Braun, her sister's former quarry from Berlin. She jumped up.

"Mr Braun, it's so good of you to come and meet us."

"Sit down, Ms Jones." He looked around, as though checking the room for enemies. "Let's keep this as low-key as possible." He joined them at the table. "I have to say I'm only here because, despite everything, I have a soft spot for your sister. And she saved me once." He continued to scan the room as he spoke. Suzanne could see he was very nervous.

"So can you help us? Do you know who's doing this?"

"Not exactly, no." He shook his head with what looked to Suzanne like genuine sorrow. "There's no word on the streets about a plot to frame Charlie. But I thought maybe we could approach the problem from the other end. Not 'who would do this to Charlie' but 'who has the capability to do this at all'. And for that, you need to talk to a friend of mine in Czechia. He's one of the best when it comes to faking evidence, especially CCTV footage. And he also knows all the other top players in the same game."

"Can't we just phone him?"

"I'm afraid not. He only works face to face. And only then, with people he knows."

"So will you come with us?"

"Not me, no." He paused and gave a rueful grin. "I'm too old to go jumping on planes at the drop of a hat. But I've asked a mutual business associate to go with you. He'll meet you this evening at nine, at FBO1 at Vaclav Havel Airport, in Prague. His name is Marek. He'll take you to meet my friend. I hope you find the answers you need."

Tomas stood and shook hands with Nathan before taking Suzanne's hand and bringing it to his lips. "Take care, Ms Jones. You are dealing with some very dangerous people."

Turning, he disappeared into the crowd.

CHAPTER 29

The flight time from Munich to Prague was less than one hour. They were due to meet Marek at nine. Nathan spoke to his pilot by phone and confirmed everything could be arranged in time. But there would be a couple of hours' delay while all the formalities were completed. They decided to stay where they were and have a late lunch/early dinner while they waited.

"Something tells me we won't get a chance to eat once we arrive in Prague," said Suzanne.

For the next hour or so, they relaxed and chatted about his family and the life they continued to lead on the rose farm in the Copper Belt; then her life with Steve in the UK. Suzanne was surprised to find how easy it was to slip back into a relaxed friendship with the tall Zambian. They made no mention of the time they'd spent together after her rescue from the kidnappers. Until the end of the meal.

"Suzanne, do you ever wonder?" Nathan cleared his throat. "Do you ever think what might have happened if I'd not gone to that business meeting that day and you'd not flown home to England?"

Suzanne regarded him steadily, although her mind was churning. Yes, of course she'd wondered. Although less so since she'd met and fallen in love with Steve. But she'd be lying if she said it hadn't crossed her mind.

"No, Nathan, I'm sorry. It was a wonderful interlude. I will always be grateful to you for looking after me when I needed it. But it was a moment in time and that's all. We both knew that."

"I guess you're right." He looked around for the waiter and gave the universal signal for the bill. "Anyway, shall we head back to the terminal? We should be ready to leave in less than an hour."

As they left the table, he strode ahead to get the door for her. Suzanne followed him, and as she did so, she couldn't help but wonder – just a tiny bit…

The flight went off smoothly and they arrived in Prague well ahead of time. Tomas had told them to wait in the bar of the private terminal, and it was there, a few minutes before nine, that they were approached by a short dark-haired man in a leather jacket.

"I am Marek. Come with me."

A man of few words, Suzanne realised. Although it could be because English was obviously not his first language. He showed them to a black SUV parked behind the terminal building and then drove at high speed towards the perimeter gates. As they were leaving, they had to pull aside out of the path of two police cars, lights flashing and sirens screaming.

"What's that all about?" Suzanne tried to catch Marek's eye in the rear-view mirror, but there was no response. She shrugged and sank back into the soft leather interior.

Once off the airfield, they joined a major highway. But instead of driving eastwards, towards the lights of the city on the horizon, they turned towards the west. Within minutes, they were deep into the countryside.

Suzanne looked at Nathan and raised an eyebrow. He shook his head in return, before leaning forward and tapping Marek on the shoulder. He flashed them a quick smile in the rear-view mirror, but said nothing.

At the next junction, he raced off the main carriageway and down the slip road, passing quickly from a well-lit highway to an unlit country lane. Suddenly from out of the darkness, bright spotlights were switched on, blinding all three occupants of the vehicle.

Marek slammed on the brakes and fought to keep control of the wheel as they slewed across the road and came to rest half on and half off the grass verge. Then the air was filled with the sound of semi-automatic gunfire.

"Get down!" Nathan screamed, grabbing Suzanne by the arm and pushing her onto the floor of the SUV, wrapping himself around her.

In less than a minute, it was all over. The gunfire stopped. The spotlights went out. There was the sound of a vehicle driving away. And then absolute silence and complete darkness.

Suzanne gave no resistance as Nathan sat up, pulled her gently back onto the seat and wound his arms tightly around her. She wasn't sure whether it was she who was trembling uncontrollably, him, or both of them. Then she remembered they weren't alone.

"Marek? Are you okay, Marek?" She pulled herself out of Nathan's arms and leaned forward over the headrest, dreading what she would see.

But the front seats of the SUV were empty. Marek had gone.

CHAPTER 30

"We have to get out of here, Nathan." Suzanne could feel panic rising in her chest. "What if they come back to check on us, and realise we're still alive?" She went to open the car door, but Nathan stopped her with a hand on her arm.

"No, wait. Think about it." He pulled out his phone and switched on the torch then leaned forward and ran his hand across the driver's seat and backrest. "See?" he said, holding his hand in front of her face. "Completely dry and clean."

"So?"

"So, no blood." He pointed to the windscreen. "In fact, no bullet holes either. I think this was meant to scare us, not kill us."

"But what about Marek?" She clutched Nathan's arm as a thought struck her. "Maybe they weren't after us at all. Maybe they were after Marek. Do you think he tried to run away and they shot him on the road?"

"I'm rather afraid our Marek was not what we thought he was. If he was running away, I don't think he'd have stopped to close the car door behind him, do you?" Nathan pointed to the driver's door. "But I'll go and check." He grinned at her. "Don't look so worried. I'll be back in a mo."

Suzanne watched the torchlight move around the outside of the vehicle and then across the road in front of them. But it was only a few seconds before he was back. "As I thought, there's no sign of Marek, dead or alive. And there's no damage to the outside of the vehicle. Whichever direction they were firing in, it certainly wasn't at us."

"I guess that's reassuring, in some way." Suzanne ran her hands down the sides of her trousers to dry the sweat from her palms. "So what happens now?"

"Now, we drive back to the airport. My pilot will be on standby and can get us airborne straight away. I told him to file a flight plan for the UK and await our instructions." Nathan crossed his fingers. "I'm just hoping Marek had the decency to leave the car keys in the ignition."

Marek had indeed done that, so with Nathan driving and Suzanne sitting close to him in the passenger seat, they returned the vehicle to the road and retraced their steps to the airport.

As they passed through security at the entrance to the private terminal, they could just see flashing lights away in the corner of the site. The security officers were tight-lipped about what was going on, but assured them it would not hold up their departure in any way.

Reaching the plane, Suzanne settled herself in the cabin while Nathan went up to the cockpit to talk to the pilot. She sat back, closed her eyes and concentrated on breathing slowly and calmly, something she had been unable to do since their car was ambushed.

Actually, when she thought back, she realised she'd been on edge from the moment Marek had met them and led them across the dark tarmac to the SUV. She didn't like to think that Tomas had double-crossed them, but it was certainly looking like his friend Marek was not as he was supposed to be.

She was just dozing off when she heard Nathan return and the plane's engines were switched on.

"Everything okay?" she asked, opening her eyes. But she could see from his frown that everything was far from okay.

"The pilot's been doing some sniffing around while he was waiting for us. All that police activity they wouldn't tell us about? Apparently they found a body at the back of one of the hangars. Looks like it's not natural causes."

"And you think…?"

"Suzanne, it's the body of a young man. He'd been stabbed. Bit of a coincidence, don't you think? That it happens at the same time as we fly in to meet a stranger. A stranger who turns out to be less than trustworthy." Nathan sat down and strapped himself in. "I think the sooner we get back to England, the better. We're waiting for clearance from the control tower. We should be taking off in around fifteen minutes."

"Then I'm going to try to ring Tomas before we leave." Suzanne pulled her phone out of her bag. "If the real Marek has been killed – and I know that's still a big if – then Tomas needs to know."

But there was no answer from the number Walter had given her for Tomas Braun. And it was still unanswered when she tried again as they landed at London City airport a couple of hours later to refuel and give the pilot a few hours' rest.

Of course, she knew it could be because it was the middle of the night and he'd switched it off.

She still couldn't get through when she tried again after an early breakfast.

And finally, when they landed at Exeter.

CHAPTER 31

"It doesn't make any sense!" Annie was prowling around the function room, running her fingers through her hair. It wasn't the first time she'd said it in the past couple of hours, and it was unlikely to be the last time, but it didn't seem to Suzanne as if anyone in the room was in the mood to disagree with her. "It's as though someone's playing games with us!"

"But pretty deadly games, by the sound of it," Rohan said. "It looks like there's at least one person been killed–"

Esther looked up from her laptop and chimed in, "Two! Don't forget the guy on the train."

"Right. Two dead bodies." Rohan nodded in acknowledgment at her comment. "Not to mention ambushing you guys in Prague. What's going on?"

Esther and Rohan were slouched in their seats at the table, across from Suzanne, and she knew exactly how they felt. Steve, still using the wheelchair albeit under protest, was next to her with his leg propped up on a stool. Nathan, seated in the corner of the room, scrolling down on his phone, had said very little once the two of them had brought the rest up to date on what had happened during their visits to Germany and Czechia.

She glanced across at him, she saw his eyes widen and he pointed to the large screen on the wall, connected to the laptop.

"Esther, pull up the BBC News website," Nathan said. "There's something you need to see."

They all watched in silence as a reporter described the scene of a drive-by shooting the previous day in Munich, not far from the airport. Several people were reported to have been injured, one fatally. The fatality was described as an elderly man, bald-headed and clean-shaven, wearing casual clothes and snakeskin boots. Police were appealing for witnesses or anyone who could help identify the man, so far unnamed.

"Tomas." It was Suzanne who broke the silence. "That's Tomas Braun." She looked across at Rohan, a catch in her voice. "I guess you can make that *three* dead bodies."

"But why?" Annie was pacing once more. "If Tomas has been killed, he can't be behind all this. And why drag you guys halfway across Europe and pretend to attack you, but not really? And what has all this got to do with Charlie being set up? It doesn't make sense."

Finally coming to a standstill, Annie checked the time on the bottom of the screen and shrugged. "Anyone for another coffee? Suzy will be back from school any minute now and I have to start thinking about supper."

There was general assent around the table. Suzanne watched as Annie left the room then turned to the others. "She's getting close to breaking point, guys. We need to sort this out." Suzanne shook her head. "But I have no idea what we do next."

The scream that ripped through the building at that moment brought them all to their feet. Rohan and Nathan were first to the door, followed by Esther.

Suzanne looked at Steve, and then at his cast. He nodded at her and pointed after the others. "Go, find out what's going on. I'll be fine here."

She hurried out of the room and across the restaurant to the bar where all the noise was coming from. But halfway across, she was accosted by a small figure racing towards her, followed by a very excited black and white dog.

"Aunt Suzanne, she's coming home. Mama Annie just got a text. Mama C's coming home!" Suzy grabbed her by the hand and dragged her into the bar, both of them avoiding the bundle of fur which was in danger of tripping everyone up in his excitement.

Nathan, Rohan and Esther were standing at the window, pointing into the car park.

Suzanne joined them just in time to see a police car draw up outside the door. As the passenger door opened and a familiar figure jumped out, Annie ran around the side of the pub and launched herself into Charlie's arms.

Looking around at the rest of the team in the bar, Suzanne realised she wasn't the only one with tears rolling down her cheeks.

CHAPTER 32

Charlie stretched out on the leather Chesterfield and patted the seat beside her.

"What a day!" Annie joined her and curled her legs under her. "I was so miserable when I woke up this morning, I could barely pull myself out of bed. All I could think about was you stuck in that prison cell. Wondering whether you were okay, whether you had enough to eat, whether I would ever see you again. If it hadn't been for Suzy, I could have pulled the bedclothes over my head and stayed there."

"Annie, sweetie, you saw me last week. You know I was eating okay. And it was Exeter, not Siberia. It wasn't so bad really."

"And then Suzanne and Nathan got back from Prague. They'd learned nothing. And no-one had any idea what we should do next." Annie swallowed hard and seemed to be having trouble keeping her voice straight. "And then, out of the blue, you came home. It's all too much to take in."

"Hey, don't cry, there's nothing to get upset about." Charlie pulled Annie closer to her, wrapping her arms around her.

"I know. It's such a shock that it's happened so

suddenly. Just like that, it's all over. At least as far as we're concerned. You're free."

"But we still don't know who killed those poor young men. Not to mention my friend Tomas. Or how they got hold of one of our knives and my keyring."

"And we may never find out. But it's not our problem, Charlie. We can leave it to the police."

"I guess you're right." Charlie was far from convinced but she didn't want to upset Annie on her first night home.

The pair sat in silence for a few moments. Then Annie wriggled around to face Charlie.

"Do the police know why it took so long for that witness to come forward?"

"She was out of the country on business, apparently. She took a flight from Bristol early on the Sunday morning and she's been in Cape Town ever since. She only returned the other day. Someone mentioned the case to her, she looked up the details and got in touch with the police as soon as she realised she'd been on the train at the time of the murder."

"Wow." Annie shuddered. "So many ways in which that might not have worked out for you. And wasn't it lucky she was filming the journey along the coast like that."

"A chance in a million, the police said." Charlie paused. "In fact, if I'm honest, it all seems a bit too good to be true."

"In what way?"

"She happened to be filming a section of the coast at exactly the same time as the murder was being committed. And she happened to catch my reflection in the window while she was doing it." Charlie shook her head. "Something doesn't smell right about the whole thing. And don't forget, Annie, this isn't just a case of mistaken identity and police mismanagement. This was a deliberate attempt to make a fake case against me, to get me sent down for murder."

"And the police were convinced straight away that the second film was genuine?"

"Apparently so. They checked the witness's story and she's really been out of the country all this time. Plus, her film shows someone sitting next to me and they traced them too. They confirmed I didn't move from my seat."

Charlie pulled a face. "So, no, Annie, I don't think it's all over for us. Not by a long mile. If we don't find out who tried to frame me – and more importantly, why – then who's to say they won't try it again. And next time, I won't be so lucky. If indeed it was luck this time."

Annie uncurled her legs and stood. "As far as I'm concerned, it's case closed. You're home. Suzanne's home. No-one I love is in danger. That's enough for me, at least for tonight." Annie stretched out her hand. "Come on, it's nearly two o'clock, time for bed. And tomorrow, we're going to contact the travel agent and think about rearranging that honeymoon we missed."

"Okay, boss, anything you say." Charlie stood and hugged Annie. "Right, I'll switch out the lights and follow you down."

"I'll check on Suzy while you're doing that."

As Charlie was locking the door to their upstairs living quarters, there was a shout from the floor below.

"Charlie, she's not here!"

Charlie thundered down the stairs and pushed past Annie, hoping against hope it was a mistake. Their daughter's bedroom, normally so neat and tidy, was in disarray. The bedclothes were thrown back and trailed on the floor. The window was wide open, as was the door to her tiny en-suite.

"She can't have gone far, Annie. Have you checked our bedroom?"

The pair raced around, checking every room, every cupboard, every space they could imagine a nearly-thirteen-year-old would fit into. They searched the beer garden and shone torches down the slope leading to the stream. But there was no sign of their daughter anywhere.

"Could she have gone up to The Falls?" Charlie knew that was unlikely but didn't want to face the reality of the situation if she could avoid it. "Maybe she's sneaked up there to check on Bertie."

Annie shook her head and pointed silently to the hook beside the front door. The bunch of keys for the pub was hanging there as always.

They thoroughly searched the car park and grounds, and the lanes and gardens close by, and took Bertie out on his lead to see if he could find the scent of the young girl he spent so much time with. But all to no avail.

Suzy Grace McLeod-Jones had disappeared without a trace.

Returning to Suzy's bedroom, Charlie spotted something they'd missed in their initial search. Poking out from under the tangled bedclothes was an iPhone in a bright pink case. Bought for her as a present on the day of their wedding, as a thank you for her hard work as a bridal planner. Certain proof that wherever their daughter was, whoever she was with, she'd not gone willingly.

As they stared at it, Charlie's phone pinged, startlingly loud in the silence. The wording of the text was stark: *We have your daughter. Tell no-one. No police or Suzy dies. We will be in touch at ten o'clock.* There was an attachment: a picture of a wide-eyed Suzy, bound to a chair, with tape across her mouth and tears rolling down her cheeks.

"Noooo!" Annie wailed and threw herself down on the bed.

Charlie took a deep breath and leaned back against the wall, steadying herself. It looked as though her suspicions were right. This – whatever this was – was far from over. Her recent incarceration was only the beginning. And the rather convenient way in which her innocence had been proved was another part of the jigsaw.

But attacking her directly was one thing. Getting at her

through their daughter was another thing completely. The game-playing had to stop.

PART 4

CHAPTER 33

"We've got to call the police. Now! We're wasting time." Charlie reached for her phone, but Annie swung around towards her, a look of horror across her face.

"No, Charlie, we can't! You saw the message. They'll kill her if we tell anyone, especially the police."

As soon as they'd discovered their daughter had been kidnapped, Charlie and Annie had woken Suzanne and Steve. The four were now gathered in the bar of The Falls, trying to make sense of what was happening.

"Charlie's right, Annie. We have to tell the police. We can't handle this one on our own." Suzanne reached across and tried to put her arm around her sister-in-law's shoulders. But Annie pulled roughly away.

"No, we need to wait. They said they'd be in touch. If they want money, we'll get it for them. We can't risk telling anyone. If Suzy's hurt..." Annie broke off, choking on the words.

Charlie and Suzanne looked at each other in consternation. They knew from experience that paying a ransom, if indeed that was what this was all about, rarely led to a good conclusion. In fact, Charlie knew kidnapping very often resulted in the victim being killed, even if the money was paid. But she couldn't think about that. And she certainly couldn't say that to Annie.

"Alright, Annie, we'll play it your way for the moment. We'll keep the police out of it – at least until we have an idea what they want and why they've taken Suzy." Charlie paused and gave her wife a weak smile. "But we're not completely helpless here. And even if we don't tell the police, there are some other folks we definitely will tell."

Charlie checked her watch. "Right, it's getting on for five. Suzanne, Esther will be up soon, so can you give her a ring in about half an hour; ask her to go and wake Rohan. Tell her we need the two of them as soon as possible. Annie, I know it's difficult, but can you get started on the breakfasts? If we're going to present some semblance of normality, we need to feed our guests at the usual time."

"And what are you going to do?" Steve asked, as Charlie picked up her jacket and grabbed the car keys.

"Me? I'm going for reinforcements. We're not completely helpless in all this." As she strode towards the door, Annie rushed after her and threw her arms around her.

"We'll get her back, Charlie, won't we?"

"Yes, of course we will, sweetie. And don't worry, I'll be back long before the call comes in." And with a wave, she was gone.

In a little over an hour, she reached the outskirts of Dorchester and drove slowly down a street of neat semi-detached houses in the suburbs. As she passed number 19, she glanced across. There was a light shining from the window on the side of the house. Charlie smiled.

"Old habits never die, do they? Always making tea before the sun rises." She pulled in to a lay-by at the end of the street, and got out of the car, gently closing the door behind her. On silent feet, she walked back to the house she'd been watching and slipped into the passage running down the side of the building. Approaching the window, she stood on tiptoe and peered in. But the kitchen was empty.

"Put your hands where I can see them. And no sudden moves." Charlie heard the quiet voice at the same time as something solid was jammed into her back. She slowly raised her arms. "Move towards the rear of the house." She did as she was told. Rounding the corner, she saw the kitchen door was wide open, light spilling out into the yard. "Inside. Sit at the end of the table where I can see you."

Charlie sat as directed and looked across at the face of her former commanding officer. "This isn't quite the reception I was hoping for, sir," she said with a wry smile, "but it's great to see you again." The short rotund man who had so comprehensively taken her unawares placed his gun on the table, shrugged and turned towards the kettle.

"It serves you right for making such a hash of that approach, Jones," he said. "I'd have heard you a mile off – even if I hadn't spotted you casing the joint beforehand." He placed a mug of instant coffee in front of Charlie and indicated the milk and sugar in the middle of the table. "Help yourself." Then Cyril Strong grinned and held out his hand. "Good to see you, Charlie. Got you then, didn't I?"

"It's been a few years. I'm out of practice. But, it's good to see you too, Lofty."

"I take it you're no longer wanted for murder then. Unless you're on the run, of course."

"No, that's all been sorted out. A witness," she used her fingers to frame the word in the air, "came forward with proof that it wasn't me. The police know I was framed, although not yet by whom."

"So, come to thank me for talking to that young detective, have you? He was very persuasive. You've got a solid friend there, Charlie."

"Yes, I know that. I'm very lucky." Charlie's smile faded as she remembered exactly why she was there. "But no, that's not it either, sir. I've come to ask you for your help, again. But not for me this time. For my daughter." In a few words, she brought him up to date with what had happened that night.

"So, we've not involved the police so far. But I'm hoping you'll agree to come and work with us. After all, you're the best abduction expert I know."

CHAPTER 34

By the time Charlie returned to The Falls, it was approaching eight am. She found Annie in the kitchen, although by the distracted look on her face, she wasn't concentrating on getting any food out. It was a good job Rohan and Esther were there.

"Charlie, where have you been?" Annie had traces of dried tears on her cheeks and she was sniffing into a crumpled tissue. Charlie gathered her into a tight hug. Partly because she felt they both needed it, and partly because she didn't want Annie to see the uncertainty on her face.

"I've been to see an old friend, from my time in the Secret Service." Annie pulled back and opened her mouth to protest, but Charlie placed a finger across her lips. "No, let me finish. This man is the best kidnap expert I've ever worked with. If anyone can find our Suzy and bring her back, it's Lofty."

"Lofty? Not Cyril 'Lofty' Strong?" Rohan looked up from the stove where he was handling multiple pans. "He told me his help was a one-off and not to bother him again. Has he changed his mind?"

"He certainly has. And don't let his outward

appearance fool you, Rohan. Inside that egg-shaped body and bald head ticks a mind like a steel trap. You wait until you see him in action."

"So where is this wonder then?" Annie didn't seem to be trying to keep the edge of sarcasm out of her voice.

"He'll be here later this morning. He's gone to collect some more team members on his way." Charlie had been delighted and not a little surprised when her former boss had not only agreed to come to Coombesford to help find Suzy but also suggested he bring a couple of additional bodies with him for support. He wouldn't tell Charlie where his former colleagues were living, but he'd offered to contact them personally and bring them with him if he could.

At ten o'clock, Charlie's phone rang. She laid it on the table, hit 'accept', and put it on speaker mode as Suzanne started recording on her phone.

"Charlie Jones, is that you?" The voice was deep, hollow, unmistakably disguised, but almost certainly male.

"Yes, I'm here."

"Good. I was a bit worried when I heard about you racing off like that into the night. I thought you wouldn't be available to take my call. Where did you go?"

"I went for a drive, to clear my head. Do you need an itinerary?"

"It doesn't matter. It doesn't affect our situation."

There was a gasp from Annie, and she dashed across the room. "Situation? How dare you refer to my daughter's kidnap as a situation. Suzy, Suzy are you there? Can you hear me?"

"Your daughter is perfectly safe, Ms McLeod. And she will remain so, just as long as your 'wife'," they could almost taste the scorn in his voice as he said the word, "does just what I tell her to do." There was a pause, then a slight chuckle, sinister in its unexpectedness. "But I guess it won't hurt to let you have a word with her. Just a minute."

There was a pause and the sound of tape being pulled off skin, followed by a little squeal. "There you go, Suzy. Have a word with your precious mothers."

"Mama Annie, Mama C, are you there?"

"Oh, Suzy darling, yes, we're both here. Have they hurt you?" Annie's question was little more than a whisper.

The evil chuckle came again. "They can't see you, silly girl. But I can report, ladies, that your daughter shook her head. I've not hurt her." There was a long pause. "And I don't intend to. I'm not in the business of hurting children."

"Suzy, speak to us," Charlie said gently.

The response, when it came, was almost a whisper. "I'm fine. I've got food and water. And they let me go to the toilet when I need to. But I miss Bertie the cat."

Charlie looked at Annie, trying to telegraph her pride that their daughter was attempting to send them messages in code, then back to the phone. "Do you know where you are?"

"Oh, nice try, Charlie, but you don't think I'm going to let Suzy answer that question, do you? Take her back into the other room." This was an aside, and was followed by the sound of a protesting Suzy being dragged away from the phone. A door opened and was slammed shut. The brief silence was broken by the kidnapper. "Right, I think that's enough for now."

"No, wait, please." The word seemed dragged out of Annie's mouth. "What do you want with Suzy?"

"Why, I've already told you, Ms McLeod. I want nothing at all to do with your daughter. And if everything goes according to my instructions, she'll be back with you very soon."

"Then what…?"

"It all depends on Ms Jones there. She's got a lot to answer for. And I've waited a long time for this moment. To return to her something she left behind." There was the sound of a fingernail tapping on a wooden surface. "But I think that's enough for now. Charlie, you have some thinking to do. I'll be in touch later today. Don't go disappearing again, now will you. I'm not going to give you any warning before I call this time. And I expect you to be there when I do."

And with a click, the call was disconnected. Annie gave out a howl and threw herself at Charlie. "What did you do? What did you leave behind, Charlie?"

"I don't know, Annie. I have no idea what he's referring to."

"Well, you'd better work it out." She pulled herself up to her full height and pointed an accusing finger inches from Charlie's nose. Suzanne reached out her arms towards her sister-in-law, but she shook her head and held her hands out to block her.

"No, Suzanne, I'm not going to be pacified this time. My daughter…" Charlie's attempt to butt in with "*our* daughter" was met with a glare and a shake of Annie's head. "*My* daughter, the child I gave birth to, is in danger and, from what I can see, Charlie has the solution. So I suggest you start putting those wonderful brains of yours to good use."

She turned and walked towards the door, throwing her parting words over her shoulder. "Because if anything happens to my Suzy, it's going to be your fault, Charlie Jones. And I'll never forgive you."

CHAPTER 35

There was a long awkward silence following Annie's outburst, punctuated by the bang of the door as she swept out of the bar. Suzanne had rarely seen Charlie in tears in the nearly sixty years she'd known her, but from the look of despair on her sister's face, she was very close to that right now.

"We know nothing. Nothing at all. What are we going to do?" Charlie slammed her fist into her palm. "Annie's right, if anything happens to Suzy, it'll be my fault!"

"Now look here, Charlie Jones," Suzanne strode across the bar and grabbed her sister by the arms, "don't you dare go soppy on me now. You need to bring your A game – we all do. And it's certainly not true to say we know nothing." She paused and looked around. "Come on, let's go into the function room. I want to get everything down on paper while it's still fresh in our minds. This Lofty Strong of yours is going to need a full report, if he's as good as you say."

"Oh, he is, Suzanne. He really is."

"Right, get hold of Esther and let's get started. She can drive the laptop while I use the flipchart. And you, Charlie, need to start thinking and talking."

By the time Cyril 'Lofty' Strong arrived a couple of hours later, the conference room walls were littered with flipchart sheets. And Esther was busy collating everything onto a single mind-map.

"So talk me through everything you know," Lofty said. Charlie pointed to the sheets but Lofty shook his head irritably. "No, I don't need to spend time reading and deciphering. Just tell me."

"We know Suzy's alive. She told us she had food, water and access to the toilet." Suzanne thought back to a time, many years before, when she'd been kidnapped in Zambia and spent some dreadful days in a hut in the woods. Darkness, insects, foul water and a bucket in which to relieve herself, changed once a day if she was lucky. Yes, it certainly sounded as if Suzy's captors were being more careful about her well-being than hers had been. And that was another thing. "We know there's more than one of them."

"How?"

"Because the one on the phone told someone else to put Suzy in the other room. And we heard a door opening and closing."

"So unless Suzy did that herself, that's a reasonable assumption."

"And we know this is about Charlie and something in the past."

"How far in the past?"

"His exact words were 'a long time'." Charlie shrugged. "Not very specific and 'a long time' can mean very different things to different people, but I think it's fair to say we're not talking about anything that's happened since we came to Coombesford."

"And anything you did when we worked together was generally under my lead," said Suzanne. "So I think we're talking back in your day, Mr Strong."

Lofty nodded. "It's an assumption until we have more

proof, but I think it's a reasonable basis to work from. Anything else?"

"We think they're still nearby. Or at the very least, still in the UK." Charlie pointed to a list of bullet points on one of the flipchart sheets. "Suzy was taken at some point between ten and two o'clock last night. The first message came in around three, from a UK phone. And the call, at ten, that was from a UK service too."

"And don't forget," Suzanne broke in, "he knew you'd driven off into the night, Charlie, so he's running surveillance on this place at the very least."

Lofty was looking sceptical. "The first message could have been sent by anyone, so that doesn't really prove anything. There's been plenty of time for a plane journey. They could be halfway across the world and we wouldn't know."

"Oh yes we would." Charlie clicked her fingers. "Suzy hates flying with a passion. We took her to Spain for a holiday when she was five and she threw up all the way there and all the way back. She swore she'd never get on a plane again." Charlie turned to Suzanne for confirmation. "Suzanne, you heard her. Did she sound like a child who'd been put on a plane against her will?"

Suzanne shook her head. "No, I think you're right. In fact, I think Suzy was very composed and was trying to send us a message."

"How so?"

"She mentioned Bertie, which isn't unexpected. Any young child in that situation might mention a pet she was missing."

"But she changed him from a dog to a cat." Charlie clicked her fingers. "That's a trick we read about in one of her books years ago. It means she's going to try to send us messages, if she gets the chance." Charlie's voice broke and she coughed to clear her throat. "That's my girl."

Lofty broke in. "Okay, so no planes. No time for a ferry; and very few trains at that time of night. It would appear they're restricted to road transport. Still plenty of time to get across the country, but hopefully we only have to operate on home ground."

"And he said he'd been waiting a long time to return something that Charlie had left behind. Doesn't that sound like he's hoping to meet up with her?"

"Possibly. Not necessarily. He could use a courier. Or an accomplice. Or even the post."

Suzanne suspected Lofty was playing devil's advocate. She decided to play along. "But if it was that easy, why wait so long – however long that may be? And why go to the trouble of kidnapping a child; especially if, as seems likely, they've no intention of harming that child? It all seems far too elaborate."

"Because they want to force me to do something I don't want to. They want me to meet with them. Exchange myself for Suzy." Charlie slowly nodded. "That's what this has been about all along. Someone – someone from my past – wants to punish me. And they've started by attacking my family."

But Lofty was shaking his head. "No, I think they started before that, Charlie. Look, you get arrested for murder on your wedding day. You were framed, obviously. But it was so professional a job, it fooled all the police specialists. And then, suddenly, a witness comes forward who can give you a firm alibi – and you're released. And on the very day you get home, your daughter's kidnapped."

Charlie was nodding once more and Suzanne suddenly realised what her sister had been thinking all morning and the conclusion that Lofty had come to straight away.

"You think it's all connected, don't you?"

"I know it is, Suzanne. And if we can only work out the connection, where this is all coming from, we can save Suzy and make this nightmare of Charlie's stop – for good!"

CHAPTER 36

It was shortly after three in the afternoon and the Jones sisters were in the function room with Lofty when the rest of his team arrived at The Falls. If Cyril Strong cut an unlikely figure as a former secret service agent and expert in dealing with kidnap situations, the two new arrivals fitted the bill much more closely. In fact they looked as if they were still operational.

"Charlie, Suzanne, meet Thompson and Rodriguez. I was hoping to bring in another colleague, Ed Winston, but he's off on a mission somewhere and I couldn't get hold of him."

"Mike Thompson." He was over six feet in height, in his late thirties, and dressed more for a boardroom than a rescue mission. His handshake convinced Charlie, if she'd needed convincing, of the strength he wielded. "Really sorry to hear about your little girl. But we'll sort this all out, don't you worry." He looked across the room at where his companion was already staring at the flipchart notes. "Rodriguez, come and say hello."

Rodriguez was slight, almost elfin, and looked like she should be on the catwalk. Stunningly beautiful, even in combat fatigues and heavy boots, she had cropped dark hair and a tanned complexion that spoke of a heritage in southern Europe or even Latin America. Yet when she spoke, it was pure Liverpool.

"Yeah, okay." She turned towards them and sketched a wave in the approximate direction of Charlie and Suzanne. "Enough with the chit-chat. Let's get this situation dealt with."

"A woman of few words, our Rodriguez," Lofty murmured, "but if you're in a jam and need someone to talk themselves into a secured building, she's definitely your woman."

"No, she's right." Charlie strode across the room and stood shoulder to shoulder with their new helper. "We've wasted enough time already. We need a plan." She glanced at her watch. "Suzy's been a prisoner for more than twelve hours. We should be hearing from her captors soon."

As though they'd heard her words, her phone rang. Everyone froze momentarily, then moved towards the table in the centre of the room. Charlie switched the call to speaker as before. Once again, the voice was disguised, but the words were chillingly clear.

"Well, Charlie, you've had some time to think. And I hope your lovely wife has cooled off."

"Cut the crap. What do you want?"

There was a chuckle at the other end of the line. "Tut tut. That's not polite." And then the laughter disappeared from the voice. "And you need to be polite to me, Charlie, if you want to see young Suzy again."

"Yes, I know." Charlie sighed. "But you need to tell me what you want. Is it money?"

"I don't *need* to do anything, Charlie. What I *choose* to do is a different matter. And no, for your information, money is not what this is all about."

"Then what? What *is* this all about?"

"Why, I thought I made that clear this morning. It's about you, Charlie. About returning something you left behind many years ago. I was hoping you might have worked out what that was by now."

"So, do you want to meet?"

"Yes, that's *exactly* what I want to do."

"And you'll let Suzy go when we do?"

"That rather depends on you, Charlie. On how you behave when we meet."

"I'll do anything you ask. Just don't hurt her."

"How many times do I have to tell you, I really don't want to hurt your daughter. That's not in *my* nature." There was a pause and Charlie thought she heard the caller drawing on a cigarette. "Right, let's get down to business. Do you know the main car park for Haldon Forest Park?"

"Yes, of course."

"Midnight, tonight. Come alone." There was a click, leaving nothing but a ringing silence in the room.

Lofty was the first to speak. "Okay, what do we know about this place, Charlie?"

"It's up on the top of the Haldon Hills, halfway between here and Exeter. It's quiet and secluded. The entrance will be closed at that time of night, so we'll have to park on the road then walk."

"What's the approach road like?"

"It's near a crossroads, so there are actually several ways to get there. But they all run through the woods and twist regularly. We should be able to get quite close without being seen."

"What are you planning?" It was Suzanne. "He said to come alone, Charlie. And he didn't say Suzy would be with him."

"But he said he might release her. So my guess is, she'll be somewhere close by." Thompson looked at Lofty. "Usual procedure, boss?"

"Yes, I think so." Lofty pointed to Charlie. "You'll go in alone and meet this guy. We'll be close by, hidden but listening. We'll find his vehicle and if Suzy's in there, we'll rescue her."

"And if she isn't?"

"Then we'll plant a tracker and follow him back to wherever he's hiding her. At least we now know one thing; they're still in the area."

"And I think we might know a few more things, boss." Charlie had forgotten about Rodriguez, she'd been so quiet up to then. "I was listening to his speech patterns, how he said things, rather than what he said. Did you notice how he emphasised the words 'need' and 'choose'?" Everyone nodded. "He wanted us to know he's the one in charge. This is about fulfilling a long-term want of his, rather than a pressing need."

"So he's not necessarily in a hurry." Lofty nodded at Rodriguez. "Good point."

"Oh, he's certainly in this for the long game, if all the planning is anything to go by," Charlie said. "Framing me for murder wasn't something he'd have set up overnight. And if, as we suspect, he was behind the situations Suzanne and Nathan found themselves in, he has a far-reaching network."

"True. But there was something else," Rodriguez went on. "When you were talking about him not hurting Suzy."

"He said it wasn't in his nature." Suzanne looked sceptical. "But can we trust him?"

"Yes, I think we can. It was *how* he said it. He didn't say 'That's not in my nature'; he said 'That's not in *my* nature'. He was comparing himself to someone else. Someone who *would* hurt a child."

Rodriguez turned and looked directly at Charlie. "And as you're the other main person in this equation, as far as he's concerned, Charlie, I think he was comparing himself to *you*."

CHAPTER 37

Charlie pulled her car up onto the grass verge close to the entrance to the car park and killed the engine. There were no other vehicles around. That wasn't surprising, given the time of night and isolated location. She assumed the kidnappers would have hidden their vehicle somewhere close by. But that was something for Lofty and his team to check up on. She had to concentrate on her meeting with the man from the phone calls.

Ever since the conversation that afternoon, her mind had been spinning. Rodriguez wasn't the only one to pick up on how the caller had emphasised '*my* nature'. She'd immediately jumped to the same conclusion. He was comparing himself to her. But that didn't help her one bit. She would never hurt a child knowingly and to the best of her knowledge, she never had. But obviously this man, whoever he was, knew something different. Or at least he thought he did.

There was only one operation, thirty years or more ago, where a child had been involved. An operation she'd worked hard to lock away in her subconscious. And she'd certainly not left anything behind. It couldn't possibly be that one.

As the one person with no need to hide her approach, Charlie had driven up through the woods with her headlights on full. Now, she climbed out of the car and slammed the door. If there was anyone waiting for her, there'd be no doubt in their mind that she'd arrived.

There was a full moon shining through the trees, its light splintered and dappled by the leaves waving in the slight breeze. Under other circumstances, it would have been a beautiful location for a romantic stroll. Charlie thought she'd love to bring Annie up there. Then with a jolt, she remembered how things stood with her new wife. She wondered if she'd ever be taking a walk with Annie again. It all depended on what happened next.

Slipping around the barrier, designed to keep cars out but no hindrance to pedestrians, Charlie took a shortcut through the gravelled skate park. She was a few minutes early, but she doubted whether the person, or people, she was meeting would leave it to the last minute to arrive. She was pretty certain they'd already be there, waiting, watching, making sure she was alone.

There was a slight crackle in her ear. "All set, Charlie. We're in position and Thompson has eyes on a vehicle hidden a few hundred metres along the road. It looks to be empty. He'll check it out once you've made contact."

"Okay." Charlie's voice was little more than a whisper, but it sounded very loud in the still darkness. She'd have to keep radio silence from then on.

When she reached the centre of the car park, she leaned against a wooden partition and peered into the darkness all around her. A shiver went through her, even though she was sweating and it was by no means a cold night. She could see nothing, and no-one, but she couldn't shake the feeling she was being watched.

Earlier, Suzanne had been concerned about Charlie placing herself in this position. "What if he brings a gun?" she'd asked several times during their planning sessions.

"Why would he bring a gun?"

"Duh. To shoot you."

"Given this man's level of planning, I think it's safe to say if he'd wanted me dead, I'd be six feet under by now." Charlie had given her sister a hug. "I'll be fine, Susu. He's playing with me. But now we've got Lofty and the team on board, we've levelled the playing field somewhat."

She had, however, given in to Suzanne's suggestion that she wear a bulletproof vest. Not that it would do her any good if someone took a head shot at her. But that thought she kept to herself.

She'd also talked to Annie before they'd headed off into the night. Her wife was outwardly fine, but there was a coolness in her eyes that filled Charlie with dread for their future if this rescue didn't go to plan. She hadn't wanted to hear the details of what they were going to do, beyond checking they were doing nothing that would further endanger Suzy's life. Charlie knew nothing short of bringing their daughter home would thaw the ice coating their relationship.

She looked at her watch again. Twenty past midnight. Something wasn't right. She scanned the area around her. Then several things happened in quick succession.

A spotlight was switched on at the other side of the car park. It highlighted a small dark vehicle that must have been there all along, but had been hidden by the shadows.

Lofty's voice sounded a note of caution in her ear. "Charlie, that's not the vehicle Thompson's watching. There's two of them. Take care. It could be a trap."

At the same time, a small voice rang out in the darkness.

"Mama C, are you there?"

"Yes, Suzy, I'm here." Charlie ran across the car park.

And in the shady spot beneath the trees, there was a click and the vehicle exploded with a deafening bang and a ball of flame.

CHAPTER 38

Charlie was at the bottom of a deep, deep lake. Everything was black, swirling. Something was holding her down, she couldn't breathe. In the distance was a bright light. If only she could swim towards that light, she'd be fine. But her limbs wouldn't work. She was going to drown. She had to start moving or it would be too late.

Gradually she felt the restrictions on her limbs loosen. And the light seemed to be moving towards her. Brighter, hotter. Her ears were ringing, there was a roaring, a popping. And the smell. A terrible stench, like meat left too long in the oven. What was that dreadful smell?

"Charlie. Charlie, come on. Wake up." The voice gradually worked its way into her mind and she came out of her nightmare and straight into a living hell.

The explosion had thrown her back across the car park, but as she sat up, she could feel the heat from the burning car.

"Suzy!" Charlie screamed and tried to scramble to her feet, only to feel herself restrained.

Turning her head she realised Lofty Strong was sitting on the floor beside her, holding her down by her shoulders.

"Lofty, let me go. I have to save her."

But Lofty kept a tight hold. "It's too late, Charlie. We tried, trust me, we tried. But it's too hot. We can't get near it. Anyone in there is beyond help."

Charlie looked up. Thompson and Rodriguez were leaning against the fence, their faces blackened from the smoke. Thompson was coughing; Rodriguez was missing a sleeve and her arm was badly burned. Both had tear streaks running down their cheeks. Charlie turned her face to her former commander's chest and sobbed.

The car was small, and the blaze didn't take long to burn itself out. The four approached and stared into the interior of the blackened wreck. It was empty. Charlie groaned.

"The boot. She must be in the boot."

"Thompson, Rodriguez, check out the information centre. See if you can find water." Lofty pointed towards the wooden hut at the corner of the car park.

Charlie lifted her head. "Dog tap."

"What?"

"There's a tap on the outside, round the back. And bowls. It's for dog walkers to use."

Within a few minutes, the pair returned with two large bowls overflowing with water. They threw the liquid over the back of the car, aiming for the lock area. Great clouds of steam arose and the air was filled with hissing, but then it died down and silence reigned in the clearing.

Charlie took a deep breath and stepped forward.

"Charlie, you don't have to do this. Let me." Thompson put his hand on her arm, but she shook him off.

"Yes, Mike, I really have to. This is my fault. I killed her."

Wrapping her sleeve around her hand, she tentatively reached out and touched the back of the car. It was still hot, but not too hot. Closing her eyes, she pressed the button and stepped back as the boot flew open. There were gasps and cries of shock from her three companions.

Charlie opened her eyes.

The body in the boot was small, curled in on itself and burned beyond all recognition. There was very little flesh left on the skeleton and even that was blackened and twisted.

Charlie felt herself sucked into a swirling void once again and she staggered back into the arms of her companions, desperately trying to hold on to her senses. But to no avail. She felt herself begin to spin and she sank to the ground. But before she lost consciousness completely, her tortured brain registered just one fact. The body in the car was not human.

By the time Charlie came round, Lofty and the others had closed the boot on the dreadful sight, returned the bowls to the hut, and were checking to make sure there would be no clue to their presence once the wrecked car with its shocking contents was discovered in the morning. The scene was strangely peaceful, despite the stench of burning plastic and flesh still hanging in the air.

"What was it?" Her words were little more than a croak, and she gratefully took Thompson's water bottle and drank deeply. "In the boot? What was it?"

"We think it was a piglet, Charlie." Lofty looked and sounded tired. Charlie was reminded that her former commander was quite a bit older than her and hadn't spent a night like this for many a year. "He probably thought the smell of roasting flesh would make us think…" Lofty didn't need to finish the sentence.

"And he was right, the bastard." A sudden thought struck her. "Tell me you got him. Please tell me he didn't get away." But the look on their faces was answer enough.

"I'm sorry, Charlie." Thompson stared at his feet, kicking the dirt with one boot. "By the time I realised he wasn't coming back to the vehicle I was watching, it was too late. I heard a motorbike in the distance, but there was no way to work out which way he went. We'd scouted the area pretty well. Either the bike was parked more than half a mile away or he had an accomplice who picked him up. We think the latter." Mike paused and shook his head. "I planted the tracker as we agreed, but I somehow suspect he has no intention of returning for that car. It's probably stolen anyway."

"Why?" Charlie ran her fingers through her hair. "Why would he set all this up?"

And as though there was a direct line from her mouth to the kidnapper's ears, Charlie's phone rang.

"Tell me, Charlie Jones, what part of 'tell no-one and come alone' did you not understand?"

"What do you mean? You must have seen me. I was standing right there in the centre of the car park."

The man at the other end of the phone growled. "Yes, I saw you, but I also saw your companions, despite how carefully they tried to keep themselves hidden. The tall guy who looks like a banker. The Latina girl who talks like a sixties pop star. And that little ball of a man who thinks he's in charge."

There was a chuckle. "Once a spy, always a spy, eh, Charlie?" But then the disguised voice hardened. "When will you realise I'm in charge here. I'm calling the shots. Go home. Clean yourself up. And await my call. And next time, you *will* follow my instructions to the letter. Take this as your final warning. If you disobey me again, it won't be a pig that fries next time."

CHAPTER 39

Suzanne looked across the conference table and caught Lofty's eye. He shrugged then shook his head. There were bags under his eyes and his face was grey in the pale sunlight. Thompson was staring at his phone screen. Rodriguez was standing, looking out of the window. Charlie was slumped in a chair with her eyes closed.

Suzanne had stayed up waiting for them to return in the early hours of the morning, but all she'd been able to get out of Charlie were the basics: no, they hadn't seen Suzy, although they'd heard her voice; and no, they'd not managed to catch the kidnapper or even plant a tracker on his vehicle, the whole thing had been an elaborate trap.

Then Lofty and the others had disappeared into the function room with their sleeping bags. Unwilling, or maybe too scared, to disturb Annie, Charlie had curled up on one of the padded benches in the bar.

It was mid-morning, and looking around the room, Suzanne suspected she was the only one who'd had any sleep.

"Okay, enough." Suzanne jumped up and seized the coffee jug. "Grab your cups and follow me. It looks like everyone needs some fresh air and a complete break for a few minutes." She pushed open the door to the beer garden and stood just outside on the patio. "Come on, you lot. Annie's relying on you. Suzy's relying on you. Move it!"

Slowly, the group started moving, Lofty and the team looking sheepish, Charlie with a glare which her sister ignored. At the last minute, she grabbed Charlie's phone and threw it on the table next to her own, shoving her sister outside and slamming the door closed.

"Hey, I need that. What happens if he calls? I don't have time for this."

"He's not going to call while we're out here, Charlie. Trust me. Now go and sit down. I need to talk to you all."

Once she'd got them seated at the table furthest from the building, Suzanne commandeered Thompson's phone and started recording. "Right, now tell me again, exactly what he said."

Bit by bit, interrupting and correcting each other, they came up with a record of what had been said on the latest call from the kidnapper. And tired brains began whirring and clicking into action.

"He described Mike as looking like a banker..."

"...but I was wearing a black tracksuit last night."

"And he said I sounded like a 1960s pop-singer..."

"...when you didn't say a word throughout the whole operation."

It was Charlie who put into words what they'd all begun to suspect. "He's got this place under close surveillance."

"And unless he's got a spy actually in the building," Suzanne continued, "he must have the place bugged."

"Shit." Charlie jumped up and pulled her sister into a hug. "I think you're right. How could I have missed it?"

"Charlie, what are you two talking about?"

"Suzanne doesn't think he's got the place bugged, Lofty. She thinks he's got one of us bugged. And it's most likely to be me."

"How have you come to that conclusion?"

"Do you remember what I said yesterday afternoon, just before that call came through? I said we should be hearing from them soon. And he rang at that very minute."

"But that's a coincidence, surely?" Thompson looked sceptical, although Lofty was slowly nodding.

"That's a possibility, true. But it happened again last night. I asked why he'd lured me to the hills, just to explode a car in front of me and make me think Suzy was dead."

"And your phone rang with the explanation right afterwards." Lofty was nodding more vigorously. "I remember thinking at the time it seemed like he was answering us."

"And he was, because he was listening to you. And it has to be Charlie's phone that's bugged, since you guys had only just arrived, from separate locations, so he wouldn't have had time to get at any of yours."

"Is it only mine, sis, or yours as well?"

"I was wondering about that. It would explain how he was always one step ahead of Nathan and me in Germany and Czechia." Suzanne rubbed her hands. "I think we're getting somewhere. So the question is: what are we going to do about it?"

Lofty held up his hand to stop the sisters' discussion. "But there's more to it than just bugging phones. If you think about what he said, he had a pretty good description of each of us. So he's also got eyes on us, as well as ears."

"Do you think he's got someone watching the pub?"

"Possibly, Suzanne, but that's going to take a lot of manpower. And in a relatively isolated location like this, it's difficult to organise without someone spotting it."

"Especially in a village, where everyone seems to know everyone else's business."

"Exactly." Lofty shook his head. "No, I think it's more likely he's got a camera or two set up, so he can watch what's going on twenty-four-seven." He paused and resumed speaking in a much lower voice. "And technology has changed quite a lot since our day, Charlie."

Thompson and Rodriguez were nodding.

"It's much easier to hide something than it used to be." Standing, Lofty yawned and stretched. "Here's what I think we should do. Everyone split up. Casual-like. We're all tired. We're taking a break. Go for a stroll around the gardens and the car park. Sit in the sun and have a coffee. Charlie, go and see how they're getting on in the bar. Suzanne, go and sort out the papers in the function room. We need to cover all the areas Thompson, Rodriguez and I have been in. Check all the likely hiding places, but be subtle. We don't want this guy realising we've sussed out his surveillance until we decide what we're going to do with it."

"But we're going to destroy it, aren't we?" Suzanne was surprised there was even a question to be considered.

"Probably not, Suzanne. If we do that, he'll know we've found the bugs and cameras, and he'll put something else in place."

"Or he'll take it out on Suzy," said Charlie.

"Exactly. But if we know they're there, we can use them to feed him false information. Use his own technology against him." Lofty stretched again. "Right, let's get to it. We'll reconvene in an hour. And make sure you grab some lunch in the meantime. It's going to be a long afternoon."

CHAPTER 40

In the end, they found two cameras: one hidden in the clematis climbing over the trellis surrounding the front door, which pointed out into the car park, and the other in the function room, tucked away in a dusty corner on one of the blackened oak beams holding up the ceiling.

Charlie had recruited Rohan and Esther to help her search the bar and the restaurant, as they were spending far more time in there than she was. Between them, they were as certain as they could be that there were no hidden cameras in there. But just to be sure, the group took to meeting outside in the beer garden. It was just as well the dry spell was continuing.

The Jones sisters started leaving their mobiles in the function room, on the table, in full view of the camera. If the kidnapper was watching, as they had to assume he was, he'd know they weren't around to take a call.

As though to prove the point, Charlie's phone rang immediately she stepped back into the room to check for messages late that afternoon. Glancing back to ensure she wasn't being observed, she pulled the door closed and pressed the accept button.

"Very clever, Charlie. It's taken a while, but I knew

you'd catch on in the end. Although if I hadn't dropped a couple of heavy hints last time we chatted—"

"We don't chat," Charlie spat. "You tell me what to do and I do it."

"That's not quite true, now is it, Charlie, as last night's demonstration proved. I told you to come alone. But you brought your little team of buddies with you."

"And you made me think Suzy was killed. Was she even there at all?"

"No, of course she wasn't. I knew you'd ignore my instructions and I was right, wasn't I?"

Charlie felt something snap and she slammed her fist on the table. "Okay, you proved your point. So why don't we end all these games right now. You said it's me you're interested in, rather than my daughter. You tell me where to meet you. I'll come alone. You can let Suzy go and we'll settle this between us. No games, no tricks, just a straight exchange."

There was a long silence and Charlie thought there was no-one still on the line. Then finally, there came a sigh.

"You know what. You're right. We've played this game long enough. I've certainly played it for a very long time. And I think maybe you've got the message. It's time for everyone to go home. Tonight. Midnight. Hay Tor main car park. By the visitor centre. And, Charlie," the voice became steely, "this is your very last chance. Come alone and I'll let Suzy go. Any tricks, any sign that you've brought anyone else with you and you both die – you and your precious daughter." There was a click and Charlie knew that was the last phone call she'd get from him.

"Charlie? What's going on?" She spun round at the sound of the voice behind her, the quiet Scottish brogue she'd missed so much in the past twenty-four hours.

"Annie, oh Annie." She crossed the room and gathered her wife in her arms. They clung to each other, and Charlie felt Annie sob into her shoulder. But it felt so good to be there together, despite everything. Finally, she pulled back.

"I'm so sorry—"

"No, it's me who's sorry. I blamed you, when I should have been supporting you." Annie swallowed and rubbed her hand across her face, wiping away her tears. "I was so scared. I still am. But I should have trusted you."

"Shh." Charlie put her finger to Annie's lips. "Let's not waste any more time." She placed her phone on the table and gently steered Annie towards the door and out into the garden, away from watching eyes and listening ears. "I'm going to need your help."

"That call? Was it from him?"

"Yes." Charlie quickly told Annie what had happened overnight, omitting the worst details that she knew she would never forget, and which she would share at some point. But not then. "But I really think he'll do what he promised and let Suzy go. It sounded like he's had enough." Charlie didn't mention the exchange she'd offered in order to secure their daughter's release. That was something no-one needed to know about. Not at that moment, anyway.

Annie picked at a loose piece of skin on a cuticle. Then she raised her head with a look of determination on her face. "What do you need me to do?"

"You need to distract Lofty and the others. They're not going to like the idea of me going to this meeting on my own. Especially as I called them in."

"And you don't think we should call the police?" Annie held up her hand to forestall Charlie's protest. "Yes, I know I was the one who argued against involving them originally, but I've been talking to Olga and she told me about the kidnappings that used to take place back home in Ukraine. It was the ones where the police were involved that usually ended better than the ones where a ransom was paid."

"She's right, but this is different. This isn't about money. And it's gone way beyond the stage where we can bring anyone else in. Last night's events certainly proved that." Charlie gave Annie what she hoped was a reassuring smile. "You keep the others busy this evening and this will all be over by breakfast time." At least it would for Suzy, she hoped. Whether she'd be sitting down to a full English with them or not was another matter.

CHAPTER 41

Charlie turned left into the tiny car park, drove to the end, and switched off the engine. She also killed the lights. The caller had insisted she come alone, telling no-one – not her friends and fellow investigators, and certainly not the police. And though every fibre of her body screamed out that she was making a mistake, walking into a trap, she and Annie complied with their wishes. She'd do anything, risk everything to get their daughter back. That was her main role these days. To keep her family safe. Whatever it took. There was no other option.

This whole situation made no sense at all. She was framed for murder, a pretty watertight case, so she was led to believe. While her friends and family were led on a wild-goose chase across Europe. Then a mysterious witness suddenly turned up and got her off the hook. No sooner had she been released and returned home, than Suzy was kidnapped.

And now, with no ransom demand, no obvious reason for what had happened, Suzy was going to be released. No, there was definitely something else behind all this. If only she could work out what it was. And the sole clue was that it related to her past and something she'd left behind.

Her thoughts were interrupted as headlights appeared at the top of a hill; far away, across the moor, but obviously coming in her direction. The lights gradually became larger and brighter until a second vehicle turned into the car park, performed a three-point turn and parked at the entrance, in the position for a quick getaway. It was a beaten-up station wagon, well out of warranty by the look of it. Charlie held her breath and waited.

After an agonising period of time that seemed like hours but was probably merely a couple of minutes, the driver's door opened and a man got out. He pulled open the back door on his side of the car and gestured. A small figure slipped out and stood waiting. Even in the darkness, Charlie could tell it was Suzy. There was something about the way she was holding her head, just like she did on the rare occasions Charlie or Annie had to tell her off.

Charlie thrust open her door and jumped out, screaming her daughter's name. A shot rang out in the darkness, echoing around the silent hills above them.

"Stop right there." The man was pointing his gun up in the air. "Make one more move and the next bullet won't go so far astray." Charlie froze as Suzy's captor continued, his Eastern European accent making some of his words difficult to understand, but the meaning clear nonetheless. "This is how it's going to work. I'm going to untie Suzy's hands. She's going to walk to the centre of the car park. You will walk towards her. You will both remain there for five minutes while I return to my car and drive away. You are then free to leave. Do not try to follow me. Take your daughter home while you have the chance. Do you understand?"

Charlie nodded, then, unsure whether he was able to see her in the darkness, cleared her throat. "Yes, I understand. We'll do what you ask."

She watched as the man put away his gun and took out a knife. Suzy shrank away from him, and Charlie heard him laugh quietly before cutting through the binding around her wrists. He gave her a gentle shove and she began walking towards the middle of the car park.

"Okay, stop, Suzy. Now, Charlie, you walk towards her. Walk – don't run."

Charlie crossed the distance between her daughter and herself in seconds and gathered her into her arms.

"Mama C," the girl sobbed. "I was so scared."

"Shush, darling, you're fine now." Charlie held her until her sobs subsided. She'd lost track of time, but looking across the car park, she realised the other vehicle had gone. And there was no sign of tail lights in either direction across the moor. Would they be able to find the people responsible for Suzy's abduction and make them pay? And why had the exchange she'd agreed to not taken place? She shrugged, and reminded herself the key thing was to get her daughter home. Everything else could wait until the next day.

Finally she decided it must have been at least five minutes since she and her daughter had been reunited.

"Come on, Suzy, let's get you home." Charlie guided her towards the car and gently placed her in the front passenger seat. Huddled there, she seemed much smaller than her age would suggest. "Pop your seatbelt on." Then walking around the front of the car, Charlie climbed in.

"Will we be able to catch them?" Suzy's voice was little more than a whisper. "Should we try to follow them?"

"I'm sure we will, poppet. But we'll worry about that later. Let's get you home first. Mama Annie is dying to see you; and Bertie has really missed you too." She reached out to turn the key in the ignition but stopped as Suzy's words hit her. "Wait, you said 'them'. But I thought there was only one man with you in the car. How many were there?"

Suzy frowned. "Two, I think. It was hard to tell. I was blindfolded whenever they were around and in the car. But I could hear them talking, just before we left to come here."

"What were they saying?"

"I don't know. They weren't speaking English."

Before Charlie had a chance to respond or process the thought that was niggling at the back of her brain, Suzy glanced behind her and screamed. There was a hissing sound from the back seat of the car. And Charlie caught sight of something in the rear-view mirror. Something out of a horror movie or a steampunk television series. A monstrous face with huge shining eyes and deep black wrinkled skin.

The world began to spin, Charlie's vision blurred. What the hell…

CHAPTER 42

Charlie had no idea how long she'd been out. But she knew a few other things. She knew she was unable to move, constrained by the ties holding both her arms and her legs to the uncomfortable wooden chair she was sitting on. She knew it was no longer night, judging by the thin beam of sunlight shining through the slats in the wall, at just the right height to blind her unless she moved her head way back against the chair. And she knew she had the mother and father of all headaches.

"I'm definitely getting too old for this game," she groaned.

"And she's back in the room." The voice allowed one more fact to fall into place: she wasn't alone. Then she remembered the events leading up to that moment, and looked around in a panic.

"Suzy! Suzy, where are you?" Charlie stared into the darkness, trying to see her captor. "What have you done with my daughter?"

"Suzy's quite safe. I told you I'd release her and I did. I left her sleeping in the car and put a message on the answerphone at The Falls. By this time, she's probably safely home in Coombesford saying hello to Bertie, her little *dog.*" The way he emphasised the last word told Charlie he'd seen straight through Suzy's comment about the cat during their first phone call.

"Who are you and what do you want?" She tried to keep her voice calm. But even she could hear the note of panic, and suspected her captor could hear it too, judging by his low laugh. It sounded as if he was somewhere to her left, in the gloom.

"All in good time, Charlie. All in good time. You're playing by my rules now, remember that."

"Playing by the rules? That implies we're still playing a game. But I thought you said the time for games was over."

"Oh, no, Charlie, this is no game. It might have been to start with, but I can assure you it's deadly serious from here on in. For you, at least."

Charlie eased the strain on her hands by twisting her wrists sideways. There was a little give in the straps holding her in place. Not a lot, but it was a start. It was time to try to draw her captor into the light, literally.

"Okay, whoever you are. You've got me. And if, as I suspect, you were behind the plan to frame me for murder, you've had me dancing to your tune for a good while now. So how about you tell me who you are and what this is really all about."

There was a long silence. So long that Charlie wondered if she was actually alone. Had she imagined the presence of another person? But finally there was a cough and suddenly, there, to her right, not her left, stood a young man. He looked to be in his late twenties or early thirties, casually dressed for hiking – or maybe a spot of hostage-taking in the wilds of Dartmoor – but wearing a black leather jacket over his tracksuit. And although she had no idea who he was, there was a disturbing familiarity about him that she couldn't quite put her finger on.

But before she could process what she was seeing, there was a slight noise to her left. For a second, she thought she was seeing double. Twins? But no, as she looked more closely, the second man who stepped out of the shadows, while similarly dressed, was much larger and well-built. His face was a different shape, square rather than heart-shaped. His eyes were so dark brown they were almost black, while the other man's were green. And there was probably a couple of years' difference in age between them. So not twins, but almost certainly brothers.

"Half-brothers, actually," said the man in the leather jacket, as though reading her mind. "Meet Kron," the man on the left bowed his head in a mock salute, "and I'm Orik."

"Kron and Orik, eh?" Charlie riffled through her memory and then shook her head. "Sorry, doesn't ring a bell. Should I know you? Would a family name give me a clue?"

"Oh, yes, Charlie Jones, I think a family name would help very much indeed. Although I'm a bit disappointed that you've not got there on your own by now. The tales of your brilliance, especially in research, are obviously overstated."

Charlie thought quickly. From the young man's words, he knew her by reputation rather than directly. And his age confirmed that anyway. Her dealings with Eastern Europe had finished thirteen years earlier, on the night Suzy was born.

At the thought of her daughter, Charlie felt a momentary glow of satisfaction that, whatever happened in the next few hours, she'd managed to rescue her daughter and return her safely to Annie's arms. So at least Annie would speak kindly of her at her funeral.

"You know how it is, boys. Life goes on; we all age. And I've been out of this game for a long time now." She attempted what she hoped was a smile in the direction of Orik, although the painful bruises she could feel around her eyes and mouth suggested it might have looked more like a grimace. "So, come on, Orik. Why not put me out of my misery and tell me who you are and why you're so pissed off with me."

"We'll be putting you out of your misery alright." Kron's voice was rusty as though through lack of use although, unlike his brother, there was no hint of an accent.

"Hush, Kron. Play nice with the lady." Orik's words lacked a trace of irony, despite the situation they all found themselves in. "She asked politely, so I think we ought to answer her question, don't you?"

Kron shrugged.

Orik grinned and Charlie could see he was building himself up for a big announcement. She hoped it made sense when it came.

"So, Charlie Jones, you asked for a family name. I could give you three guesses, but you've made it clear you've had enough of playing games." He glanced across at his half-brother then whispered to Charlie conspiratorially behind his hand. "And to be honest, I'm not sure how much longer I can keep control of Kron. He's not killed anyone for a while now, and he gets very grumpy when that happens."

Orik paused, drew himself up to his full height, then bowed to Charlie. "We're half-brothers, as I said; sharing the same father. Our family name is Laska."

Charlie felt like she'd been hit by a steamroller. But Orik hadn't finished. "Yes, I thought that name would ring a bell. Thirty-one years ago, you knew our father Alban. You knew him very well indeed, didn't you? And in case your maths is as poor as your deduction skills these days, I'll save you the trouble. I'll be thirty-one on my next birthday. And that birthday will be on–"

"The seventeenth of September," murmured Charlie.

Orik gave a growl. And his voice, if possible, became icier than ever.

"So you do remember. I'm not sure whether that makes me feel better or worse. Hello, Mommy dearest."

CHAPTER 43

"They told me you were dead!"

The words were out of Charlie's mouth before she had a chance to process the fact that the person holding her prisoner, who'd kidnapped Suzy, and who apparently was also responsible for framing her for murder, was in fact her son. Maybe if she'd been thinking more rationally, she'd have tried to deny all knowledge of him; to convince him he'd mistaken her for someone else. Instead, her gut reaction was too quick.

But Orik didn't appear to hear her. Partly because she only whispered. Partly because he was still talking. But mainly because the words he was saying to her were exactly the same as hers to him.

"They told me you were dead!" Orik looked across at Kron for confirmation, and his half-brother pulled a face and nodded.

"They did, yes. It seemed the best explanation. A tiny baby, abandoned by his mother, to be brought up by his father and his family."

"A family," Orik interrupted, "where might was right and everyone was out for themselves. And where differences were mocked, rather than being celebrated.

How do you think I felt, this little boy with green eyes and fair skin among a tribe of dark-eyed olive-skinned folk?"

"But you survived?"

"Yes, I survived. By becoming the biggest and baddest in the crowd. One day, when I was about twelve, I got fed up with being taunted and teased all the time. So I lay in wait for the largest of my cousins. I knew he always came home across the fields after school – if he went to school at all. So I used vines to trip him up, and a boulder to beat him over the head."

"You killed him?"

"No, I didn't kill him. He was alive when I left him and still alive when my uncles found him later that evening. But he was never the same again. He recovered physically – in time – but his brain didn't work in the same way ever again."

"And the punishment for this attack?"

"There was no punishment. Our family didn't work like that. No-one had any proof that I'd done it – and he swore he didn't see his attacker. But everyone knew. And from then on, whether it was through fear or respect, the teasing stopped. And my father started training me up for the family business soon after that."

"I thought Alban was out of the picture these days."

"Oh, he is. My father – your erstwhile lover – is a shuffling wreck who remembers nothing of his glory days. He spends all his time in the garden watching the fish in the pond, or inside, staring out of the window. Alban's days are definitely over." Orik slapped his chest. "It's Orik's time now."

"Your father must be very proud of you." Charlie hoped her comment sounded sincere, although she suspected the brothers would pick up on the edge of sarcasm in her tone.

"Oh, he was eventually. But it was so hard trying to make him notice me. And just think how different life might have been if I'd had a mother's love and care while I was growing up." He pointed at Charlie. "If I'd had *your* love and care, in fact."

He smiled coldly. "Do you know, Mother, we celebrated your birthday every year. And said a prayer for you to watch over us from heaven. And then, all of a sudden, a few years back, some woman in a bar mentioned Rose Fitzpatrick and how she'd done the dirty on her. Well, it's such a distinctive name that my ears pricked up. I bought her a few drinks, asked a few questions and realised we were talking about the same woman. My mother, Rose Fitzpatrick, otherwise known as Charlie Jones, who I'd thought was dead, and who I've been venerating all my life, was actually alive and well and living an easy life in England. I'd lost my mother as a baby, not to illness or bad luck, but to abandonment and cruelty. I decided that day I'd find you and make you pay. It's taken several years of planning and preparation, but that day has finally come."

A woman in a bar? Who'd been betrayed by her? Who could that be? But Charlie pushed that to the back of her mind. She could work through that later, when she got out of this situation. If she got out of this situation, that was. But first, she had to persuade her son – that phrase was going to take some getting used to – that she hadn't wilfully left him to a life of crime in Eastern Europe, but she'd been tricked into thinking there was nothing left to keep her there when the job was finished. Yes, that had to be her first priority.

"Orik, I'm sorry you were lied to. I'm sorry you had such a terrible start in life, and I can understand why you feel so resentful. Why you feel you deserve some retribution. But you have to believe me. We were both lied to. Do you really think I would have walked away and left a tiny baby in that place, in that situation, if I'd known what was really going on?"

The young man was standing with his back to her, but he'd stopped pacing and his stillness told her he was listening to her. Glancing across at the other man in the room, she could see Kron was focused on her, his eyes glittering in the candlelight. But she would think about him later. Now, she had to concentrate on Orik. She held her breath.

Finally, he spun round to face her.

"Alright, Charlie Jones. Alright, Mother. You have five minutes to convince me I'm wrong and you deserve to live."

PART 5

CHAPTER 44: ALBANIA, 1993

I'd been under cover for about fourteen months. And Alban's woman for just under a year. He wasn't the target of the operation. None of his relatives were. After all, the new family business was only just getting started.

Alban's father-in-law turned to crime when he found there were no jobs to be had after the Second World War. He started with a bit of black market trading; meat and milk from the farm in return for other staples they couldn't afford to buy. It was Alban who began dealing in drugs. He bought from the major suppliers, the ones who shipped them in from the Middle East and the Far East, and he was gradually setting up a distribution network across much of Eastern Europe.

But as far as my bosses were concerned, he was only a middleman. The ones we were after were the big boys. If we could take them off the board, it would be far more effective than just stopping the distribution on the ground. So although I would ultimately put the Laska family out of business, I was never going to betray Alban directly.

In the March we had a major breakthrough. I finally managed to identify who Alban was dealing with. I got the information back up the line and there was a plan in place to trap the main players and bring down the supply chain. My bosses knew I'd be suspected once the plan went through and told me I needed to get out.

But on the day of my planned extraction, I realised I was pregnant. Although, it wasn't me who realised first.

Alban's mother had never liked me and, although she managed to hide it well, she didn't trust me either. She'd gathered enough evidence to suggest I was up to something, and she arranged for Alban and me to have tea with her that afternoon.

Firstly, she served hot black tea and sweet sponge cakes, all smiles and soft words. That in itself should have given me a clue. But I was too focused on preparing to leave and I let my guard slip. Next she fed enough sly comments into the conversation to make Alban suspicious of me. He said very little, but I could see him looking at me, thinking, trying to put everything together.

And then just as I thought the whole thing was going to explode, she dropped the real bombshell. I don't know how she knew about the baby, but she did. And as soon as she mentioned it, I knew she was right. I'd been so busy, I'd missed all the signs. But there was no denying I was expecting her grandchild, Alban's second child.

And at that moment, my chance of escaping, getting out of the country, disappeared. I became a prisoner in her house. Not only was she always there, often in the same room, but there was also at least one guard at the door and another patrolling outside. And I think they were drugging my food, so I slept soundly every night and was less of a flight risk than during the day.

For six months, I saw no-one apart from that spiteful old woman, and occasionally one of her daughters. I was reasonably well treated, but I was still a prisoner. I never heard from my bosses. How could I? And I was only dimly aware of the planned operation going ahead. Later, I found out it was a complete success. But at the time, there was nothing.

As the months went on, I began to worry about the birth itself. Would I be left on my own in that deserted farmhouse? Would Grandma be my midwife? Maybe her daughters would be called in to help. I had no illusions about my own future, but didn't think they'd allow any harm to come to the child. After all, that was the whole reason for keeping me prisoner for so long, wasn't it?

But in the event, it was much more professional than I'd expected. One night, I went to sleep in my bed in the farmhouse and the next morning I awoke in a private clinic. White walls, bright lights, nurses in uniforms and plimsolls that squeaked as they walked the corridors – I especially remember those squeaking footsteps. So my concerns about the birth itself were eased.

I assumed all the staff were in Alban's pay – or at least the ones who dealt with me. They were polite, they smiled at me when they were in the room, but none of them spoke English and if I tried to talk to them in their own language, they either ignored me or went to get one of the women from the family.

Then finally, came the seventeenth of September. I went into labour the evening before and my child was born as the first rays of daylight appeared on the horizon. It was a difficult birth and I knew something was wrong right away.

There was a blessed relief from pain, but there was a silence, where there should have been a crying infant. I could hear the midwife and the nurses talking softly, but I couldn't understand what they were saying. Then I heard a door open and close. They were all gone; my baby was gone; I was alone. I was so tired, I didn't care about anything and I drifted in and out of sleep for hours.

When I finally awoke, it was evening. There was a tray of food on the bedside table – cold meats, bread and cheese. That was reassuring, since I'd assumed they would kill me once the child was born.

A little while later, a nurse I'd never seen before came

in to check on me. She said nothing until, as she was about to leave, I grabbed her arm.

"Nurse, please, tell me, where is my baby?"

She stood and steadily looked at me, and I thought I saw the hint of a tear in her eye and sympathy in her face.

"Your baby is dead," she said. "Too much trauma. Could not survive." Then she turned and left the room.

CHAPTER 45

It was the light, shining directly in my face, that woke me. I groaned and covered my eyes with my hand. Where was I? What had happened? And why did I feel such a dull ache in my stomach? For a long blessed minute or two, there were only questions. And then, like a wave crashing onto the beach in the middle of a storm, reality hit me, as it had several times before. I was in the clinic, I'd given birth – but my baby was dead.

I thought back to the moment when the nurse had broken the news. The shock had held me rigid until the nurse's footsteps had faded into the distance and all was silent. But then the silence was broken by a long low wail, like an animal in pain. And it had taken a while for me to realise the sound was coming from my own mouth.

The tears, when they came, were unstoppable. There didn't seem that much water in the world, let alone in my body. I'd sobbed for hours before drifting off into a troubled sleep. And while I'd lost track of time, I had an idea I'd passed several days in this way. Crying, drinking and eating the cold food left for me as a pure survival instinct, and sleeping fitfully. But the previous night had been different. I'd fallen into a much deeper and more peaceful sleep – a sleep from which I'd just awoken.

And with that awakening came a realisation. For the past six months, I'd been kept prisoner by Alban and his family. Partly because of the operation I'd been spearheading, and the damage done to their business. But mainly because I was carrying Alban's child. Now that child was no more. My usefulness to the family was gone. And all that was left was my betrayal. Which meant I was in deadly danger. And needed to get away.

I had no idea where in the country I was. They'd drugged my food on the evening I was transported to the hospital. And I was still weak from giving birth. But I had to try. The only alternative was to wait for them to come and kill me. That was not an option I was willing to consider.

Although I did wonder why they hadn't come for me already.

From the direction of the sunlight, I calculated it to be early morning, around seven o'clock. I must have slept for around twelve hours. Climbing out of bed, I pulled open cupboards and drawers, but they were all empty. I glanced down at the hospital robe. There was no way I would survive outside in that, even in late summer.

Listening at the door, I realised how silent this place was. Was I the only patient? Had the clinic, in fact, been specially prepared for me? That seemed unlikely, but we were talking about Alban's child here, so anything was possible.

I pulled open the door and peeped out. My room was at the end of a short corridor, off which there were just four doors in two pairs. At the other end I could see a glass door leading to a small vestibule and then to another set of doors and green countryside. So definitely a much smaller building than I'd thought. And there was no-one in sight.

Slipping out of my room, I tried the door to my right. It opened into a tiny kitchen. There were meats and cheeses in the fridge, and bread on the table. Bottles of water sat to one side of the sink. I recognised the food that had been left for me each day. But no ingredients for other meals, and no cooking utensils.

Across the corridor, I found a storeroom filled with medical supplies and cleaning materials. Plus, in a cupboard at the back, packs of doctors' scrubs. I grabbed a couple of bags, and pulling them open, found a set that fitted. Not much thicker than the hospital robe, but a better protection for my dignity.

As I approached the other set of doors, I glanced towards the vestibule. I shrank back against the wall and felt sweat trickle down my spine. I was not, as I thought, alone in the building. The nurse who'd given me the news about my baby's death was sitting at a desk facing the outside door, talking on the telephone. So, leaving by the front door didn't look like a viable option after all, at least at that moment.

I wondered if I should return to my room and wait for the chance to overpower the woman when she next brought me food. But I decided to check the last two rooms first. One was a tiny changing room, where to my delight I found a row of lockers. Exchanging my scrubs pants for some thicker trousers, I pulled a jacket off the peg behind the door. It was too tight for me to close the buttons, and the sleeves were a tad short, but over the scrubs tunic, it looked okay. And I wasn't going to a fashion parade anyway.

The best find was a pair of stout walking shoes, luckily fitting reasonably well. They were slightly too big, but they'd do.

Taking clothes which I assumed belonged to the woman currently sitting in the foyer was a risk, but I had to hope that I'd be away from the building long before she realised what was happening. Pushing down all feelings of guilt, I rifled through the woman's purse. A handful of notes and a few coins went into my pocket.

At the last moment, I peeked into the final door. The tiny room was full of barrels; barrels that were wired together. On top of the nearest one was a block of explosives and a digital clock. A clock that showed twenty minutes and fifteen seconds.

As I stared at the sight in front of me, one part of my mind urged me to run, while another part desperately searched for a solution to the situation.

The seconds ticked away. Fourteen, thirteen.

I knew then why there was no-one around and why they'd not come to kill me. An explosion this size would destroy me, my body and all evidence. I wondered if the nurse was aware of what was happening. I certainly hoped so. Despite what she was involved in, I didn't want anyone else to die.

But for myself, I knew it was too risky to go out of the front of the building. I had to move. And I had to move now.

I ran softly back to my room, pulling the door to and locking it behind me. Then I raced across to the window and pushed hard. It didn't move. The window was locked, there was no way out and by my reckoning there was around sixteen minutes left before the whole building went up.

CHAPTER 46

The bathroom. That might be better. And separated by yet another door from the foyer, there was maybe less chance of the nurse hearing what I was doing. But the window in the bathroom proved to be equally immovable.

There was a tiny pane at the top that opened outwards, but it was too small for even a child to squeeze through, let alone a fully grown woman. And the frosted glass was threaded with wires. So smashing it was likely to yield an unsatisfactory conclusion. No, the only option, if I wasn't going back out into the rest of the building, was in my bedroom.

I returned to the main room and checked the window once more. Tightly locked, and with no give in the frame, it looked like pushing it out wasn't going to work. But it was only single glazed. And there were no wires. Much easier to break. Could I smash it and run away before the nurse came to investigate? The door was locked from the inside, but that wouldn't hold off a determined shoulder for very long.

Sounds from outside caught my attention and I peered through the slats of the plastic blind. A car pulling up, a horn blowing. A swarthy young man jumping out of the driver's seat and beckoning impatiently to someone out of sight by the front door.

The nurse appeared around the corner of the building and glanced across towards the window of my room. I pulled back, fearing for one terrible moment that I'd been seen. But then two car doors closed in quick succession. And the vehicle sped away.

There had been no time for the nurse to visit her locker, so she wouldn't know I'd stolen her clothes and money. And now I was apparently alone. Should I just make my way to the front foyer, open the door and walk away? Something in me wanted to do that. To take the easy way out. But my sixth sense told me that wouldn't work. The door would be locked. They wouldn't have been daft enough to leave it open. And I had only minutes, possibly even seconds, before the building blew.

Making sure the car was out of sight, I ripped down the blind and, grabbing a chair, swung it at the window with all my might. There was a smashing sound and a rush of fresh warm air through the hole I'd made. Enlarging it rapidly with a copy of the Bible from the bedside table – a nice ironic touch on their part – I checked the money I'd salvaged from the nurse's locker was safe in my pocket, climbed onto the chair, jumped through the window and rolled across the ground. I clenched my teeth as I felt shards of broken glass rake my face and arms. But I was free. I could worry about a few cuts later.

A small stand of trees in the distance, on the side of a hill, looked like a good starting point. I rose to my feet and took my first couple of steps towards freedom. Only to feel the ground rock beneath me as a dull roar filled my ears. When the building behind me exploded into a cloud of dust and flame, I was lifted from my feet and thrown across the rough scrubland. I landed flat on my face, arms outstretched to break my fall, and mouth full of dust.

Judging by the faint sirens in the distance, it was only a matter of moments before I came back to full consciousness. Looking over my shoulder, I could see flames shooting from the remains of my prison. And I was so close, I could feel the heat on my back.

Too close. I was way too close. And still out in the open.

Stumbling to my feet, I bent low and raced across the open ground towards the trees. If I could only get in there, hopefully I'd be able to hide. I guessed Alban or one of the family would be along soon. They'd tell the authorities it was an empty building, used for storage, an unfortunate accident. I very much doubted they'd mention the one occupant they thought was in there. Maybe they were hoping there'd be nothing left for anyone to find. Maybe they had a story ready if a body – or at least some sort of human remains – was found. A tramp, hiding in the building. Looking for a warm place to sleep. Or maybe they'd just pay their way out of things.

The one thing I was certain of, they'd not admit to keeping a young woman prisoner while waiting for her to give birth. And for once, their duplicity might work in my favour. So long as they didn't specifically go looking for proof of my death, I had a chance of getting out of this region, out of this country.

All I needed to do was find a main road and friendly car. I'd hitched many times in this part of the world. There was always someone willing to give you a lift in return for a few leks. And so long as I avoided lorry drivers or lone males in cars, I should be okay.

A family was best. Children were happy to chat to strangers. And parents were happy for someone to absorb the incessant chatter, especially on long journeys. "Are we there yet?" sounded much the same, whatever language it was whined in.

And I had enough currency to get me a long way down the road. I had a fleeting moment of concern that I might have deprived the nurse of the means to feed herself and her family. But then I remembered how she'd run from the clinic, leaving me to die, and decided a couple of days without food was far less than she deserved.

CHAPTER 47

With my hearing muffled by the explosion, head thumping and pain suffusing my whole body, I continued my stumbling journey across the open ground. The sirens were getting closer. The road ran along the margin of the field I was crossing. If the emergency vehicles arrived before I reached the trees, I was in clear sight. I had to keep running.

The sound of engines competed with the sirens, so loud I could hear them despite the effects of the blast. I looked back across my shoulder. The road was still clear. And in the other direction too. Maybe I had time to reach the trees. Just maybe.

But when the first vehicle appeared, it wasn't, as I expected, along the road. With a roar and a smashing of foliage, a huge black shape burst out of the trees almost in front of me. Without thinking, I threw myself sideways down a small slope, and rolled into a dry ditch.

There was a fallen tree stretched across the top and I crawled into the space below it and held my breath. Peeping through the branches, I was in time to see what it was that had come through the trees. Not a car; certainly not an emergency truck. It was a massive piece of farm equipment, a digger of some kind. By now, it was across the field and nearing the smoking ruins of the clinic. I could only see the rear of the cab and the back of the driver's head. Plus the passenger sitting beside him.

But I didn't need to see any more to know who it was in the farm vehicle that was careering across the ground. The stark stripe of white stretching from the crown to the nape of the neck was all I needed. Alban. Alban Laska had come himself to make sure his former lover, the woman who'd betrayed him, and then had borne his child, was safely dead and buried in the explosion.

I knew he hadn't seen me. If he had, he'd have made the driver turn his transport around and mow me down. Alban was looking for absolute proof. I had to get out of there.

Sirens passed by as the emergency trucks finally arrived.

Checking the road was clear and there were no more surprises on the way, I hauled myself to my feet and, at a crouching run, finally made it across the rest of the field and into the trees. I'd hoped to rest there for a while, but the arrival of Alban changed all that. I had to get as far away as possible. Now.

There was a path through the trees gradually winding up the hill. It wasn't the direction I wanted to go. I knew I had to get down to the valley and find a safe way onto the road. But it was the only path I could see, so reluctantly I started climbing.

At the top of the hill, the trees stopped and the view opened up for miles. In the far distance, out on the horizon, I could see the outline of what looked like a city. There were huge apartment blocks, factories from whose chimneys billows of smoke and steam issued, and over the whole area, a pall of smog. Yes, definitely a city. But which one I couldn't tell, from where I was.

Much closer, at the bottom of the hill, was a small village, with others dotted on the wide green plain between me and the horizon. I searched for signs that it was somewhere I knew (and therefore was likely to be known) but that didn't seem to be the case at all.

Alban's compound was on the edge of a small town. Built on a large piece of land, bordered by roads on two sides, and a river winding around the rest of the perimeter, it was well made and well looked after. Fences of barbed wire, not to mention the guards on the gate, kept out sightseers. But no matter how far I looked, I could see nothing that resembled the compound at all. Maybe my luck was changing. Maybe I was so far away that no-one would know about the Laska family, their history and their way of life. But in that case, what was Alban doing riding around the countryside in a digger? Unlikely as it seemed, there had to be some connection between him and this village.

The village was tiny, just a few houses, and a farmhouse. The road entered at one end and carried on at the other, heading straight towards the far-distant city. There was a tiny church, built of wood as were all the buildings, in the centre of the village. And that was it. Little in the way of outbuildings, nowhere obvious to hide.

And I didn't think hiding was a good idea anyway. My gut told me the only way I was going to get out of this alive was to keep moving, make it to the city where I could lose myself in the shadows while trying to decide what to do next. But the city was so far away, twenty to thirty miles, I estimated. It would take forever to walk there, if I could even make it that far.

The path down the hill towards the village was bordered by a high hedge, hawthorn, brambles and other shrubs. The last sort of foliage to have to hide in. But what choice did I have?

Crossing to the other side of the hedge, away from the path, I pressed myself into the undergrowth and began creeping down the hill. Occasionally, someone would come out of one of the houses. Each time that happened, I stopped. But they never looked up.

Slowly, slowly, I moved down the hill towards civilisation and possible safety. Or possibly not.

CHAPTER 48

At the bottom of the hill, the path merged with the road through the village: packed earth, not tarmac, but clearly used for vehicles rather than the feet that mainly used the path. The hedge petered out and there were no more trees. I felt as though there were eyes gazing at me from every corner, every window.

Bending low, I crossed an expanse of farmyard. In the rainy season, it would be a sea of mud. But now, at the tail end of summer, the mud was baked into hard ridges. Hard on the feet, but easier to cross than when wet.

A huge barn lay at the other side of the yard, its doors wide open. A glance around confirmed there was no-one in sight – at that moment – so I slipped inside, exchanging the hard white daylight for a soft gloom that instantly made me feel less vulnerable.

Along both sides of the barn were stacks of boxes filled with vegetables: kale, cucumbers, tomatoes. In one corner, bulging sacks were piled up. An odd potato or two lying on the ground gave a clue to their contents. To one side, I spied a ladder leading up to the hayloft and hauled my tired and aching body up the rungs.

The loft was full of straw bales. Threading my way

through them, I reached the back wall. An unglazed window gave me a clear view of the village street and the road leading out of town, towards the city.

Adjusting the position of a couple of bales, I built myself a small cave; hidden from the window, hidden from anyone who climbed the ladder. With a sigh, I curled myself into a ball and closed my eyes.

The sound of a lorry woke me. Darkness had fallen and I didn't need the rumbling of my stomach to tell me I'd slept the best part of the day away. Peering from the window, I saw headlights in the distance, moving through the village. A lorry drove past the barn, stopped and reversed through the open doors. Exhaust fumes filled the air and I held my breath for as long as I could, trying not to cough.

Peering through the gaps in the floor of the loft, I watched as both doors of the lorry opened and two young men jumped out. They were dressed like farmhands.

"Oh, you've arrived then, have you?"

A voice made me jump; the two young men swung round as a middle-aged woman entered the barn.

"Now, Ludmilla, don't scold us," said the driver with a grin. "We had trouble getting this old thing started." He patted the bonnet of the truck. "Had to give her a bit of a service. But she's fine now."

"Hmm," sniffed Ludmilla, who I assumed was the farmer's wife or maybe even the farmer herself. "Now you're here, we'd better get you loaded up." She glanced up at the hayloft and I recoiled in horror, but she didn't seem to see anything. "I'm assuming you're going straight back to the city. Not going to spend hours sleeping in my loft this time?"

The driver shook his head. "No, tempting as the offer is, Ludmilla, we'll go right back, otherwise we'll miss the market. It's only a couple of hours. We can sleep tomorrow."

For the next fifteen minutes, the two men loaded boxes and sacks into the back of the truck. By the time they'd finished, there was barely an inch of spare space left. But I knew this was my best chance of getting away. If I could only get down without being seen. And in the end, it was so easy, I couldn't believe my luck.

"Come over to the farmhouse before you go," said Ludmilla, as the final boxes were slid into place. "I've made a basket for you to take back. Only coffee and snacks, but it'll help keep you awake."

Listening to the sounds of the three voices as they faded across the farmyard, I slipped out of my hiding place and down the ladder. I ran to the rear of the truck and hauled myself up into the crowded storage area. Climbing across boxes, I reached the sacks of potatoes. I tried to force my way behind them, but they were so closely packed, it wasn't possible. There was nothing for it, but to perch on the top of the sacks. I resigned myself to a very bumpy ride indeed. I just hoped no-one would look too closely at the truck before it began its journey to the city.

Footsteps heralded the return of the two men. I flattened myself, making sure only my dark clothing was visible. I closed my eyes and held my breath. But all was well. There was a bang as the tailgate was pushed into place and the bolts slid across. Then two doors opened and slammed, the engine started and my journey to freedom continued.

As the lorry slowed, turning out of the farmyard, a gust of wind caught the canvas at the side nearest where I, propped up against the back of the cab, was seated. For a brief instant, I found myself looking out across the farmyard, lit by a full moon and brilliant stars in an otherwise inky black night. And straight into the eyes of Ludmilla as she stood at the door to the farm building watching her produce leaving for market.

I jumped and turned my head, hoping the other woman hadn't been able to see me in the gloom. But somehow, the look on her face suggested she knew there was a stowaway in the lorry. And that she knew exactly who it was.

As the lorry turned into the road, and the canvas fell back into place, the last thing I saw was Ludmilla taking down a walkie-talkie radio from a hook next to the door.

CHAPTER 49

I held my breath, waiting for the crackle of a radio in the cab, for the squeal of brakes and running feet as the driver and his companion came to discover me stowing away in the back of the lorry. But all I heard was the sound of wheels turning on the pitted road, and as the distance between the village and the lorry increased, I realised I had a slight reprieve.

Maybe the guys didn't have a radio. Maybe Ludmilla wasn't trying to reach them. Maybe she thought there was a better way to deal with the runaway she'd spotted. That was it. I knew with a certainty that brought dread to my heart, Ludmilla was contacting Alban or one of his loyal family members. So although I had a brief respite, that was all it was.

I had no way of knowing where I was in relation to Alban's compound. I hadn't been able to spot it when I'd scanned the plain from my vantage point at the top of the hill. With a bit of luck, it was the other side of the city. In which case, they'd be waiting for me when the lorry arrived.

But what if that wasn't the situation? What if Alban was *behind* me? He'd been at the clinic to inspect the results of the explosion. And although he was in a lumbering digger at that time, there was no way that was the only vehicle at his disposal. And one of Alban's cars would be able to outrun this old lorry any day of the week.

I couldn't afford to wait until we reached the city. Two hours, the driver had said. That was far too long, far too much time for my enemies to catch me. I had to get out, as soon as possible, and find an alternative route to safety. I needed these guys to stop, maybe to break into that picnic basket Ludmilla had provided. Then I'd slip out of the back, hide until they'd driven on, and think again.

The opportunity I'd been waiting for arrived in little more than thirty minutes. The lorry ground to a halt. Everything was silent for a moment, then I heard a whistle in the distance and a slow clicking that gradually increased in volume and speed. Peeping through a hole in the canvas, I saw we were parked at a level crossing, waiting for a massive goods train to pass.

I crawled across the sacks, squeezed past the boxes and, checking there was no-one in sight, climbed over the tailgate and lowered myself to the ground. There was a slight jarring in my ankle as I landed awkwardly, but it was nothing major and I knew I'd have to ignore it. I was in for far more than a sprained ankle if Alban found me.

There was a shed by the side of the road, a few metres from where we were parked. In seconds I was around the back of it, flattened against the rotting boards.

The train seemed to go on for ever, but finally the last carriage sped past, the signal changed to green, and the gates on the level crossing opened. With a crunching of gears, the lorry started up and drove across the tracks. As I watched from my hiding place, the tail lights dwindled and then disappeared. All was silent and very, very dark.

I pondered my options. There was a small railway station two hundred metres down the line. The freight train hadn't stopped there, but it had slowed. There were unlikely to be many trains stopping there at night, but if any other freight trains came through, maybe I could hitch a lift. Except, I had no idea which direction was the right one. If I guessed correctly, I could be in the city in less than an hour. But if I was wrong, I could be heading who knew where – and quite possibly back towards danger. No, I didn't think the train was a good option.

Could I steal a car? Maybe a motorbike? That would be a quick journey, and I knew the way to the city – follow the lorry across the plain. But that risked putting yet another target on my back. Not only would Alban be looking for me, but so would the police.

It looked as though hitch-hiking or stowing away again were my only options. But before I did anything else, I desperately needed something to eat – and maybe some rest. I gazed around me. On this side of the tracks, there was nothing apart from this little shed. But on the other side, I could see a handful of buildings, including a church. So a village at the very least. I began walking.

The church was the first building I came to. I pushed the heavy oak door, more in hope than in expectation, but once again, luck was in my favour. The door opened easily and I slipped inside. To begin with it seemed pitch black, and I waited a few moments for my eyes to become acclimatised. Then I spotted a flicker of light in a side chapel. Candles, burning in front of a statue of the Virgin Mary.

I ran to the chapel and grabbed a fresh candle from the box, lighting it from one of the others and throwing a quick apologetic look at the benign face gazing down at me. Then I turned away and explored.

To the right of the altar, I found the door to the vestry. There was a small kitchen off to one side and there, in front of me, the answer to my prayers – or at least some of them. A kettle, a jar of coffee, and a box full of cookies. Obviously the priest of this parish had a sweet tooth.

I took a deep breath and reached for the kettle.

CHAPTER 50

"Someone looks like they've been making themselves at home."

It wasn't the gentle voice breaking into my dreams that surprised me so much as the Irish accent. I wondered if I'd dreamed the past terrible six months and was really back in the UK. But as I opened my eyes and took in my surroundings I realised it hadn't been a dream at all.

The small fusty-smelling vestry, the empty mug next to my chair, the last few crumbs down the front of my jacket. And not least, the tall imposing figure in black looming over me. No, the accent might be Irish, but the surroundings were very definitely Eastern European. I scrambled to my feet.

"Father, I'm so sorry. I was really hungry, but I only meant to stop for a little while. I must have fallen..." My voice faltered and my explanation came to an end as I watched the look on the priest's face turn from concern to horror. Glancing down at the chair I'd been sleeping on, I saw a deep red stain spreading across the cushion.

"My child, you're hurt. Were you attacked?"

I shook my head. "No. At least not this time." I paused and took a deep breath. "My baby. I had a baby a week or so back." I realised I had no idea even what day it was. And suddenly it all became too much.

I was Charlie Jones, undercover agent with many years' experience under my belt, who prided myself on never crying. But now, I collapsed into the arms of a total stranger who, like me, was far from home, and sobbed on his shoulder.

I had no idea of the time, or even whether it was the same day, when I woke. I had vague memories of the priest, who'd told me his name was Father Gerard, leading me to his presbytery, next door to the church, and helping me upstairs to a tiny box room at the back of the building. I remembered quiet voices on the landing outside the door, and being undressed by an elderly woman who smiled at me but simply shook her head when I tried talking to her.

My wounds had been treated, gently, and then I'd been helped into bed. And although all my senses screamed I had to keep moving, had to keep trying to reach safety, I'd given in to my desperate need for sleep.

I thought there had been moments when I was awake; drinking soup from a spoon held to my lips by the same old woman, but that might have been a dream. Certainly, I was not as starving hungry as I had been when I reached the church. But why I'd slept so deeply and for so long, I didn't understand.

Rising stiffly from the bed, I spied the clothes I'd stolen from the clinic folded neatly on a chair by the window. They'd been laundered and smelled fresh and clean. I quickly pulled them on. The notes and coins I'd stolen were lying on the bedside table. Pushing them back into my pocket, I crept across the floor to the door and pulled it open. There was a man speaking in the hall below. From the accent I could tell it was Father Gerard.

"Yes, I have her. She's fine. A bit beaten up, hungry and tired, but we've dealt with that. She should be fine to travel tomorrow." There was a pause, and I realised he was talking on the telephone. From the sound of it, the person at the other end commanded respect or even fear. Father Gerard continued. "Yes, I'll bring her in tomorrow. We should get to the city about noon."

My stomach churned. I'd thought my luck had changed. I'd really thought I was safe. A man of the cloth, for goodness sake. But it sounded as though, yet again, I'd stumbled across one of Alban's far-reaching tentacles. I was going to have to run again. Or was I?

If this man was going to take me just where I wanted to be, maybe I should play along for the moment. And then, when we reached the city, that would be the time to make a break for it. Much better than trying to escape on foot again in the middle of nowhere.

I heard Father Gerard end the call and drop the telephone receiver back onto the cradle. As I pushed the door wider, a floorboard creaked and the priest looked up the stairs directly at me. He smiled.

"Charlie, you're awake. And I must say you're looking much better. How are you feeling?"

Confusion stunned me. How did this man know my real name? A name I'd not used, and barely thought of, for more than a year. Then I remembered a snippet of conversation the previous night. As he'd helped me from the church to his house, Father Gerard had asked what he should call me. And something had stopped me giving him my undercover name. After all, if anyone from Alban's family was sniffing around, they'd be looking for Rose Fitzpatrick. And automatically, I'd told him my real name. In which case, who had he been talking to on the phone? Who in this country knew me as Charlie Jones? Maybe I wasn't about to be betrayed after all.

I swallowed my confusion and smiled back at him. "Not bad, Father, not bad at all."

He looked at his watch. "You're just in time for supper. Do you want Vlora to bring it up to your room, or would you care to join me downstairs?"

"I'll come down, if that's okay with you."

"Delighted to have some company, my dear."

I plodded downstairs and realised that although I was stronger than I had been, the past few days, not to mention giving birth, had really taken it out of me. Even if this priest was going to try to hand me over to Alban when we reached the city, this brief time in his home in the country gave me a chance to recover my strength for the trials still to come.

I decided to let Father Gerard – I wondered if that was really his name, or whether he was even a real priest – think I was still unaware of his plans for me. I would have a decent dinner – the smell of roast lamb wafting from the kitchen was enticing – and another night's sleep.

"Something smells wonderful, Father," I said as he ushered me into the dining room. "I'm starving."

Maybe I could even persuade him I needed a couple more days to recover. That way, I would be better able to deal with whatever I faced next. And somehow, I had a nasty feeling my ordeal was far from over.

CHAPTER 51

The dinner was as delicious as the aromas from the kitchen had promised. Father Gerard might be an ordained minister (although I was still reserving judgement on that) and he might be living in the middle of nowhere in one of the poorest countries in Europe, but he certainly kept a decent table.

As well as the roast lamb, there were new potatoes, delicately sliced green beans and chunks of carrots all cooked to perfection. Plus a mint sauce that took me right back to my mother's Sunday dinners. Although the rather good red wine that was served with this meal would have been considered far too much of a luxury for that little house in Devon.

"Your cook's done a wonderful job, Father."

"Vlora? Yes, she really spoils me." He rubbed his stomach that was starting to strain ever so gently against the dark fabric of his cassock. "And I'm afraid it's beginning to show. But I do love my food." He looked across at my empty plate. "If you've had enough, I happen to know we've got a rather nice apple and blackberry pie for dessert."

I wondered about the origins of this paragon in the

kitchen. She didn't speak English, nor did she seem to speak the local language either. Just who was she? And where had she come from? Maybe I'd be able to steer the conversation in that direction later.

No outside observer would have been able to spot the undercurrents in the situation that evening. Father Gerard made no attempt to quiz me on my story and why I'd wandered into the church in that state. When I'd tried to explain the previous evening he'd held up a hand to silence me.

"Hush now, child. I'm sure you have your reasons, but I'm not going to pry. All I need to know is that you're in a bad way and need some help. And that's what my job calls for, after all. But as for more than that — well, it's probably better you don't tell me anything. Then if anyone asks, I can truthfully say I know nothing."

Similarly, my one attempt to find out the background of an Irish Catholic priest running a parish in such a bizarre place was gently but firmly deflected.

Instead, the conversation across the dinner table was light-hearted and erudite. We touched on books, music, politics and even theology. Under other circumstances, I would have found it relaxing and thoroughly enjoyable. But deep down, I knew this was just a minor interlude.

It wasn't until we rose from the table after several hours of eating, drinking and pleasant conversation that Father Gerard raised the topic that had been at the front of my mind all evening.

"I've got to drive into the city tomorrow morning. If you're feeling strong enough, I can give you a lift. You've not told me where you're headed and I don't want to know, but I suspect you're more likely to find what you're looking for in a crowded location, rather than an isolated one."

I nodded. "You're right, Father. And a lift to the city would be very helpful." I marvelled at how he managed to turn what was obviously a decision on his part into a choice for me to make. This man was good. What would have happened if I'd said no, I didn't want to go? Would he have forced me, or changed his plans? Perhaps I'd test that question out the following morning.

"Right you are then. I want to leave by ten at the latest. Will that be okay?"

"No problem." I headed for the stairs. "Goodnight, Father."

"Goodnight, my child. And God bless you."

The combination of heavy food and good red wine meant I had no trouble getting to sleep as soon as I climbed into bed. However, I was awake again by four and lay in bed feverishly going through options in my head. Run away? Steal the car and drive to the city on my own? Tell Father Gerard I felt ill and wanted to stay at the house longer?

None of these options seemed sensible and I decided in the end to go along with my original plan; to drive into the city with the priest the next day (or later that morning, I corrected myself) and take the first opportunity to escape.

I'd seen the vehicle, an old Citroen, and I was fairly sure it didn't have central locking. So I should be able to get away at a traffic lights. In fact, once we reached the outskirts of the city, I would jump out the first time we came to a halt.

At just before ten, Father Gerard put the car into gear and drove away from the presbytery and the temporary reprieve I'd been enjoying. He tried to engage me in conversation at the start of the journey, but maybe sensing my mind was elsewhere, he soon gave up trying and concentrated on driving instead.

It was a straight road across the plain, and the smudge on the horizon gradually increased in size and then resolved itself into large modern-looking buildings. Ninety minutes after we'd started driving, the countryside gave way to residential areas, at first an odd house or two, but soon we were passing Soviet-style blocks of flats and industrial complexes.

"Not long now," Father Gerard said. "I'm going to drop you in one of the suburbs. I think you'll find what you're looking for there."

I panicked. My time was running out. Any minute, we'd reach our destination and Alban or one of the family would be waiting for me. I had to get out, now.

As the car turned into a wide tree-lined street, full of very grand houses, I took hold of the door handle and gently began pushing it down. Father Gerard slowly braked the car and came to a halt. At the other end of the street, two large armoured vehicles screamed into view. And behind them, a huge tractor parked across the junction, effectively turning the street into a dead end.

Father Gerard slammed the car back into reverse, threw his arm along the top of my seat and peering back over his shoulder, gunned the engine.

"Keep your head down, Charlie!"

I had no time to work out what was going on before he swore violently, in a most unpriestly way.

Turning round, I saw another tractor slotting itself into place at the entrance to the street. We were trapped.

CHAPTER 52

Father Gerard braked sharply, threw the car into a three-point turn and headed directly towards the tractor. I dug my fingers into the dashboard. At the last moment, he swung the car up onto the wide pavement, colliding with planters and a small sapling in the process. We scraped along the railings in front of one of the houses, and forced our way, with inches to spare, between the advancing tractor and the corner of the building. With a squeal of tyres on tarmac, we were out.

Except we weren't.

Parked a few hundred yards along the road was another armoured vehicle. A fourth one appeared in the distance behind us. And suddenly we became aware of a clattering sound above our head. A helicopter? A small plane? I couldn't see. But whatever it was, someone was firing down on us.

Bullets sprayed the road all around us. We swerved from one side to another. By some miracle, nothing hit the car. The vehicle in front of us made no attempt to stop us and we were past in seconds. Looking back I saw it begin to give chase, but keeping back, as though escorting us, rather than trying to catch us. I suddenly realised what they were doing.

"We're being herded, Father. They want us to keep going, but they're choosing the route."

"Yes, a common trick of theirs. They're driving us where they want us. Somewhere quiet, no doubt."

"But who are they?" I'd seen all of Alban's cars in the past. There had been nothing like this. This was definitely on a much larger scale.

"All in good time, Charlie. All in good time. Let's just get out of here first."

We were approaching a road junction, where our minor road crossed a major street, heavy with midday traffic. The signal was on green. Father Gerard approached the junction slowly then, at the last minute, as the light changed from green to red, he shot across the junction, narrowly avoiding being hit by the stream of traffic coming from either side. The junction was then crowded with slow-moving traffic and our pursuers were stranded on the other side.

We turned left into a narrow lane, then right into an even tighter one, before shooting out onto a broad avenue leading to a bridge across a wide river. On the other bank, I could see what looked like a row of empty warehouses.

"The old shipping quarter." Father Gerard pointed with his chin. "We should be able to hide there for a while."

We crossed the bridge, turned onto the wharf, and then into a huge hangar-like building. And not a moment too soon. The plane that had been following us – not a helicopter after all – burst over the horizon and flew along the river.

"I think we're safe for the moment." Father Gerard climbed out of the car and stretched, before walking across to the huge sliding doors which he pushed to. "No point in letting the world see what we're doing in here."

I joined him at the front of the building. The sound of the plane was fading and suddenly we were surrounded by silence.

"Who *are* you, Father Gerard?" He turned at my question and smiled at me.

"Just someone like you. Someone trying to make things better in a bad world."

"So, you work for—"

He held up a hand to stop me. "That's not important. All you need to know is there's a whole network of folks across the region, some on the books, some not."

"But I had no idea. I was convinced…"

"…that I was working with Alban Laska? Going to hand you over?" He shook his head. "On the contrary, Charlie, we were just a couple of streets away from a British safe house when we were ambushed."

"And how did you know about me?"

"Oh, you're famous around here, Charlie. Although, to be honest, everyone thought you were dead, after you went silent back in March. That's why no-one came looking for you."

"But why didn't you tell me when I first turned up at the church?"

"You know the answer to that one. The less we know about someone and the less anyone else knows about us, the safer we all are. If they'd captured either of us, we'd not have been able to give anything away."

I sighed. That made sense. Although I'd have slept better if I'd known I was in a safe house rather than with one of Alban's associates. Then a thought occurred to me. "But who *are* they? The people chasing us? I've spent the past year or more with Alban and his family. They're minor league. They don't have the sort of vehicles and arms we've seen today."

"I rather suspect someone close to the folks further up the food chain got wind that you were still alive. That operation back in March did some serious damage to the distribution network and resulted in some very dangerous people being sent to prison. But rumour has it there are remnants of the gang still around, and they're out for blood. Your blood, I'm afraid."

I shivered. It looked like avoiding Alban and the family was suddenly the least of my worries. "So what happens now?"

"We should be safe here until nightfall. Then we'll make our way back across the river and try to reach the safe house on foot. I don't want to risk the car, they'll be looking for it. Once you're there, the powers that be can organise an extraction team. You should be back in the UK before the end of the week."

"But what about you?"

"Oh, I'll be fine. I'll go back to my parish and make sure Vlora is safe. Then I'll quietly shut up shop and slip away." He smiled into the distance. "Maybe I'll even go home for a spell. It would be good to see the Wicklow Mountains once again."

Then he rubbed his hands. "Right, we might as well make ourselves comfortable, if we're going to be here for a while. You'll find a basket in the trunk that Vlora packed for me. She always makes far too much, so there should be plenty for both of us. Then we'll get a few hours' shuteye. It's going to be a long night."

CHAPTER 53

It was just after midnight when Father Gerard shook my shoulder to wake me. We'd found a pile of old sacks in the back of the warehouse and although they were musty and smelling somewhat of fish, we'd managed to make ourselves reasonably comfortable after doing justice to Vlora's packed lunch.

Last time I'd glanced across at my companion, he'd been fast asleep with his mouth open and gentle snores rising into the air.

Now, however, he was all business.

"Rub this on your face." He handed me a lump of mud he'd presumably scraped up from the edge of the river. In the six months I'd been kept prisoner, I'd lost my tan and knew my face would gleam in the moonlight. I grimaced at the smell, but did as I was told.

He pulled a lighter out of his pocket and, shielding it with his hand, showed me a map he'd scribbled on an old greaseproof bag.

"We're not going back over the main bridge. Too open, too easily surveilled." He indicated to a point back downstream. "There's a small pedestrian bridge here, but next to it, there's a rail crossing. We'll go over that. It's the last thing they'd expect."

"Is it safe? What about the trains?"

"There shouldn't be any at this time of night." He shrugged. "And I think it's a risk we'll have to take. Once we've reached the other side, we'll work our way through the back streets and approach the safe house via the rear entrance."

He shoved the map into my hand. "Here, in case we get separated. You should be able to find your way with this." Standing, he pulled me into a brief but tight hug before sketching a quick blessing in the air above my head. "Bless you, my child. And safe journey."

I nodded, smiling my thanks, too full of emotion to say anything. We took a final look around our temporary home in case we'd missed anything, made sure the car was secure until Father Gerard could come back for it, and headed out into the night.

The moon, a few days past full, was hazy but there was sufficient light to see by. We moved swiftly downstream, flitting from one pool of shadow to the next. As far as I was aware, there was no-one around.

When we reached the train crossing, we climbed up the slope away from the river and found our way to the edge of the track. A narrow walkway, barely wide enough to stand on, stretched along the side of the rails, across the bridge and into the night. The metal frets lining the track provided occasional handholds.

Initially, the walk was easy. We moved quickly, single file, with Father Gerard leading the way. But as the bridge rose high over the river, the wind, little more than a breeze at ground level, became a roaring monster that tried to push us off our narrow path and onto the train lines.

It was just as we reached the pinnacle of the bridge and I was looking forward to a gentle walk down the other side that I became aware of another noise that gradually eclipsed even the wind in its ferocity. A train!

There was a train approaching the bridge. Glancing

back, I saw a pinpoint of light in the distance that grew as it approached. Father Gerard turned back and looked at me in horror. We both turned towards the outside of the bridge, wrapped our arms around the nearest metal strut and clung on. Then the monster was upon us.

As with the train I'd watched at the level crossing when escaping from the lorry, it was a goods train made up of thirty or more closed wagons. So no passengers to look out of the window and spot the madmen clinging to the bridge. Just second after second, minute after minute of extreme noise and air rushing past us. It seemed to go on for ever.

And then it was gone. With a haunting whistle floating back through the night, as though bidding us a safe journey.

I continued to cling to the strut, shaken and shaking, until a voice called me back to reality.

"Charlie, come on. Let's move."

We finished the second half of the crossing in a much shorter time than the first. At the base of the bridge, we stumbled, almost rolled, down the slope back to the embankment before sinking to the ground, our legs no longer able to hold us up.

For the best part of ten minutes I lay in the dark, waiting for my heartbeat to return to normal. Then I clambered to my feet. "Shouldn't we move?"

There was no answer from Father Gerard, who was sitting hunched over, his face in his hands and his shoulders shaking.

"Father." I touched him on his shoulder. "Are you okay?"

"Oh yes, Charlie. I'm just fine." He looked up and whatever emotions I'd expected to see on his face, it wasn't joy and laughter. "That was fun, wasn't it?"

"I'm not sure fun is how I would describe it." I held out my hand to help him up. "I thought you said there wouldn't be any trains."

"There shouldn't have been. I guess we were unlucky with that." He rubbed his face with his hands and shook himself. "Okay, let's get moving. I need to get you to the safe house, pick up the car, and drive back home before daylight." And giving me a cheeky grin and a jaunty wink, he set off into the night.

CHAPTER 54

On silent feet, I followed Father Gerard through back streets so narrow that on occasion, we could touch the walls on either side by stretching out our hands. There were no houses on these streets and very few front entrances to buildings. There were unmarked doors with no handles on the outside. Huge communal garbage dumpsters, sometimes overflowing, were always stinking. Even so late at night, the heat from the summer's day still radiated from their dented lids. An occasional hiss or yelp followed by a rush of small paws told us we'd disturbed the neighbourhood cats and dogs.

I lost all awareness of where we were. Our journey earlier that day had been rapid and filled with adrenaline. Now, the tension was just as palpable, but the silence and the fact that we were on foot made everything seem as though it were happening in slow motion.

We saw no-one on the journey, which took the best part of an hour, with frequent stops to check we weren't being followed. At one point, we had to pass through a brightly lit passageway. Father Gerard took off much faster than I would have expected for a man of his age and lifestyle. I struggled to keep up with him.

When we reached darkness once more, we hunkered down in a doorway to catch our breath, and I raised a subject that had been niggling me since we'd been forced to flee the safe house that morning.

"How did they – whoever they are – know we were going to be there at exactly that time?" I didn't want to go down this road, but I knew I had to. "Who did you tell we were coming to the city today?"

"Only you and I knew. I told Vlora I was going to take you to the railway station up near the border so you could catch a train." Father Gerard looked askance. "Why, what are you saying?"

"I'm saying our reception committee was too big and too well-organised to have been there on spec. They had to have prior warning." I thought hard. "How about a tracker? Could your car be bugged?"

"If it was, don't you think they'd have found us in the warehouse soon after we took cover?"

"Good point." So that really only left two options. Either Father Gerard was a traitor – the way he'd behaved since that morning told me that wasn't the case – or there was a leak on the British side. Maybe the safe house wasn't as safe as we assumed. "Who did you speak to at the safe house?"

"The duty officer." Father Gerard stopped, then shook his head. "No, I've known Brian Filson for years. He's saved dozens of people. There's never been any suspicion about him."

"Maybe there's cause for suspicion now." I shrugged. "Look, all I'm saying is that we need to be careful. We mustn't let our guard down when we get there. Until we know what's going on." I shivered. The breeze was starting to build, and the sweat from our run was drying cold on my skin. "Come on. Let's keep going."

We reached the wide street with the old houses about ten minutes later. Peering around the corner, I saw no sign of the vehicles used to close off our exit that morning. But we caught a glint of dark metal, a car parked under the trees at the end of the street. Father Gerard tapped me on the shoulder and pointed to an alleyway running along the back of the houses.

I followed him to the first building in the row, and watched as he tugged at a rusted gate in a set of railings running along the whole of the block. We slipped down a short flight of metal steps and through a door hanging open at the bottom.

"Where are we? This isn't the right building. And why is the door open?" I could feel my heart rate rising as I wondered if I'd been wrong in clearing Father Gerard of any suspicion. Was this an elaborate trick?

"Shh. This leads to the cellar which runs all along the row of buildings." He looked at me as though he could read my mind. "And in a place like this, a locked door attracts far more attention than one that's hanging off its hinges." He turned and disappeared into the building.

Following him, I found myself in a darkness so deep I wondered if I'd gone blind. There was a click and a small torch was pushed into my hand. I glanced up at the walls, but there were no windows through which our lights would be seen. We hurried down a long echoing area. Every so often it was blocked by a wall of bricks, but in each case, a narrow opening was hidden in the deepest corner. This was obviously a well-used passageway.

As we reached the fifth or sixth section of the cellar, Father Gerard held up his hand to stop me. He pointed to a short flight of steps leading up to a solid-looking wooden door. Climbing the stairs, he took a large key from his pocket and fitted it into the lock. It turned silently, and he opened the door, switching off his torch and signalling for me to do the same.

"And some doors we definitely do keep locked," he whispered in my ear as he waited for me to pass him. He relocked the door behind us then pointed up the concrete staircase.

On the third-floor landing, we turned left and approached a door labelled 34. Father Gerard used another key from his bunch and the door swung open.

It was like walking into a little piece of home. To the right of the front door, a small kitchen held evidence of someone preparing supper. A filled kettle sat on the stove, although it was cold to the touch. There was a box of Tetley teabags open on the worktop, next to a mug decorated with red, white and blue stripes. A milk jug and sugar bowl were nearby.

Opposite the kitchen was a tiny bathroom. Further down the hallway, to the left and the right, doors opened out into bedrooms, each containing two neatly made single beds. One even had a candlewick bedspread over it. At the end of the hallway was a lounge, the width of the whole apartment. Tastefully decorated, if slightly dated, with Laura Ashley wallpaper and matching fabric on the sofa and armchairs.

The only jarring note was the middle-aged man seated on the sofa, eyes open in terror above a strip of tape across his mouth. His legs were splayed wide and on the floor between his feet lay a bundle of dynamite sticks, taped together. A timer strapped to the bundle displayed 5:00 in red numbers.

As we walked into the room, there was a click and the numbers started counting down.

CHAPTER 55

"Brian, my God, what have they done to you?" Father Gerard surged forward, but I grabbed him and held him back.

"No, wait, we need to check this out before we get any closer." I looked across at the other man. "It's Brian, right?" He nodded. "Okay, Brian, we're going to get you out of this, but I need you to work with me. Can you do that?" He nodded again.

"Is anyone still here in the apartment?" He shook his head. "And are there any other devices, do you know?" He shook his head a second time and a trickle of sweat ran down the side of his face and fell onto his collar.

I breathed slightly more easily, tiptoed forward, and ripped the tape off Filson's mouth before crouching down in front of the deadly device.

"Can you defuse it, Charlie?" Father Gerard was leaning over my shoulder.

"I don't think so. It's not an arrangement I recognise." The device wasn't big but it would cause quite a bit of damage if it went off in this small room. I stood and walked across to the window. It was open and beyond it was an iron fire escape, presumably serving all the floors on the building. Peering round the curtains, I spied a pocket-sized park across the street. "I think our best option is to lob it over there." Father Gerard joined me at the window and grunted his agreement. "There's no-one around." I checked the timer. Less than two minutes left.

"Let me, Charlie." Father Gerard gave me a grin. "I was top bowler in the seminary's cricket team. You get Brian sorted out and we'll find out who did this to him."

Father Gerard climbed through the window onto the fire escape and held his hands out for the device. With extreme care, I picked it up and walked towards him. I watched as he raised his arm and leaned as far as possible over the side of the railing. Then I hurried to the kitchen, grabbed a knife from the block, and ran back to release Filson's restraints. In the distance, we heard an explosion, and the windows rattled.

Filson wiped the sweat from his forehead with his shirt sleeve. "I thought my time was up there."

"What happened?"

"I don't know how they found me. But they were waiting on the fourth-floor landing when I arrived. They said very little, but I'm pretty sure they were connected to the group you helped put away earlier in the year."

"So not just connected to Alban Laska, then?"

"Oh, definitely not. Much more sophisticated than that. They grabbed me, tied me up and left me as you found me. And rigged the explosives so the timer only started when you arrived." His face clouded over. "I have a nasty suspicion our phone line's been compromised. We're certainly going to have to find new accommodation." He looked around the lounge. "Pity really, I quite like this place." He rubbed his hands. "But our first task is to sort out your arrangements." He held out his hand and shook mine. "Welcome back, Charlie Jones. It's good to see you're still alive."

"I wouldn't be here at all if Father Gerard–" I broke off and looked around. "Where is he?" We raced to the window. The fire escape was empty. And as I stared across the road at the little park, with an untidy crater where the central flowerbed had been, I realised what Father Gerard must have known before he volunteered to deal with the device. There was no way even a champion bowler could have made a throw that long. He must have run down the fire escape and carried the device across the road. But run out of time.

While I no longer shared the beliefs that Father Gerard lived his life by, I whispered a silent prayer for my new friend who'd saved my life on more than one occasion in the past few days.

PART 6

CHAPTER 56: DEVON, JULY 2024

A slow hand-clap pulled Charlie out of her memories and back into the cavernous barn on the wilds of Dartmoor. But when she looked at her son, he wasn't moving. Orik was staring down at his shoes, a puzzled look on his face. It was his half-brother Kron who was applauding, and as she turned towards him, he gave her a mocking bow.

"You tell a good tale, Charlie Jones, I'll give you that. You almost had me convinced for a while."

"But every word is true, Kron, I swear."

"Oh, I've no doubt it is, in your mind at least. But it doesn't alter the fact that you betrayed my father. As a result of your testimony, he spent years in prison and was never the same again." Kron paused to light a cigarette and took a deep drag before finishing. "And despite what my brother said, your eloquent story-telling isn't going to save you. You used the word 'retribution' a little while ago. And that's exactly what we're looking for."

Charlie felt despair wash over her and desperately thought about what she could say to make this man – these two men – change their minds. But help came from an unexpected quarter.

"Kron, wait. I grew up thinking my mother had died

when I was born. It was only recently I found out that wasn't true. And I hated her for it. I wanted to make her pay for deserting me. Not just by killing her, but by making her suffer first. A spell in prison to see what our father went through. The anguish of losing a close family member. And finally, giving herself up for her child, something she didn't do first time around."

Orik paused and shook his head. "But now I find out she was also lied to. By the same people who lied to me. My father – your father – and my grandmother." Orik shook his head. "Don't you see? They took everything away from me, and from her. Now, Charlie and I have a chance to get to know each other. To make up for lost time." He looked as though he couldn't believe what he was saying. "I have to let her go."

He walked over to Charlie and pulled a knife from his belt. She shrank away from him, still unsure whether she could trust his words or not. But with a shy smile, he slit the ties binding her wrists and then bent to release her legs as well.

"Noooo!" There was a roar from Kron and he raced across the barn and pulled Orik away, throwing him to the ground. The knife slipped from his fingers and slid under Charlie's chair. "After all the work you put into this! After the time and expense of framing her for murder. Breaking into The Falls to steal the knife and keyring. Setting up the cameras and bugging her phone. The fake CCTV. Arranging for someone to film the whole journey so she would be released when you were ready to move on. Then kidnapping her daughter. And finally holding her prisoner. Do you really think we can let her go and walk away from this? Are you crazy?"

"But you can! I won't tell anyone." Charlie had no idea whether she was speaking the truth or not. She'd worry about that later on. For now, she had to keep them talking. "Why don't you untie me and leave me here? Walk away. I'll wait here for an hour, longer if you like, so you can get away. And I won't come after you."

She took a deep breath and realised she meant every word. "Suzy's safe. I'll be free. We can forget all about this. You can go home and you'll never hear from me again." A tiny voice whispered in her ear that she was about to lose her son for the second time, but she couldn't afford to worry about that.

"See, Kron, it'll be okay." Orik climbed to his feet and reached out, laying his hand on his half-brother's arm. "She won't say anything. We can go home."

But Kron was shaking his head, a slow final movement that sent shivers down Charlie's spine. "She may be able to convince you with her lying tongue, little brother, but I'm made of sterner stuff. No, this ends now!" Kron pulled a gun from his belt and pointed it directly at Charlie. "Say goodbye to your mother, Orik."

"Stop!" With a scream, Orik threw himself forward, as Kron pulled the trigger and Charlie closed her eyes. There was a muffled roar and a groan. She opened her eyes to see Kron holding on to Orik, who was sinking to the ground, a dark red stain spreading across his chest.

"Orik, what have you done? What have *I* done?" The older man gently laid his brother on the floor and leaned over him, desperately feeling for some sign of life.

Charlie felt under the chair and grabbed Orik's knife. Kron was distracted momentarily, but she knew that wouldn't last for long. She sliced through the ties binding her ankles to the chair and then sat absolutely still, waiting for the circulation to return to her feet.

Kron was sobbing.

"You need to call an ambulance. Where's your phone?" Charlie asked, although she could see from where she sat that it would be pointless.

Kron gave a howl and climbed to his feet. "He's dead, bitch, and it's your fault. Yet again, you've destroyed my family. Now, you will pay."

He raised the gun again. Charlie dived to the ground,

directly towards Kron, kicking the chair in the opposite direction at the same time. He fired wildly, and Charlie heard a bullet thud into the wall behind where she'd been sitting seconds before.

As he turned and levelled the gun towards her, she drove the knife deep into the muscle of his calf, and jumping up, knocked the gun out of his hand and kicked it into the darkness in the corner.

Without pausing to see what damage she'd inflicted, Charlie stumbled across the barn and threw herself out the door. She could hear Kron swearing inside. A heavy wooden bar stood leaning up against the wall nearby. On either side of the door were rough wooden cups.

Picking up the bar, she dropped it into place. The door was secure, at least for a while. Hopefully long enough for her to get away from here – wherever here might be. And that was her immediate challenge. Where was she?

CHAPTER 57

Charlie had no idea what time it was, but despite the lack of moon and stars, the darkness was not as impenetrable as she'd expected it to be. In fact to one side, where the countryside plunged away downhill, there was a faint suggestion of light beginning to show. So around four-thirty, she guessed. And now she knew which way was east.

There was a farmhouse across the other side of the yard. It was in total darkness. Whether that meant it was deserted or the occupants were still sleeping was an unknown factor, but Charlie didn't feel exchanging one building for another was a sensible approach.

Much more useful was the car parked to the side of the barn. Muttering a silent prayer to a God she wasn't sure she believed in most of the time, Charlie ran across to the vehicle. All the doors were locked. Her hope not only for open doors, but for keys left in the ignition, was not going to be fulfilled. And from the sounds of banging and splintering wood, Kron was not far from breaking out of the barn.

Charlie took a quick look around. The road was clear and ran from the farm gate towards the plain below. But on foot, she was no match for a vehicle. And she'd heard no other traffic while she'd been in the barn. She would be better off going across country, at least until she could find a busier road or some other sign of civilisation.

So she had two options – uphill or downhill. Downhill would be easier going, but it was open countryside, with very little cover. In the other direction, there were lots of trees, far more cover. But the path started climbing just outside the gate of the farm.

Charlie gave a sigh, resigned to a stiff climb, reminding herself that at least she didn't have a knife wound to slow her. She ran across the yard, out of the gate and into the trees.

Behind her, there was a grating sound and a crash. Kron was already on her trail. Without pausing to look, she headed uphill at a gentle trot. And to her delight, she heard an engine start up and a vehicle drive away. Was she going to make it to safety before he realised he was driving in the wrong direction?

After a steep climb of twenty minutes or so, the path petered out and the trees gave way to a flat hilltop. Huge boulders in an untidy pile reared over her head and Charlie realised she was on one of the tors. But which one? None of the surroundings seemed familiar. It had gradually got lighter as she climbed and, even though she was looking west, there was enough daylight to see by. Although nothing she could see gave her much comfort.

The countryside tilted steeply downhill once more, but as before it was open, with no trees and very little in the way of cover, apart from an occasional stone wall or small pile of boulders. More to the point, there was no sign of safety or civilisation: not one building or even a road.

She hadn't been back in Devon for long this time around, but she remembered from her childhood, tales of people who got lost on Dartmoor, who'd wandered around for days until they'd finally been found by Search and Rescue or, more likely, had starved to death. So, no point in trying to find her way out in that direction. To her left, in a southerly direction, the ground finished in a line of rocks and fell away into a deep quarry.

Turning to her right and walking around the tor, she spied, between the open countryside she didn't want to chance and the trees she'd just climbed through, a more gentle slope that led down to a tiny car park on the side of a road. A road that stretched across the moor and therefore must lead somewhere. That was more hopeful.

If she made her way down there, she could wait for a car to pass and hopefully persuade the driver to give her a lift. In fact, as she peered down in the gloom, she realised there was a car already parked down there. An early morning walker maybe? She took a few steps in the direction of the slope when a voice stopped her.

"I knew you'd end up here. Taken you longer than I expected. You must be slowing down, Charlie Jones. But I guess age catches up with all of us sooner or later."

Kron stepped out from behind the tor, between her and the path to safety. He was limping, and his trouser leg was soaked with blood, but the gun in his hand, which he was pointing directly at her head, was as steady as the boulders in the tor he'd been hiding behind. He leaned back against the rock and smiled coldly at her.

"So, nowhere to run to, Charlie Jones. Only one path, down that hill, and you have to get past me to reach it. What are you going to do now?"

"Oh, I don't think I'm going to do anything, Kron," she said, gazing over his shoulder, "I don't need to. My friends are going to do it for me."

There was a crunch of feet on the path just below them.

Kron whirled around and fired wildly. There was a frightened whinny and the sound of galloping hooves as the two ponies Charlie had spotted raced back down the path. It was only a momentary distraction, but it was enough.

Charlie slipped off the top of the hillside and disappeared from Kron's view. But instead of racing for the trees, she slid between two huge boulders and began to climb the tor.

Kron was right about one thing; Charlie wasn't going to run any further. This thing had to finish right here, right now.

CHAPTER 58

As the sound of hooves faded to nothing, silence descended on the tor. Charlie desperately tried to keep her breathing as quiet as possible as she moved, toehold by toehold, up the side of the giant boulder, feeling with her fingers for each nook and cranny that she could use to haul herself up.

It had been growing lighter, and finally the sun broke from behind the hills to the east and she found herself spotlighted on the side of the tor, just as Kron rounded the corner a mere twenty feet below her, gun still in his hand. All he had to do was look up and she was finished.

Kron stopped and looked wildly around. Time stood still. Then Charlie's foot slipped and a single pebble rolled from beneath her heel and fell to the ground. Kron looked up, and smiled slowly. Raising the gun, he pointed it straight at her and pulled the trigger. Charlie threw herself off the tor right into the bullet's path, knowing it was probably all in vain. But her movement was enough to startle Kron and she felt the bullet zip past her ear as she fell.

She landed on her pursuer and her momentum threw the two of them to the ground. The gun flew from Kron's hand and disappeared over the edge of the cliff. Charlie heard it fall many feet below them. Kron twisted from beneath her, threw her on her back. Straddling her body, he clamped his knees around her chest and pushed her hands above her head. She tried to knee him in the back, but couldn't reach him.

"You're a hard woman to catch, Charlie Jones." His voice was little more than a grunt and he was breathless from their fight, but Charlie understood his words. Holding both her wrists with one massive hand, he reached down and pulled a small knife from his boot. "But you're not going to escape from me this time."

Charlie twisted her head towards the arm that was holding her wrists and sank her teeth deep into the flesh. There was a howl and she tasted blood. His grip loosened slightly, enough for her to yank her wrists free. Her fingers reached for his face and she dug her thumbs into his eye sockets and twisted.

Kron screeched and dropped the knife as his hands flew up to protect his eyes. Charlie threw him sideways and hauled herself to her feet, grabbing the knife as she did so. Kron was kneeling on the ground, blood trickling from his bitten wrist, covering his streaming eyes with his hands.

Charlie looked at the knife and the defenceless man before her. Another Charlie, in another time, would have taken the advantage, would have plunged the knife into his eye or his neck. But that Charlie was long gone, and she didn't want to see her ever again.

She walked to the edge of the plateau, far enough away from her assailant, in sight of the path leading down to the car park.

"Get up, Kron." Her voice, even to her, sounded cold.

Kron stumbled to his feet. "Help me, I can't see."

"Yes, I know. Here's what's going to happen. I'm going to guide you down to the car park and we're going to get in your car and I'm going to drive you to a medical centre where you can get help." She gestured with the knife, although she knew he couldn't see it. "Right, follow the sound of my voice. And if you try anything, I'll walk away and leave you to find your own way out of here. Is that clear?" Kron nodded. "Okay, walk forwards. You'll have to trust me, but I give you my word, I'll guide you safely down to the car park."

It took a long time and many pauses, but eventually the two made it down the side of the hill and into the tiny car park. Charlie had wondered what would happen if any cars passed; how would they interpret a woman with a knife calling out instructions to a blinded man who was shambling behind her? But luckily, the moors were still deserted.

At the edge of the car park, Charlie called a halt.

"Throw me the car keys."

The huge man thrust his hand into his trouser pocket and pulled out a bunch of keys. "How can I throw them when I can't see?"

"Fair point. Throw them in the direction of my voice."

The keys left Kron's hand, but travelled barely a couple of feet before they hit the ground. Charlie sighed and moved towards them, stepping very gently so Kron couldn't hear where she was. But as she bent to retrieve the bunch, there was a flurry of movement and Kron dived towards her.

Charlie sidestepped and the man's momentum carried him across the car park until he collided with his car and bounced backwards, landing awkwardly on his side.

"I'm glad to see your eyesight's recovering, Kron." Charlie strode towards him and kicked him hard in the side of the head. He groaned and went still. She ran to the car, unlocking it as she moved. Wrenching open the boot, she found just what she needed, a bag of cable ties.

By the time Kron came around, he was propped up against the side of the car, tightly bound at the ankles and with his hands behind him. Charlie was leaning against the bonnet, staring at him.

"Oh good, you're awake. I took the liberty of searching your pockets." She waved his phone in front of him. "But I couldn't put you inside on my own. You're too heavy for me to lift. Up you get." She hauled him to his feet, pulled open the rear door on the driver's side and pushed him down onto the seat, before rolling down the window and slamming the door on him. Leaning in through the open window, she held up the mobile phone once more. "There's no signal here, so I'm going to go and find one."

"But I thought you were going to take me to the hospital. You gave me your word."

"Don't whine, Kron, it doesn't suit you." Charlie grinned and shook her finger at him. "I promised to bring you safely down to the car park, that was all. There's no way I'm staying in an enclosed space with you, even if you are tied up. But don't worry. I'm sure the police will get you checked out before they complete the formalities."

Blowing him a kiss, Charlie Jones pushed the car keys and phone into her pockets, and walked away.

CHAPTER 59

"Lofty, it's me. Is Suzy safe?" It had taken Charlie twenty minutes to get a phone signal. Her first instinct was to call Annie, but she didn't want to do that until she knew whether Orik had spoken the truth. And looking at the low level of charge left on the phone's battery, she only had time for one call.

"Yes, she's fine. A bit teary but Annie's looking after her. Last time I looked, they were frying chips and flipping burgers while little Bertie yipped and growled at anyone who went near them. But what the hell happened to you, Charlie? What possessed you to go off on your own like that?"

"Long story. Can we save it until later? I need you to pick me up. And we've got a prisoner to hand over to the police." She paused and looked around her. "Trouble is, I'm not sure where I am."

"Describe your surroundings, everything you can see. We'll find you."

The phone died, just as Charlie was describing the tor she could see in the distance. She had no idea whether she'd given Lofty enough information. She certainly hadn't managed to give him directions from her current position back to the car park where she was holding Kron prisoner. With a sigh, she settled herself against a rock at the edge of the road. It was less than an hour's drive from The Falls to the centre of Dartmoor. She'd give them ninety minutes to sort out her location and get there. Otherwise she would have to try hitching a lift.

In the event, it took thirty-seven minutes. There was a roar of an engine, a squeal of tyres, and a spray of gravel as the vehicle swerved to a halt half on the grass verge. Even before it stopped, the passenger door flew open and Suzanne jumped out. She threw herself at Charlie and the sisters hugged each other tightly.

"I've been so worried. Why did you go off like that?"

"It was the only way, Susu. He knew every move we made. He'd already caught us out once and I couldn't risk us ignoring his instructions a second time. Annie understood."

"What? Annie knew you were going off on your own? How could she?"

"Because our daughter was in danger and we had to do whatever it took to get her back."

There was a cough behind them. Lofty was leaning against the side of the car, tapping his watch. "We can go through all the history – and the recriminations," he raised an eyebrow at Charlie as he said that, "when we're all safely back at The Falls. Charlie, you mentioned a prisoner? Where is he?"

Charlie walked over and shook Lofty's hand. "You're right, and I know I owe you an explanation." She turned and pointed up the road. "It's about a mile and a half, or a bit more, that way. I walked it in twenty minutes, so it shouldn't take us very long to drive."

"Okay, come on then." Lofty walked back to the driver's door. Then he grinned at Charlie. "But next time you ask me for help, Charlie Jones, we're going to put a tracker on your person, rather than just on your car!" He jumped in and started the engine before Charlie had a chance to respond or even process the fact that her friends had suspected she might need keeping tabs on, and had made provision for it.

Charlie climbed into the front passenger seat and Suzanne got into the back of the car.

"Right, before we go anywhere, Charlie, perhaps you should let us know exactly what we should expect when we get there. I take it your prisoner is the kidnapper?"

"One of them, yes. Not the guy who was on the phone. He's dead." Charlie swallowed hard and realised there was such a lot she was going to have to explain once they all got back to The Falls. "This one's his brother, and of the two, I reckon he's probably the more dangerous. He's tied up in the back of his own car."

"But we're going to hand him over to the police, aren't we?" The question came from Suzanne, and Charlie turned to answer her.

"We certainly are. But that's going to take some explaining. They're going to think it's a hoax to start with. And we'll have to explain why we didn't call them as soon as Suzy was kidnapped."

"But your name must be known to every police officer in the country."

"True. And they'll all know about the murder on the Plymouth-bound train. A murder I can now solve for them." Charlie nodded. "Maybe you're right, Suzanne. But I think I'll try to get hold of Derek Smith, rather than just dialling the emergency services. It will be quicker in the long run."

In the event, it was a moot point.

"Are you absolutely sure this is the right place, Charlie?" Lofty asked a few minutes later. They'd arrived to find the car park deserted.

"Yes, I'm positive." Charlie pointed up the hill to the nearby tor. "Look, that's where we fought. We came down there together. He tried to attack me over there," indicating an area where the gravel was scuffed and scraped out of place, "and once I'd knocked him out, I dragged him across there to his car. You can see the heel marks in the dust."

She raked her fingers through her hair and screwed her eyes tightly shut. "Shit! Shit, shit, shit." She kicked out at a stone lying nearby then turned to look at Lofty and Suzanne. "I'm sorry, guys. It looks like he wasn't secure enough. He's gone. And we have no idea where to find him."

CHAPTER 60

"She's fast asleep, poor mite." Annie flopped down in a garden chair, blew her fringe out of her eyes and picked up her drink. Steve Ford, stretched out on a lounger, resting his leg in its plaster cast, opened his eyes and smiled at her as she went on. "And Bertie's curled up at her feet, dreaming doggie dreams. Charlie will have a fit if she finds hairs on our quilt."

"Suzy's not in her own room then?"

"No, I've left her in our bed for the moment." Annie felt her stomach lurch as she tried to imagine everything the young girl had been through in the past few days. "She went to her own room quite happily when I first put her to bed, but woke up screaming soon afterwards. Now she won't even go over the threshold."

"Kids are very resilient. I'm sure she'll be fine in a little while."

"I certainly hope so. I'd hate to think those bastards had caused permanent damage." Annie looked across the beer garden to where a tall figure had appeared around the side of the pub. "I wonder who this is."

Annie watched as the stranger approached. He was smiling shyly, but seemed to be quite wary, glancing around him frequently. He also appeared to be limping slightly.

"Good afternoon. Ms McLeod?"

"Yes, I'm Annie McLeod." Annie stiffened. Given everything that had happened, she wasn't going to welcome a stranger into her home. "What can I do for you?"

"I'm looking for Mike Thompson and Rodriguez. I'm a friend of theirs. My name's Winston, Ed Winston."

Annie felt herself relax. "Yes, of course, Mr Winston. Cyril Strong mentioned he'd contacted you. I'm afraid no-one's here at the moment. Mike and Rodriguez have gone for a hike up the Teign Valley, I believe. They should be back in a while." Annie pointed to a spare garden chair. "Why don't you join us and wait for them."

He shook her hand and dropped into the chair. "I heard you had a bit of a situation here. I've come to offer my help."

"That's very kind of you, but I'm delighted to say it's all been resolved. Our daughter's been returned to us, and my wife's on her way back from Dartmoor as we speak." Annie stretched and yawned. "All this sunshine is making me sleepy. I think I'll make us a jug of iced tea while we're waiting. Steve?"

"Mm, please. Although you're going to have to bring it down here to me, I'm afraid. Those stairs are still too much." He turned towards the newcomer. "No soft carpeted ones inside, sadly." Steve then pointed to Ed Winston's trousers. "Looks like you're having trouble with your leg too, Mr Winston."

"Ed, please." He rubbed his knee and winced. "Yes, I pulled a muscle in a training exercise at the weekend. It's taking a while to recover." He stood. "But I'm fine. I'll come and help you with the drinks, Ms McLeod."

"Okay, if you don't mind. And call me Annie. Come on, the kitchen's upstairs. It's a bit of an upside-down place."

"But a lovely spot by the stream." Winston followed her up the outside staircase and into the huge glass-walled lounge. "Wow, what a beautiful room."

"Yes, we're very proud of it. The view's always been stunning, but originally you had to stand and look through tiny windows to see it. One of the first things we did when we moved in was to have that wall put in."

Annie crossed through the open-plan kitchen to the fridge.

"What can I do to help?"

As she turned, she was surprised to find Winston standing right behind her. She'd thought he was still just inside the door. This man was surprisingly light on his feet, despite his size and apparent injury to his leg. "Nothing for the moment. You just sit and admire the view. You can carry the tray downstairs for me in a few minutes."

"Where's Mama Annie?"

Annie picked up her daughter's voice through the open kitchen window. Looking out, she saw Suzy standing with her uncle Steve. Bertie was prancing around at her feet.

"I'm up here, poppet," she called down to her. "We'll be down in a minute. Do you want some juice?" But at the sound of her mother's voice, Suzy raced towards the stairs. Her feet could be heard pounding up the steps and, seconds later, she skidded to a halt in the doorway.

Winston had returned to the window and was staring out across the fields and hills towards Dartmoor in the distance.

"I woke up and wondered where you were." A slight frown creased Suzy's soft forehead and her bottom lip trembled slightly. Annie realised her daughter was going to need a lot of support and cosseting in the coming days, possibly weeks. She ran across the room and gathered the young girl into her arms.

"It's okay. Uncle Steve was right outside your door. And you had Bertie with you for protection." She gently turned her daughter towards the room and their visitor, who was still staring out of the window. "Suzy, this is Mr Winston, Ed. He's a friend of the people who helped find you and bring you home."

"Hello, Suzy." Winston turned from the window and smiled.

Annie felt her daughter go rigid in her arms.

There was a moment of complete silence. Then Suzy screamed.

CHAPTER 61

Charlie stared at the space where she'd last seen Kron, tied up in his car. She was inwardly cursing herself for leaving him awake, alive even. What an idiot. She really was getting too old for this kind of thing.

"You know, Charlie, it's not true to say we have no idea where to find him." Lofty was the first to speak. "He didn't pass us on our way here. So he must have gone in the other direction." Lofty pointed along the road that stretched away from them across the moor. "How much of a head start do you think he'll have?"

"It could be an hour or more, I guess. Although it's probably a bit less than that. He was pretty well trussed up, so I'm assuming he had another hidden knife." She punched her fist into her palm. "Why didn't I search him properly?"

"It might not have been on him. It was probably hidden in the car. That's what I always used to do."

"Yes, I remember." Charlie nodded. "And I'd taken the car keys with me, so he'd have had to find a way of starting the car. Unless he had a spare set. I didn't check."

"I wonder why he went in that direction," said Suzanne.

"To avoid me?"

"But if he was trussed up, he wouldn't have been able to see where you'd gone, surely. And he was in a car while you were on foot. It would have been the ideal opportunity. He could have knocked you down and got away unobserved."

"Gee, thanks, sis. Glad you're playing for my team." But Charlie's grin faded as she realised exactly what had happened. "The farm! He's gone back to the farm. His brother's body is there. He wouldn't want to leave him behind." She jumped back in the car. "Come on. I'm sure I can find it. We can catch him there."

They drove along the road, stopping at each turning, every side road, while Charlie tried to orientate herself. Finally, she spotted the wooded path she'd climbed to reach the top of the tor. And a little way down a track they could see the farmhouse, although the barn wasn't visible from where they were.

"We'll leave the car here." Lofty drove past the turning and pulled onto the side of the road. "No point in spooking him."

As she got out of the car, a familiar smell reached Charlie and she looked across the roof at her sister, whose look of consternation reflected exactly what she was thinking. She raced down the slope, heedless of the calls from Suzanne and Lofty to take it slowly.

She pelted across the farmyard, only coming to a halt as the barn came into view. Or at least, what was left of it. The roof had collapsed, as had the door and one of the walls. Flames leapt through the gaps, licking at the surrounding grass and threatening to set the whole area on fire. But it was what she could see inside the burning building that really shocked Charlie. She approached as close as she could, until the heat became unbearable.

The fire must have been started from the edge of the building and was moving inwards. In the centre of the barn stood a table, surrounded by bales of straw and piles of timber. On the table lay a body. A young man in a black leather jacket. His arms were folded across his chest.

He looked as though he was just sleeping. But as she watched, the first flames licked the side of the table. There was a whoosh, a flash and an explosion. Charlie closed her eyes against the sight and the sound. When she opened them again, the body and the table were gone.

Orik, her lost and found son, was gone.

Charlie imagined what might have been, if things had been different. Her head told her there was no way she and her son could ever have been anything but enemies. But her heart wanted so badly to believe otherwise.

"Charlie?" She felt someone pull at her sleeve and turned to face Suzanne. "It's okay." Charlie smiled at her sister. "I'll explain later."

"He's not here, Charlie." Lofty came around the side of the barn. "There are no vehicles around here. And the farmhouse is locked up and empty. There's a pile of post just inside the door. Looks like they've been gone for a while. What do you want to do now?"

"Let's go home, guys." Charlie felt all her energy drain from her, removed by a sleepless night, the trauma of finding and then losing Orik, and then capturing and losing Kron. "We're not going to catch him now. There's too many places he might have gone."

They reached an area where the networks were working, so Charlie borrowed Suzanne's phone to ring Annie. But there was no answer.

"She must have turned it off. Maybe they're having a nap. I guess both of them have missed a fair bit of sleep in the past few days." She held out the phone to Suzanne. "Can you try Steve? Give him a message. Tell him we're on our way back. Should be there in around forty-five minutes."

But Suzanne was unable to reach her husband either. However, a quick call to Rohan ensured the message would get through.

Suzanne ended the call and threw the phone into her bag. "Of course, they knew you were safe, Charlie, as well as Suzy. I guess everyone's having a rest now the drama's all over. Looks like we're going to have to wake them all up when we get back."

CHAPTER 62

Rohan tried Annie's mobile, even though Suzanne had told him they couldn't get through. Still no response. That really was strange. He glanced up at the huge backwards clock above the bar. Just after ten. Everything was ready for opening at eleven. Then he caught sight of the house phone on a windowsill in the corner.

Picking it up, he checked the list on the card displayed next to it. Yes, there was an extension for The Folly. It was rarely used, but he knew there were extensions both in the upstairs lounge and inside the door leading to the downstairs sleeping quarters.

The phone rang for a long time. Rohan counted to nine rings and was about to give up and walk across to see what was going on, when the phone was answered.

"Hello?" It was a male voice. Rohan remembered Steve Ford limping across the garden with Annie and Suzy after breakfast.

"Steve, it's Rohan. I'm trying to reach Annie–"

"Rohan, thank God. Can you get over here now? I think Annie's in trouble. They're up in the lounge. There's a stranger with them. Says he's a friend of Lofty and the others. But I've just heard Suzy scream."

"I'll be right over. Don't do anything until I get there."

Rohan dropped the phone back into the cradle and raced through the door behind the bar, along the corridor and through the back door, slamming it to behind him. As he crossed the beer garden, a small bundle of black and white fur limped towards him, whimpering.

"Bertie, what's the matter, old boy?" The little dog was shivering violently and there was blood around his mouth. Rohan picked him up and ran on towards The Folly.

Steve Ford was about a third of the way up the outer staircase, hauling himself from one step to another, and groaning as he did so. The door at the top of the stairs, kept open all day long during the summer months, was shut.

"Steve, what are you doing?"

The older man turned to look at Rohan with an anguished look on his face. "I heard Suzy scream again and Bertie barking, then the poor little chap was thrown down the stairs and the door slammed shut. I couldn't sit there doing nothing."

"Come back down and tell me what's going on up there." Rohan helped him back down the stairs and into a chair, and Steve brought him up to date on the arrival of Ed Winston.

When the story was finished, Rohan shook his head. "I've never heard of an Ed Winston. I've no idea who he is. Lofty's on his way back here with Charlie and Suzanne. He didn't mention anyone else coming to join the team – and the other two didn't say anything before they headed off for their hike."

Rohan walked towards the stairs. "I don't like this at all. I'd better get up there and see what's going on. Keep an eye on Bertie, will you. I don't want him getting hurt again."

Rohan tiptoed up the stairs. Reaching the landing at the top, he dropped to a crouch and peered through the small round window in the wall next to the door. Suzy and

Annie were sitting on the sofa. Suzy was sobbing quietly. Annie, who had her arms wrapped around her daughter, was dry-eyed, but pale and shaking.

To start with, Rohan couldn't see anyone else. What was going on? But then a shadow crossed the glass and the third occupant of the room came into view. He was a large swarthy-complexioned man who limped as he walked towards the women.

The man was definitely a stranger as far as Rohan was concerned. Of course, it wasn't unusual to see strangers around The Falls. Pubs played host to strangers every day of the week. But in The Folly, that was different. That was the McLeod-Jones family home. A stranger here wasn't normal, especially given recent events. And the stranger was holding a gun.

Annie turned her head and looked straight at Rohan. Her lips twitched slightly, but she gave the merest shake of her head. It was only a slight movement, but enough to catch the attention of Suzy. And a young girl is much harder at hiding her feelings than a grown woman. Her face lit up in a huge smile.

The stranger, seeing the direction of Suzy's gaze, spun towards the window. Rohan ducked out of sight. Had he been seen? He didn't think so. He held his breath and counted to ten. There was no sound from inside the room. Slowly, he raised himself to his feet and took a step back towards the stairs.

The door flew open and the stranger appeared, pointing the gun directly at Rohan's chest.

"Whoa." Rohan put his hands in the air. "No need for that, mate. Put the gun away. Let's talk."

"The time for talking's done. I have nothing to talk to you about. I'm waiting to see Charlie Jones."

"Charlie's not here but she'll be home soon. It's Ed, isn't it? Why don't you let Annie and Suzy go. In fact, why don't you come and have a drink in the bar while you wait."

"No, the woman and the girl stay here. We are preparing a little surprise for Charlie. But you need to go. This is your final warning." The man fired the gun.

Rohan threw himself sideways. There was a sharp sting on his right arm and he realised the bullet had not completely missed him. He felt his foot slip off the top step.

Grabbing for the handrail, his fingers grasped empty air.

He heard Suzy and Annie scream and Steve shout out.

Rohan went over the handrail then was tumbling through the air, landing with a crash on the patio below, his head hitting an ornamental granite boulder at the edge of the flowerbed.

CHAPTER 63

As Lofty reached the village of Coombesford, Charlie gazed out of the window, drinking in the sights of the place she and her family called home. The late-morning sun shining through the leaves dappled the grass of the village green, and ducks squabbled gently on the pond. But as they drove past the primary school, Mike Thompson stepped into the road and flagged them down.

"We've got a hostage situation up at The Falls. Or at least in The Folly. There's a guy with a gun, and he's shut himself in the upstairs lounge with Annie and Suzy."

"Noooo." Charlie threw herself out of the car and began to run across the green. But Thompson stepped in front of her, held up his hands and blocked her way.

"No, Charlie, wait. Listen to me. *Listen to me*. Whoever he is, he's got a gun."

"I know who he is." Charlie was pushing at Thompson, trying to get past. "I've spent the past twelve hours either chasing him or being chased *by* him." When her pushing didn't have any effect, she swung a punch at him, but he easily deflected her fist.

"And you know exactly what he's capable of, Charlie." Lofty had joined the struggling pair and took Charlie by her shoulders, turning her to face him. "I know it's hard. But if you go charging in like the proverbial bull, someone's going to get killed." He let go of her shoulders and drew himself up into a military stance. "So snap out of it, Jones, and do what you've been trained to do."

Charlie took a series of long, slow deep breaths, then looked up and nodded.

Thompson briefed them on what had happened so far. "When we got back to The Falls, it all seemed too quiet for a lunchtime, and the front door was locked. There were a couple of regulars just pulling into the car park, but we told them there was a gas leak and sent them home. The back door of the pub was closed as well, so we went across to The Folly. We found Steve already over there. He was stuck at the bottom of the stairs."

"And Kron Laska?"

"So that's his name. Well, Mr Laska has shut himself upstairs with Annie and Suzy." Thompson paused. "And I'm afraid Rohan's hurt. He was at the top of the stairs, Laska shot him and he fell over the bannisters. He was on the patio and while we were there, Steve was helping him inside the building out of the firing line. He's going to be fine, but could probably do with some medical attention."

"Have you called the emergency services?"

"Not yet. We wanted to wait until you arrived. We've blocked the entrance to the car park, so no-one else will go up there. And Rodriguez has gone into the school to make sure the kids are all kept inside over lunchtime."

At that moment, the fourth member of the team appeared through the school gates and gave them a thumbs-up.

"Right, here's what we're going to do." Lofty spoke quietly, but his colleagues were alert and taking in his instructions. "We're going to have to call an ambulance for Rohan. And if they find out they're dealing with a gunshot wound, they'll inform the police, even if we don't. But getting an armed response team set up and in place is going to take far too long. So, the four of us will get down there and tackle Laska on our own. Suzanne, you wait here, give us ten minutes to get into position then call the police and the medics."

"But what about Steve…"

"Steve will be fine, Suzanne, I promise." Charlie squeezed her sister's hand then turned back to the rest of the team. "I've got an idea. If we go through the grounds of Mountjoy Manor, we can approach The Folly from the rear of the building, where there's no windows and Laska won't be able to see us until it's too late." She pointed to the car. "We'll drive up there, it'll be quicker."

Moments later, they arrived at a set of ornate iron gates, fortunately wide open, and slewed to a stop, gravel flying, in front of Olga Mountjoy's large manor house.

"This way." Charlie led the group down a narrow path through an overflowing shrubbery. Luckily there was no-one around. She didn't want to waste time explaining to Olga why there was a team of pseudo-commandos rampaging through her garden. They ran across the manicured lawns and down the slope to the stream at the bottom of the garden.

Standing at the top of the waterfall, they gazed downstream to where the thatched roof of The Falls was visible through the trees. "It's a bit of a climb, but it's okay if you take it steady. I find it easiest to go down backwards."

She launched herself over the side of the hill, using rocks, saplings and plant roots to steady herself. Within a couple of minutes, she was on the ground. Thompson and Rodriguez soon followed. Lofty made heavy weather of the climb and Charlie remembered belatedly that her former commander was in his early seventies. But finally, he too was at the bottom.

"Okay, Charlie, lead the way." Lofty was wheezing slightly but otherwise showed no ill effects from the past few minutes. They hurried up the slope to the little house and slipped through the open front door into the main bedroom, putting their fingers to their lips as they passed Steve who was tending to Rohan. "We need a better idea of the situation before we go any further."

He pointed to Rodriguez. "You're the lightest on your feet. Can you climb up the stairs and see what's going on? Don't let yourself be seen, either by Laska or the hostages."

Rodriguez nodded and slipped out of the door.

"Boss, it's me he's after," Charlie said. "If I go upstairs to talk to him, maybe he'll let the others go. He let Suzy go."

"And maybe he won't." Lofty was shaking his head. "From what you've told me, Charlie, it was the other brother who let Suzy go. This one's a different proposition altogether. He might just kill everyone."

"Why would he do that? He'd never get out of here alive."

"I suspect that may well be his plan. His brother's gone. He's committed murder and kidnapping, so he's going to be a hunted man. He knows he's running out of options."

"And if he's going down, he's taking me, my friends and family with him. Is that what you're saying?"

"Yes, Charlie. I rather fear that's exactly what he's planning."

CHAPTER 64

Rodriguez returned within a few moments, with news of both the hostages and Rohan.

"Annie and Suzy are sitting on the sofa. They appear to be unhurt, although both are visibly upset."

"Are they tied up?"

"No. I guess the presence of a man with a gun in the room is enough to keep them quiet and unmoving."

"Good point." Lofty turned to Charlie. "Is that outside staircase the only way in and out of the top floor? Or is there any other way you could get the hostages out, if I can distract Laska?"

Charlie shook her head. "No stairs inside. There's a fire ladder attached to the big window in the kitchen. But it's all folded up. It's not possible to get them out that way. It would take too long."

"So it looks like I'll have to negotiate with him." Lofty rubbed his hands across his bald head. "It's been a while, but I used to be good at this."

Everyone turned as the door opened. It was Steve. His hands were covered in blood.

"Rohan's conscious, and able to stand. I've managed to stop the bleeding for now. It's only a flesh wound, thank goodness, but it's going to need stitches."

"Great news, Steve." Charlie turned towards Thompson and raised an eyebrow. Thompson nodded. "Mike will help you get him back up to the pub. Suzanne's up there now, waiting for the ambulance to arrive." Charlie grabbed a lead from a hook by the door and called Bertie to her. "And take this little chap with you, will you?"

Within moments, the small procession had reached the other side of the beer garden and was crossing the patio. At the same time, sirens in the distance reassured them that medical help was on its way. Charlie gave a deep sigh of relief and smiled at Lofty. The pair, accompanied by Rodriguez, went outside. Lofty gestured for Charlie and Rodriguez to remain hidden while he approached the bottom of the stairs.

"Laska. Kron Laska. Can you hear me?" Lofty waited a few seconds then tried again. "Kron Laska. This is Cyril Strong. I'm a friend of the family. I'd like to talk. Can I come up?"

There was the sound of a door opening. Charlie peered around the side of the building. The door was indeed open, but the top landing was empty.

Lofty tried again. "Kron, what can we do to help resolve this situation? What do you need?"

"I *need* Charlie Jones up here right now." As far as Charlie could tell, the voice came from close to the door, although Laska still kept out of sight. "That's the only thing that will 'resolve this situation', as you put it."

Charlie stepped forward with an apologetic look towards Lofty. "I'm here, Kron. I'll come up and talk to you. But you have to let my family go."

"I'm not interested in your family, Charlie Jones. Only in you. You come up here and your family can go free."

Charlie began walking up the stairs. Halfway up, she paused. "Okay, Kron, I'm here. Let my family go and I'll come the rest of the way up."

A small figure appeared in the doorway. Appearing to

receive a gentle push from inside, Suzy came onto the landing, glancing back over her shoulder all the time. Charlie felt a huge weight begin to lift. "Suzy, it's okay, come down."

"But Mama Annie–"

"Hush, Suzy, I'll sort it. You go all the way down." Charlie gave her daughter a hug as she passed her on the stairs then watched as the girl reached the bottom and ran full tilt towards her aunt who had just crossed the beer garden. Then Charlie turned back and continued climbing the stairs. "Kron, I'm here. You can let Annie go now."

An arm reached out and pulled Charlie inside.

"All in good time, Charlie," Kron said, "all in good time. We have some talking to do first."

"You're going to have to talk to both of us then!" The voice from the doorway was unexpected and Charlie spun round. Suzanne was stepping into the lounge. Charlie opened her mouth in protest, but her sister held up a hand to silence her. "No, Charlie, you're not doing this one on your own. We're sisters. We'll sort this out together."

"So sorry to break up this family reunion." There was a sneer to Kron's voice that sent icicles down Charlie's spine. "But can I remind you it's me who decides what's going to happen next?" He waved his gun at Suzanne. "You, over there on the sofa." Then he turned to Annie. "You, come here."

Charlie watched as her wife gave her a big somewhat-tearful smile and, rising to her feet, crossed the room and stood beside her. All three women looked towards Laska, waiting for him to make the next move. But it seemed to Charlie that for the first time since she'd met him, her son's half-brother was indecisive, uncertain what to do next. Finally he shook his head. "You know, I've always believed that flexibility is important. And this is a time to be flexible."

In a sudden move that caught even Charlie by surprise, he grabbed her by the arm, shoved her out onto the landing and slammed the door shut. There was the sound of a bolt being rammed into place. Charlie hammered on the door, but Kron ignored her. As she watched through the glass pane, he used his gun to push Annie across the room and back down onto the sofa, next to Suzanne. Only then did he turn towards the door and raise his voice to address Charlie.

"As you probably guessed, Charlie Jones, my plan was to kill you and myself, up here in your little love nest. But that would be too easy, over too quickly." He paused and seemed to be struggling to get his words out. But when they came, they were chillingly clear. "I had to watch my brother die. And it was your fault. Now, in return, you will watch your sister and your wife die. And there's not a thing you can do to stop it."

Opening his jacket, he revealed for the first time the pack of explosives strapped to his chest. Charlie watched in what seemed like slow motion as he dragged a detonator out of his pocket.

CHAPTER 65

When the impact of Kron's words sank in, a wave of panic swept over Suzanne. She felt Annie clutching at her arm and knew her sister-in-law was experiencing the same thing. And somehow, that calmed her. She squeezed Annie's arm and gave her a smile she hoped conveyed a confidence she didn't necessarily feel.

Charlie was still hammering on the door and this was distracting Kron's attention, but Suzanne knew that wouldn't last very long. She rapidly scanned the room and considered their options. The fire exit was too unwieldy to open unnoticed. So their only exit from the room would be via the main external door. The door that was not only bolted, but currently blocked by their captor.

"We have to talk to him. Get him away from the door and distract him," she muttered without moving her lips or turning her head. "Follow my lead." Annie nodded.

It went quiet outside. Charlie had gone, and Suzanne hoped she had a plan. But for the moment, they were on their own.

Suzanne raised her voice to attract his attention. "Kron, you don't have to do this." He swung around towards her, gun in one hand, detonator in the other. "There must be another way out of this."

"No. No, there really isn't." He shook his head. "My brother is dead. I killed him."

"But it wasn't your fault. It was an accident. The police will understand that. Charlie was a witness."

"Your sister was our hostage. We kidnapped her daughter. How will the police understand that?"

Annie broke in at this point. "But you didn't harm her. She's my daughter too. And she told me you were kind to her all the time she was with you."

"Of course. Why would we hurt a child? We're not monsters. That's not what this is all about."

"So what *is* it about, Kron? Why don't you explain it to us? Make us understand what you wanted to do? And then, maybe we can help you."

"I was only a baby when Charlie Jones came into my life." Kron was still pointing the gun at them, but he'd slipped the detonator back into his pocket. "She was supposed to be part of my father's gang. A disaffected British student who'd run away from home and was looking for adventure in a foreign land. And she played her part so well. My father became besotted with her. My grandmother didn't trust her. Tried to warn him. And finally, she found proof that Charlie was a spy. But by that time, it was too late. Charlie was pregnant."

There was a gasp from Annie, while Suzanne finally realised the significance of the funeral pyre she'd found Charlie transfixed by earlier that day. So much she didn't know about her sister. So much to talk about. But that would have to wait until later. If there was a later.

"And that baby was Orik?" Suzanne thought she knew the answer to the question already but needed to keep him talking.

Kron nodded. "Yes. My baby brother, Orik." Kron swallowed hard. "They told us Charlie was dead. We grew up believing that. And then three years ago, we learned it was all a lie. Orik thought his mother had deserted him as a new-born and swore to get revenge. Retribution, he called it."

"But Charlie wouldn't have done that, Kron. She's not a monster either."

"Oh, yes, she was blameless in that, as it turns out. She was told he had died. She didn't even know Orik's name. So my brother's quest was in vain and he died for nothing." Kron shook his head. "But she *was* to blame for what happened to my father and the rest of the family. That *was* her fault. And that's why I'm here. That's why she has to suffer." He pulled the detonator out of his pocket again.

At that moment, several things happened at once. Annie slipped from the sofa in a dead faint, Charlie smashed the glass of the door with a brick, and Suzanne swung her foot up and slammed it into Kron's damaged leg. Bellowing, he dropped the detonator and grabbed at his knee.

Suzanne hauled a lamp from the table and brought it down across the back of his head, giving him an additional shove with her foot at the same time. He went flying across the room, landing with a groan in the corner, and was still.

"Annie, are you okay?" Charlie had managed to open the bolt through the broken window and was through the door and across the room in an instant.

As Suzanne watched, Charlie gathered Annie to her and hugged her.

"Yes, of course I'm fine," came a muffled voice. "Let me go, Charlie." Annie was grinning through her tears. "Suzanne was doing a fine job keeping Kron talking, but I saw you creeping back upstairs with that brick and thought a little additional distraction wouldn't go amiss."

"It certainly worked. Well done."

"Although you and I need to have a serious talk about your past, Charlie Jones."

Charlie looked abashed, but Suzanne spotted a slight

twinkle in Annie's eye and knew everything was going to be okay.

"That's going to have to wait until we sort out our erstwhile captor." Suzanne stood and turned towards the corner. But it was empty. Kron was gone. "Where is he?"

They ran out onto the landing. Across the grass, just before a stand of trees, Cyril Strong was helping Rodriguez climb to her feet. The pair walked slowly back towards The Folly.

"What happened?" Suzanne found her voice first. "Where is he?"

"He disappeared into the trees!" Cyril pointed downstream. "When he came down the stairs, we were about to grab him when he showed us the vest he was wearing. He grabbed Rodriguez and dragged her with him." Cyril shook his head. "There was nothing I could do. I couldn't risk him setting off the explosives."

"When we got near the trees, he punched me, I fell, and he made a run for it." Rodriguez shook her head. "I'm sorry, Charlie. We've let you down."

"It's not your fault." Charlie smiled ruefully. "We knew he was good at getting out of tight spots. We should have tied him up while we had the chance." She shrugged. "But, he can't have got far, the state he was in. And the police will be here soon."

"But he's still armed, Charlie. And he's desperate. We need to warn everyone." Suzanne turned to go down the stairs. But Annie's voice stopped her.

"What's that, under the table?" She went back into the lounge, bent and pulled out a small black box with a switch, a flashing light and a button. "Charlie, it's the detonator. So he's not so dangerous as we thought." She stopped and then held the box out to Charlie. "Can't you…?"

Charlie stared at the device in Annie's hand, a series of conflicting emotions crossing her face. Suzanne watched as her sister had one of the most important conversations of her life, with herself. Finally, she shook her head.

"No, Annie, I can't do that. The old Charlie Jones might well have pushed the button. But not any longer. To kill Kron like that would be wrong, cowardly. It would make us no better than him. Not to mention we don't know who else might be in range of the explosion."

Charlie reached across and gently flipped the switch. The flashing light went out. Wherever Kron was, his explosive vest was no longer a threat to him or anyone else.

CHAPTER 66

The sound of an engine made them rush back outside. A battered old Land Rover burst out from under the trees at the side of the stream and tore up the slope and across the beer garden, leaving scattered tables and chairs in its wake. It disappeared around the side of the pub, but they could still hear it crossing the car park, crashing through the temporary barrier and turning onto the road. They caught a final glimpse of it as it raced south, towards Chudleigh.

"Shit!" Charlie realised that yet again, this situation was far from over. "Are the police here yet?"

"Not yet, but shouldn't be long. The ambulance crew called them as soon as they saw Rohan's injury." Lofty grinned. "He's going to be fine. The bullet only clipped his arm."

"But, in the meantime, Kron's got a head start!" Charlie thought rapidly. "I assume the car's still up at the manor?"

When Lofty nodded, Suzanne groaned. "He's gone then. We've lost him."

"Not necessarily, sis." Charlie ran down the stairs and grabbed a bunch of keys, throwing the words over her shoulder. "You tell her, Annie." She raced across the garden and stopped outside the shed she and Annie had been wrangling about so often. The shed Annie wanted to convert into another accommodation unit. The shed housing her pride and joy.

"Although I don't get to use you as often as I'd like, old girl," Charlie muttered as she pulled on her helmet and climbed onto her Harley-Davidson Sportster. Taking a deep breath, she turned the key and then released it as the engine roared into life. Within seconds, she was thundering along the road.

Kron didn't know the area, as far as she was aware, apart from his surveillance of The Falls. So she had to assume he'd stick to the main road for the moment, rather than turning off and risk ending up in the cul-de-sacs of a modern housing estate.

So when she reached Chudleigh, she kept going straight through the town, mentally apologising for her excessive speed. She hoped no-one recognised her or her bike. Passing through the traffic-calming chicanes, she stepped up the speed.

As she flew down Station Hill, she wondered if Kron would have turned onto the busy A38. And if so, which way? At the last minute, she spied the Land Rover in the distance, making a sharp right turn in front of a tractor into the Teign Valley road.

Now she had him. The road was nine or ten miles of narrow carriageways and wicked bends. There were a few turnings leading off the main road, but they were sufficiently spaced out that she'd be able to spot him if he took one.

And Charlie knew this road. Their favourite pub/restaurant, when they needed a break from The Falls, was in a tiny village two-thirds of the way along. She'd driven this road many times in the past five years, in all sorts of conditions.

So Charlie was fairly confident, as she adjusted her speed to the needs of the road, that she was going to be able to catch Kron within a short distance. What she would do when she caught him was something she'd not worked through. But she'd play that bit by ear. At least, while he was driving, he couldn't shoot at her.

The road was fortunately quiet at that time in the early afternoon. The last thing she needed was extra traffic getting in the way. Reaching the long wide sweep above Huxbear Barton, she flew around the corner, expecting to see the vehicle directly in front of her. But the road was empty. She slammed on the brakes. Where had he gone?

Then she heard the roar of an engine from behind the hedge surrounding the garden of an isolated cottage a little way down the road. The Land Rover burst back out into view and rocketed off in the direction they'd come from, swerving wildly as Kron struggled to keep the vehicle on the road.

As it disappeared around the first of a series of tight bends that carried the road high above the River Teign, the vehicle lurched to the right and slammed into the rocky hillside. The collision threw it back across the road, directly into the river's barrier, which crumpled and split apart. The Land Rover was launched through the air, crashing into the river below it.

Charlie started her bike and approached the scene. Switching off her engine, she gazed down into the river. The Land Rover was on its roof in the shallow water which flowed gently either side of the vehicle. There was no sign of movement. An arm stretched out through the open window lay palm upwards, as though asking for help. But the bank was too steep, completely inaccessible. There was nothing Charlie could do but stand and watch.

This time, finally, she would make sure he didn't disappear.

In the distance, Charlie Jones heard the sound of police sirens.

EPILOGUE

"And you really had no idea your son was still alive?" Suzanne asked the question, but Charlie could see from their eyes that Rohan and Esther wanted an answer as well.

"No, of course not. I believed the nurse when she told me the child was dead. Do you really think I could have turned my back if I'd even suspected?"

"Not for one moment, sweetie." Annie wrapped her arms around Charlie and hugged her tightly to her.

The police had recovered Kron's Land Rover from the river and confirmed the single occupant was dead. There had followed a long afternoon of questions – some official, some less so.

They were back home now. Charlie had showered and eaten; she had told her tale multiple times; and Annie had finally persuaded everyone else to either return to their homes (locals) or go to bed (visitors). Lofty, Thompson and Rodriguez had disappeared in the same way as they'd arrived – quickly, quietly and with little fuss. Even Suzy, who'd refused to leave Charlie's side from the minute the police car had returned her to the car park of The Falls, had given in to exhaustion and was safely tucked up in her bedroom.

The five friends were having one final drink before calling it a night.

"So, what happens now, Charlie?" This time it was Rohan who took the lead.

"The police want to talk to me again. They've got a lot to untangle. After all, we're talking about four major crimes here: the murder on the train; Suzy's abduction; my imprisonment and assault; and today's home invasion."

Charlie paused and reached out for Annie's hand as she returned from checking – again – that Suzy was safely in her room. "And then we're going to take that trip to Latin America that was so rudely snatched away from us."

"About that, Charlie," Annie said, glancing anxiously downward, as though she could see through the floor into Suzy's bedroom. Charlie squeezed her hand.

"It's okay, I know what you're going to say. And it's fine by me. If Suzy wants to come with us, she can. I know you don't want to let her out of your sight." She paused and grinned. "Although, how we're going to deal with her hatred of flying, I'm not sure."

"Maybe we should switch from planes to ships." Annie winked. "I've always fancied crossing the Atlantic in style."

"That's certainly an option. We'll see what she fancies tomorrow." Charlie paused. "Of course, she might feel spending a month with Olga at Mountjoy Manor is preferable to tagging along while her two mothers celebrate their marriage."

"*Euch.* Gross." Annie's imitation of their daughter's current favourite expression was spot on, and the five friends laughed together.

"Precisely. So we'll give her the choice." Charlie stopped talking and looked around the room at her closest family and friends. Then she nodded to herself and stood, as though what she was about to say warranted a degree of formality. "But one thing I've learned from the past few weeks; I'm really finished this time."

"Finished, Charlie. What does that mean?" asked

Esther.

"It means, Esther darling, no more adventures. No more late-night chases across the moor. No more fighting." She rubbed her hands down her body, much of which she knew was covered in bruises, and winced. "Definitely no more fighting. I'm getting way too old for this."

Charlie took Annie's hand once more. "I'd never try to tell you what to do, Annie, but as for me, I'm done with solving murders or investigating crime. Time to settle down and concentrate on the family and The Falls."

Annie jumped up and hugged her. "Delighted to hear it. I'm very happy to agree with you. No more crime-fighting for either of us."

Rohan and Esther were looking at each other, aghast.

"But what about...?" Rohan began.

"What happens if...?" Esther started at the same time.

"If there's another murder in Coombesford, Esther?"

Esther nodded at Charlie, who smiled gently at her. "You guys are perfectly capable of investigating on your own. Rohan's an ex-policeman, for goodness sake. And your IT skills are even better than mine." Charlie looked at Annie and raised one eyebrow. Annie smiled back. "So that's it, guys. We'll still be around, running this place, but the Gang of Four is officially now a Gang of Two. And we know you'll do just fine on your own."

Charlie glanced at her watch. "And now, Esther, I think it's time you and Rohan headed back to the farm. Your dad will be getting up soon, wanting his breakfast."

As she watched the couple walk across the garden, hand in hand, Charlie thought hard about her next words. Taking a deep breath, she turned to face Annie and Suzanne.

"I've kept a lot of secrets from you guys in the past. And I'm sorry. Ask me whatever you want. I'll answer all your questions. The time for secrets is over."

ENJOYED THIS BOOK?

Reviews and recommendations are very important to an author and help contribute to a book's success. If you have enjoyed *Retribution!*, please recommend it to a friend or, better still, buy it for them as a birthday or Christmas present. And please consider posting a review on Amazon, Goodreads or your preferred review site.

ABOUT THE AUTHOR

I was born and brought up in Birmingham. As a teenager, essays and poetry won me an overseas trip via a newspaper competition. Despite this, I took scientific and business qualifications and spent more than thirty years as a manufacturing consultant, business owner and technical writer before returning to creative writing in 2006. I have written short stories and poetry for competitions, gaining a few wins, several honourable mentions and some shortlisting along the way. I am published in several anthologies.

Under the Chudleigh Phoenix Publications imprint, I have published six collections of short stories, including two co-authored with Sharon Cook. I also write non-fiction, including a series on business skills for writers and self-publishing.

My debut novel, *Gorgito's Ice Rink*, was runner-up in the 2015 Self-Published Book of the Year awards. These days, I write crime: the *Jones Sisters* thrillers; and cozy crime in the form of the *Coombesford Chronicles*.

I am a member of several writers' groups including the Crime Writers' Association; ALLi (The Alliance of Independent Authors); and Authors in a Pickle, which grew out of the Women in Publishing community.

You can find out more about me and my writing on my website, by clicking the QR code.

OTHER BOOKS BY THE AUTHOR

Coombesford Books
Murder at Mountjoy Manor
Villainy at the Village Store
Calamity at Coombesford Church
Coombesford Calendar volume I
Coombesford Calendar volume II
Coombesford Calendar volume III

The Jones Sisters series
Counterfeit!
Deception!
Corruption!

Other fiction
Gorgito's Ice Rink
Flashing on the Riviera
Parcels in the Rain and Other Writing

Co-written with Sharon Cook
Life is Not a Trifling Affair
Life is Not a Bed of Roses

Non-fiction
Sunshine and Sausages

The Author Business Foundations series
Part 1: Business Start-Up (ebook only)
Part 2: Finance Matters (ebook only)
Part 3: Improving Effectiveness (ebook only)
Parts 1-3 (print only)
Parts 1-3 Workbook (print only)
Part 4: Independent Publishing

Printed in Great Britain
by Amazon